2008

started calling my grandmother by her first name when I was thirteen. It was the summer before Grandpa died, and Dad and I were spending the month of July with them in Woodacre, California. They owned a cedar-shingled cottage there where they'd go for weekends and vacations, and after Grandpa retired from Berkeley, they moved into it permanently.

My grandmother was an artist who was known primarily for her paintings and photographs. She was always mentoring a few art students, and one of them had a show opening in San Francisco during our visit. My grandmother took me with her.

The show was in SoMa at a garage that specialized in hybrid and electric vehicles, and doubled as an art gallery. A red plug-in Prius was elevated on a lift at the back of the garage, which had the cleanest polished concrete floors I'd ever seen. I had expected to see paintings hanging on the walls, but this artist made wire sculptures. They hung from cables that stretched across the space, twirling slowly in the air like graceful dancers made of silver mesh. Other sculptures were installed on stands scattered across the floor. Most were abstract in form, but some resembled female bodies or animal-like shapes: arms and tails extended, or elongated heads that seemed to look at you, even without eyes.

I was the youngest person there. As soon as we arrived, my grandmother was pulled away by a stranger, and then another one, and after a few minutes of awkwardly hovering a few feet away, I retreated to the rear of the garage by the Prius. Nearby, two couches were arranged around a sky-blue shag rug, and I sat down by myself while more people came through the garage's huge open doors.

I could see the traffic whooshing by on Mission Street in the dusk. As Saturday evening settled into Saturday night, growing shadows blurred the city's hard edges and turned them into soft-focus suggestions. I had been to plenty of art galleries before but not a Saturday night opening, and I'd dressed up for it in a teal-and-white sundress along with a carefully applied coating of lip gloss. Sitting on that sofa, I felt grown-up, almost.

I lost track of my grandmother in the gathering crowd. It was mostly women, mostly casually dressed in jeans and tees or tank tops, sneakers or boots, along with a smattering of all-black ensembles. Many of them had bare arms covered with tattoos: flowers or pinup girls or intricate abstract designs. A couple of women, one with pink hair, sat across from me on the other couch and set down small paper plates of cheese and grapes, while they toasted each other with clear plastic cups of white wine. I thought about making a plate of cheese for myself, but before I could get up, a Black woman with very short hair sat down beside me.

"This seat's not taken, is it?" she asked.

"No," I said.

"Thanks." She held a plate of cheese and grapes, too, but instead of wine she had a small bottle of Pellegrino. She twisted it open and took a sip.

I could see the brown skin of her scalp where her hair was faded in on the sides. I didn't want to stare, so I lowered my gaze. She was wearing black jeans and black motorcycle boots.

"Joan West is supposed to be here tonight," the woman said. "Have you heard of her?"

I looked up. "Yeah, she's . . ." Her right eyebrow was pierced, and her eyes were sapphire blue. The edges crinkled as she smiled at me, and suddenly I didn't want to admit that Joan West was my grandmother. It wasn't that I didn't want to be connected with her, but this woman was speaking to me as if I were an adult, like her. To be Joan West's granddaughter made me a child, which I didn't want to be. "She's great," I said. "I like her work."

"Yeah? What's your favorite?"

My grandmother's most recent paintings were quite different from her previous work, but I liked them. Long, golden sweeps of light across doorways and honeyed wooden floors. When I looked at them, I thought of her and Grandpa on their deck in Woodacre in the late afternoon, the smell of wild grasses in the sun.

"I like her Time series," I said.

She nodded. "Very meditative. I really appreciate her photography. The shots of her children especially."

I knew the ones she was talking about. The pictures of my dad and Aunt Tammy when they were kids in Colorado. "Yeah, I've seen those," I said. "People say they're not about her children, but about the way we think about childhood."

The woman's smile broadened. "You know a lot about Joan West's work. Are you a fan?"

I realized I had put myself on a path toward directly lying about who I was, rather than simply skirting the truth with careful omissions. It was a little exciting.

The woman's smile softened as she looked at me, as if she knew I wasn't telling the whole truth, but she wouldn't push me. It was as if we were co-conspirators, and the thought of conspiring with her sent a nervous thrill through me. I wondered who she was.

"Yes," I said. "I'm a fan."

She nodded as if she had expected me to say that. "Joan's been a big influence on a lot of artists here in the Bay Area. She should be way more famous than she is."

I felt shy as I asked, "Are you an artist?"

"I am," she said, as if it surprised her.

"What medium do you work in?" I'd heard my grandmother pose this question to others before, and I thought it made me sound mature.

The woman blinked, her smile disappearing for half a second before it returned. "Metal and wire. Sculpture mostly."

"Sarah! There you are."

We both looked up as my grandmother came toward us. She was wearing a purple-and-gold-patterned blouse that draped around her in some complicated way that created wings when she opened her arms for a hug. The woman sitting next to me rose to her feet and embraced her.

"Thank you so much for coming," she said.

"Of course I came. I'm so happy for you." My grandmother saw me watching and said, "I see you've met—"

"Hi, Joan," I said quickly, standing up and smoothing down my dress. I flushed as my grandmother gave me a funny look.

The woman grinned. "Yes, I think I've met one of your biggest fans," she said.

My grandmother seemed a little puzzled. "Aria, this is Sarah Franco. She's the artist featured here tonight."

Metal and wire, she had said. I was embarrassed that I hadn't put that together.

Sarah extended her hand to me. "Hello, Aria. Nice to meet you officially."

"Likewise," I said. Her palm was rough, her fingers a little scratchy.

I wondered whether my grandmother was going to explain who

I was. We didn't look related because she was white and I'm half Asian, although there was something similar about the shapes of our faces.

"I'd better go get ready," Sarah said. "I have to make a speech."

My grandmother squeezed her shoulder. "I'm looking forward to it. And congratulations."

"Thanks. Nice talking to you, Aria," Sarah said, and then she headed off toward the front of the garage.

My grandmother looked at me with an amused smile. "Shall we go up front and get a good spot? I want to be sure to see everything." She put her arm around my shoulders, and I knew she didn't mind that I'd called her Joan, and maybe she even thought it was funny.

During Sarah's speech, she thanked my grandmother for mentoring her over the past five years, for pushing her to go beyond her comfort zone. The audience applauded when Sarah pointed out my grandmother standing beside me, and when she stepped forward to acknowledge their applause with a smile and a wave, she looked beautiful and wise. I felt a keen sense of pride to be related to her—to *Joan West*. She was my grandmother, yes, but she was more than that, and it seemed inadequate to call her by a name that said nothing about her accomplishments.

From that night on, she was Joan to me. When my dad told me I was disrespecting her, my grandmother laughed and said, "We're on a first-name basis now."

Barely a couple of weeks after my dad and I returned to Massachusetts, Grandpa was diagnosed with fourth-stage pancreatic cancer. It all went so fast.

In mid-August, we flew back to California. Dad took a leave of absence from Wellesley College, where he taught. Aunt Tammy and her family came up from Pasadena, and we all stayed in a vacation rental near Woodacre. A hospital bed was set up in my grandparents' bedroom and Grandpa spent more and more time there, while nurses came and went twice a day.

Dad and Aunt Tammy kept scurrying back and forth—from the kitchen to the bedroom to the grocery store and back—as if they were trying their hardest to hold the world together with their bare hands. Joan sat at Grandpa's bedside and read to him, everything from the latest astronomy papers to his battered old Robert Heinlein science fiction novels. Sometimes I sat with them, and Joan's voice would lull me into a half-waking dream of rocket ships and the boys who flew them.

Grandpa died in September. It was one of those perfect, golden days in Northern California, the air warm and weightless, the light like slowly melting butterscotch. Dad had made plans to grill steak for dinner because Grandpa said he wanted some, even though he wasn't eating much anymore. He never ate it.

The memorial took place at the Unitarian church in Berkeley that my grandparents had gone to in the two decades they lived there. It was full of Grandpa's former colleagues from Berkeley's astronomy department, where he'd been a professor, but plenty of Joan's friends came, too. Afterward, when I was waiting in the church vestibule for my parents, I saw Sarah Franco, the artist from the garage show. She was dressed all in black, with a black button-down shirt and polished black oxfords. She came over to me and told me she was sorry for my loss, and I realized then that she'd always known I was Joan's granddaughter.

2013

D ad and I took a 6:00 a.m. flight from Boston to San Francisco. Our seats weren't together because he'd bought the tickets last minute, but I was relieved to be alone. I got a window way in the back, only a few rows up from the toilets.

As soon as the plane took off, I reclined my seat and stuffed the tiny airplane pillow against the edge of the window, trying to make myself comfortable enough to sleep. The plane smelled like bathroom cleaner and somebody's egg-and-cheese bagel. The constant hum of recycled air seemed to press against me, pushing me deeper into the hard plastic window shade. I began to imagine my body passing through it, envisioning my skin and bones as individual cells and then singular atoms and then only photons—energy itself. And each photon, each tiny particle of light, could be instantly inside the wall of the airplane and simultaneously beyond it. My whole body could be suddenly outside, thirty thousand feet above the earth's surface. I imagined the whirling air around me, nitrogen and oxygen and water vapor in the clouds and in me, the dawning sunlight scattered by microscopic particles of water and the atoms of my body.

I slept in that unsettled way I often do on planes, half dreaming, half awake. I still remember one of those dreams. It has stayed with me my entire life. I'm in the woods; the trees seem too tall to be real. I look up and up and can't see their tops, only their feathery, dark green needles draping down and down. My grandmother is there, wearing a smock splashed in gold and blue and green. She holds a brush loaded with fuchsia paint and begins to sweep it across her torso, as if she is her own canvas. She notices that I'm standing nearby and raises her eyes to look at me.

She says: *Don't worry, something will happen.*

And then I'm on a beach, and someone is handing me a shell. Pink and white, coiled tight.

I say: *Is this something?*

The airplane shuddered and I jolted awake, and the captain came over the speaker and said, "We've reached some expected turbulence over the Rockies, so I've turned on the fasten seat belt sign. Please return to your seats."

The pillow slid down from the window. A bright white line shone from the bottom of the shade, and I inched it up, wincing against the sunlight. When my eyes adjusted, I looked out and down, and far below me the Rocky Mountains looked the way they do on topographical maps: wrinkled blue and brown, unreal.

If only, I thought. If only this wasn't real.

Morning traffic was heavy as we left the San Francisco Airport rental car center, and Dad was silent as Google Maps navigated us onto the freeway. I stared out the window as we passed Colma and Daly City, continued up the stop-and-start length of 19th Avenue, then through Golden Gate Park and the Presidio. Finally, we reached the Golden Gate Bridge, glowing red in the sun. To the right, the glittering bay and Alcatraz; to the left, the blue of the Pacific beyond the suspension lines, and then we were swallowed by the rainbow entry of the Waldo Tunnel through the Marin Hills.

I wasn't supposed to be here. I was supposed to spend the summer on Martha's Vineyard with my friends, not in the remote woods of Marin County with my grandmother. The interior of the car suddenly felt airless, and I fumbled for the button to unroll the window. Traffic noise and warm dry air blasted inside. It smelled like Northern California: brown grass and sunshine and something else, some kind of tree or plant that grew here, and I remembered Grandpa taking me out on his precarious rooftop deck on late-summer nights to look at the stars. An ache inside me. He died five years ago, and I still missed him.

"Smells like California," Dad said loudly over the rushing wind. They were the first words he'd spoken since we got in the car.

I glanced at him, and maybe because I had been thinking about Grandpa, I noticed how Dad looked like him. His eyebrows were bushy in the same way. "Yeah," I replied.

Dad gave me an eager smile. "You always loved visiting here."

I knew he was trying to get me to feel better about this summer, but I didn't feel better and I didn't want to pretend like I did.

"It's too bad we never visited here with your mother," he said. "She has family here, too."

I felt like I must have known this before, but even so, it surprised me. "Who?" I asked.

"Some cousins. They're out in the East Bay, but I think they used to live in Chinatown." He looked at me encouragingly. "You should ask your mom."

Now I knew what he was trying to do: get me to call her. But she had a phone, too. She could call me if she wanted.

We exited 101 North at Sir Francis Drake Boulevard, which we took all the way to Woodacre. The road passed through well-manicured suburbs with relatively tasteful strip malls at first, but bit by bit the strip malls became more worn-out, and the trees and hedges became

13

wilder and less trimmed. We drove past Safeway, the last supermarket before Woodacre, and Sir Francis Drake High School, and then we went through the little hippie town of Fairfax, and at last the road broke out into open space. Brown hills dotted with green oak trees rose up on either side as the road wound between them, and all was laid bare beneath the wide blue sky. It felt like an entirely different world from the New England we'd just come from, where one town merges right into the next, and the sky always seems to be held at bay by trees and buildings.

Just past Spirit Rock Meditation Center, Dad turned left onto Railroad Avenue, which led into Woodacre. It was barely a town—a post office and a market and that was about it. The road narrowed and lost its center stripes, curling up and around the hills. The air smelled of sunbaked wood and grass, and the wind had hushed so that we could hear the birds singing. At last we rounded the final bend, and Dad pulled up behind my grandmother's car, an old Honda Civic, in a gravel-covered pullout at the side of the road. Just ahead of the pullout was the green-painted gate that led up to the cottage.

After Grandpa died, I thought my grandmother might move back to Berkeley, where her friends were, but she had stayed. She had adopted a dog—a black lab that she named Analemma—and told everyone she preferred the remoteness of Woodacre.

Now I climbed out of the car and followed my dad to the trunk, where we pulled out two big suitcases and two backpacks. Dad was only staying for a couple of days before flying north to the Deer Bay Writers' Colony in Washington, where he was spending the rest of the summer. He was supposed to finish his second novel there, but it was six years late by now, so I had my doubts. As I lugged my suitcase toward the gate, the reality of my summer began to sink in. I was staying here. *Here.*

I unlatched the gate and clumsily shoved the suitcase through. I heard a dog start barking. Analemma.

"I'll get that," Dad said. "Will you take the backpacks?"

He held them out, and I took them without meeting his eyes, but I saw the expression on his face: that sad hesitance he'd worn almost continually since that day a month ago.

I turned away and started up the brick steps to the house. It was built on the side of a hill, so you had to climb up a meandering, mossy brick path to access it. Along the way were several terraced gardens planted with ferns and hostas and flowers that could grow in the shade. A wheelbarrow filled with a tray of flowers was parked beside one of the garden plots, and a water bottle was perched on a nearby bench as if the gardener had stepped away for a moment.

Around the next bend the house came into view. The front door was painted turquoise blue, and it was opening already. Analemma shot outside, a blur of shiny black fur, and I had to drop the backpacks on the brick patio and kneel down to greet her, slobbery tongue and soft floppy ears and wriggly muscle.

"Hey, hey," I said, laughing.

"Analemma, come," my grandmother said. Ana's ears perked up and she glanced back at Joan for an instant as if she were contemplating disobeying her, but Joan snapped her fingers, and Ana went. Then my grandmother smiled at me and held out her arms. "Aria," she said. She was in her seventies, but you wouldn't have known it by the way she looked. She was wearing faded jeans rolled up at the ankles, Birkenstocks, and a loose red-and-orange peasant blouse. Her gray hair was trimmed in a short, stylish cut that revealed dangling bronze earrings.

I got to my feet and let her enfold me in a hug. "Hi, Joan." She smelled like coffee and lemon-scented soap, and as my arms went around her I felt a loosening within me, and for a horrifying second,

I was afraid I would start to cry. I suppressed the urge, but when I pulled back, my grandmother gave me a sympathetic look and kissed me on the forehead as if I were a little girl.

"We're going to have a good summer," she said.

I didn't have time to respond, because behind me Dad was arriving with my big suitcase, and then Analemma bolted forward, and Dad had to squat down to greet her. Joan told me I would be staying in the guest room. Dad would have to take the sofa bed for the couple of nights he'd be here.

Because the house was built on a hillside, the interior was on three levels, with most of the living space on the second floor. I carried my suitcase upstairs and rolled it through the living room, with its vaulted pine ceiling, Joan's painting *Southern Cross* on one wall, and into the guest room. The double bed was covered in a patchwork quilt that looked like it was about a hundred years old; I recognized it from every previous visit. Over the bed were three black-and-white family photos, though they didn't look like anyone else's family photos.

There was one of Dad and Aunt Tammy as kids, double exposed so that their faces appeared to be echoed inside each other's. One shot of Grandpa and Dad, when Dad was a teen, both looking directly at the camera with exactly the same curious expression on their faces. And a self-portrait of my grandmother, taken when she was much younger, her reflection floating in a window.

I heard Dad and Joan and Analemma coming upstairs, and Joan called, "Come and have lunch."

Analemma dashed into the guest room and bumped my hand with her wet nose. "You want me to come?" I said, rubbing her ears with my fingers. She gave a soft woof, so I followed her out into the living room.

Dad had left his suitcase by the cold woodstove across from the purple velvet sofa. In the kitchen, lunch had been laid out on the round wooden table: a big bowl of salad with olive oil and balsamic vinegar, a take-out rotisserie chicken, a loaf of sourdough bread, and a pitcher of iced tea.

"Help yourself to food and let's go sit on the deck," Joan said, taking out plates and silverware.

I had only eaten a stale bagel on the plane, and as I watched Dad cut into the chicken, I realized I was starving. I piled salad and chicken onto a plate and tore into the bread, and Joan gave me a glass of iced tea. I took my lunch out to the deck, which opened off the kitchen and had a view of the Marin Hills through the trees. Gently rolling golden-brown waves beneath a powder-blue sky. It was warm but not too hot, and the air was dry. Northern California summer.

"Matty, you sure you don't want to stay a bit longer?" Joan asked as she sat down.

"Sorry, I can't," Dad said between bites of his salad. "The timing has been difficult this year."

He was being diplomatic, but I knew it was my fault.

"I have to get some work done today, too," he said. "Do you mind if I use your studio to write?"

Grandpa had built an art studio for my grandmother on the highest part of the property, so that she could get as much natural light as possible. But after Grandpa died, she had moved most of her work into the house, into his office, which was on the third floor along with their bedroom.

"I haven't been in there for a while," Joan said. "It's probably covered in dust."

"I don't mind the dust. I just need a room." Dad took a swig of iced tea and looked at me. "Ari, you need anything else before I get to work?"

"No."

"We can talk about your plans for the summer," Joan said.

In the distance I heard the front door close, followed by footsteps crossing the wooden floors. Analemma, who was lying in a pool of sunlight on the deck, thumped her tail against the floor as a person in dirt-stained cargo shorts and a baseball cap came out onto the deck.

"All finished?" Joan asked.

I figured this was the missing gardener.

"Yep. All done."

I gave the gardener a second look and realized she was a woman, although if you didn't pay too close attention it would be easy to mistake her for a man. She was boyish, with short hair beneath her Giants baseball cap, dressed in what looked like boys' clothes. She was probably in her twenties. Both her forearms were dark with tattoos; I couldn't make them out, but the designs looked intricate.

"Steph, this is my son, Matthew, and my granddaughter, Aria," Joan said. "Matty, Aria, this is Steph." Joan went back into the kitchen, where I saw her rummaging through her purse.

"Nice to meet you, sir," Steph said to my dad, extending her hand to him as if they were man to man. As she came closer I saw some of the tattoos more clearly. A snake, maybe, or fish—something with scales.

"You helping out my mother?" Dad asked.

"I do a little yard work," Steph said.

"She's good," Joan called from inside. "You know all my neighbors want to hire you. You could have a monopoly on Woodacre yards if you wanted."

"Thanks," Steph said.

Joan came back with a check and handed it to her. "Same time in two weeks?"

"I'll be here," Steph said. She glanced at me. "Nice to meet you, too. Your grandma's told me a lot about you."

I felt the tiniest bit self-conscious. "Oh yeah? You know she lies."

Joan's mouth quirked into an impish grin. "Everything I said was true," she insisted.

Steph smiled and pocketed the check. "I wouldn't doubt it. I'll see you in two weeks." She gave me a quick look as she left, as if she wasn't quite sure what to make of me.

It wasn't like I was struck by lightning or anything, but I remember that last look, that fraction of a moment before she left. I remember thinking *I wish you were a boy*, because then my summer would be a lot more interesting.

This is why I was spending the summer in Woodacre instead of on Martha's Vineyard: A boy took some topless photos of me and posted them on Tumblr. The photos got around, and somebody spray-painted *slut* on my locker, which meant the school counselor got nosy and called me in to her office. I wouldn't tell her what the graffiti was about, so she poked around on her own and found the photos somehow, and then she called my dad and told him.

I came home from school one afternoon to find my dad waiting for me in the living room, where he sat me down and forced me to tell him about the whole thing. Even though I warned him not to look at the photos, I think he did. He couldn't meet my eyes for days after that.

That might have been the end of it, except my dad then called my mom in Vienna, where she was playing the title role in *Tosca*. My parents divorced when I was six, and I suppose it was my dad's duty as a parent to tell her what had happened, but the second he told me he was calling her, I knew it wasn't going to end well. I had to listen to her yelling at me over the phone about how I had no respect for myself and she was ashamed of me.

"It could've been worse. At least it's just my top," I said flippantly.

"I don't know how you can joke about this," my mom said. "How could you let your boyfriend take pictures like that?"

He's not my boyfriend, I thought. But I said, "You don't understand."

"Then explain it to me."

But I couldn't.

After that call, my summer plans completely unraveled, and before I knew it, I was on that plane to Woodacre, to spend the summer before college under my grandmother's supervision.

I'm telling this all wrong. I should start over.

The boy's name was Jacob Krieger. He took the photos during Haley's big party in mid-May. Haley Pierce was one of my best friends, along with Tasha Lewis. I'd known Tasha since second grade, and Haley since she moved to Wellesley in seventh grade. In eighth grade, we became a trio. Because Tasha was Black, I was Asian, and Haley was white, Haley's parents treated us like the multicultural promised land and were always encouraging us to do things together. But the three of us moved in somewhat different circles in school (Haley was a swimmer, Tasha was a debater, and I did Science Olympiad), although there was always an overlapping area—the intersection of our Venn diagram. In March of our senior year, Tasha and Haley had a falling-out I didn't understand, and for a while we no longer overlapped. Our intersection was empty.

Then Haley had the idea to throw a house party before prom and senior week—the last party of our high school years, the kind we'd all remember at reunions to come. And we intersected again. It felt like old times, with the three of us lying on Haley's king-sized bed, making a YouTube playlist on our phones while talking about who to invite.

Jacob was an automatic choice, along with all the guys on the lacrosse team, because they overlapped with Haley's swim team circle.

He had a reputation for being a partyer and a commitment-phobe, but in that charming way that guys can get away with. He looked kind of like Chris Hemsworth, but less built. I knew who he was, but before the party, I'd never given him much thought. It wasn't that he was out of my league; our leagues were simply different.

The day of the party, I walked over to Haley's to help set up. Her house was only about a mile away from mine, but it was in a different universe from the condo my dad and I lived in behind Central Street. We dealt with drafty windows and old doors that either stuck or didn't quite close. Haley lived in a mansion on a hill. It looked like a classic white colonial with black shutters, but it had been extensively remodeled. Everything inside was new and seemed to be made of marble or glass.

When I arrived at the foot of the long driveway, I saw Tasha's red-and-black Mini Cooper already parked at the top. It was early evening on a Saturday in May, and it finally felt like spring. It was just warm enough to wear shorts, and the trees were thick with white and pink blossoms. I headed for the gate to the back patio, where I knew Haley and Tasha would be setting up for the party. Haley's mom had taken us to Whole Foods the day before, and she'd paid for huge amounts of guacamole and chips, fancy cheese and crackers, organic sodas, and bottled water. Haley's mom had even gotten us a bunch of prosecco to celebrate our upcoming graduation. We expected people to sneak in beer and liquor, and we expected Haley's parents to look the other way. As long as nobody drove drunk, it would be fine. We were seniors and deserved to let off some steam.

As I came around the side of the house, I saw Haley and Tasha before they saw me. They sat facing each other on the edges of two loungers. Haley was saying something and leaning toward Tasha, one hand outstretched. Tasha was looking at her through her oversized sunglasses, so I couldn't see her eyes, but there was a weird stiffness to her face. I wondered if they'd had a fight. But then she caught sight of me and jumped up.

"There you are!" Tasha said, looking relieved. She pulled a bottle of prosecco from the giant cooler nearby. "Let's have a toast!"

"Hey, Ari," Haley said. She got up and grabbed three red Solo cups from the party supplies, passing them out.

Tasha poured in generous slugs of fizzing prosecco and said, "To graduating."

"To partying," Haley said.

"To us," I said. We knocked our plastic cups together and drank, but I noticed that Haley and Tasha avoided looking at each other.

The party officially started at eight o'clock, but it didn't really fill up till almost nine. A lot of people came, spreading out over the backyard and going in and out of the basement, although "basement" was a misnomer. It was an entire floor dedicated to entertainment that opened directly onto a lower patio. There was a kitchenette with a wet bar stocked with prosecco and the sneaked-in booze, a home theater with velvet seats where music videos played on a big screen, a game room with Ping-Pong and foosball tables for increasingly drunken gaming, and a lounge area with squishy sectionals for conversations that would lead to hookups.

By the time Jacob noticed me, I was pretty drunk. I left Tasha and Haley dancing in the home theater while I went to get some water. As I was digging in the fridge, Jacob asked me to grab a bottle for him, too, and then we had to edge around the crowd in the kitchenette, and we ended up trapped in a corner of the lounge watching one of Jacob's teammates attempt to down way too much beer way too fast.

Jacob leaned over and said in my ear, "I always wanted to kiss you."

I almost wasn't sure I'd heard him correctly, but the sensation of his breath on my ear was unmistakable. A shiver went through me involuntarily.

I could have said *You're lying, you've never thought about me before this minute.* I could have said *That's a terrible line.* I turned toward him, intending to give him a withering look, but the expression on his face stopped me. A small grin on his mouth, a sparkle in his eye, all mischief.

"You're always so mysterious, Aria West," he said.

"I'm not mysterious," I said, but I felt flattered. I wanted to be mysterious.

"I've known you since, what, sixth grade? How come we've never hooked up?"

I thought I should be offended by his question, but the feeling of flattery only seemed to intensify. In the lounge, they were chanting for his lacrosse buddy to drink faster. Strains of "Blurred Lines" floated out from the home theater. I didn't say anything in response, which only made Jacob lean close to me again, his mouth practically on my neck as he whispered, "We don't have to talk if you don't want."

He must have felt the shiver go through me again. I was a little irritated by my body for responding when I wasn't sure if I wanted it to, and then I thought, *Why not?* This could be the twist of the night for me—even the twist of the year. Ever since sophomore year, I had made it my rule to never hook up with anyone from school. I knew that was one reason Jacob thought I was mysterious. But now, school was almost over.

I didn't say anything, but I turned my face to his, and I let him kiss me.

There were a couple of guest rooms tucked in the back of the basement. We found one of the empty ones and locked the door behind us. I pulled his shirt off before we even made it to the bed. I was wearing a white off-shoulder tee printed with a gold tiger, with a lacy red bra underneath. His fingers fumbled a little on the clasp, so I took it off for him. His skin was warm and his body was firmly muscled, and I wanted him physically in a way I hadn't felt in a while. There was something transactional about it, but that's what made it work for me. I was under no illusions that he'd want something more with me, and I didn't want anything more from him. Just this experience, on this bed, his body above and against me, my hands pulling him in.

When I reached for the waistband of his jeans, he told me to wait while he got out a condom. But when I lay back against the pillow, he had his phone in his hand—he must have taken it out of his pocket—and he snapped a bunch of photos.

"What are you doing?" I said, putting a hand up over my face. Even then it didn't occur to me to cover my breasts.

"You look so beautiful," he said. "I just want to capture the moment."

The day after the party, the photos appeared.

Haley sent me the link. I was at home, watching mindless TV to get through my hangover, when her text made my phone vibrate.

Someone sent me this. You're in these pics. WTF?

I clicked through without thinking, and when the first photo loaded, a shock of heat went through me. I sat up abruptly. There I was on the bed in Haley's basement, one arm over my head, looking straight at the camera as if I'd posed for it. There were four photos, almost identical, as if he'd kept his finger on the red shutter button and snapped them off within a second or two.

The number of likes on the post clicked up as I was looking. The heat that had flushed my body seemed to pulse through me now, my blood surging with each heartbeat.

I had told him to put the phone down before we continued, and he had. But it hadn't occurred to me to ask him to delete these.

A cool, snarky voice inside my head commented, *At least you look good*. And I did. I had sexy hair and bedroom eyes, my lips were puffy from kissing him, and my breasts looked fantastic. But as the likes kept going up, a nauseating feeling took hold of me, a groundless, falling sensation that made me think I was about to vomit. I ran to the bathroom and gagged while bending over the toilet. My phone clattered onto the tile floor, barely missing the toilet bowl. Two hundred and fifty-three likes and counting.

Everything happened pretty quickly after that. I was supposed to go to Martha's Vineyard with Haley after graduation. Her parents had invited me to stay with them at their Edgartown house through the Fourth of July. By then, Tasha would be back from her marine ecology internship in Thailand. Her parents had a summer house in Oak Bluffs, also on the Vineyard, and I was going to stay with them till August. Then I was going to California to see my grandmother for a couple of weeks before coming back to get ready for college.

My dad had been relieved when the plan came together, because he'd been accepted at the Deer Bay Writers' Colony in Washington State, and he wanted to be there the entire summer. Martha's Vineyard was the perfect plan. I'd have one last summer with my friends before we all scattered to different colleges in the fall. Haley was going to NYU, Tasha to Spelman, and I was starting at MIT.

But the day after *slut* was painted on my locker, Haley's mom called my dad to say that unfortunately they were not going to be able to host me on the Vineyard. Haley told me it was because her mom had seen the pictures, recognized the seashell lamp on the nightstand next to me, and realized the photo had been taken in their basement.

I tried to convince my dad I could stay at home by myself until it was time to go to Oak Bluffs with Tasha, but then Tasha called and explained that her mom was taking her to France for a couple of weeks after Thailand, so I couldn't stay with them anymore.

"I'm really sorry," Tasha said gently.

And just like that, my parents decided I'd spend the whole summer with my grandmother. No amount of arguing could convince them that I would be fine on my own, that I hadn't done anything wrong.

Jacob didn't seem to get punished at all. In fact, he only seemed to get more popular. Somehow the fact that he had managed to get my shirt off made him someone the other guys looked up to, but the fact that I had taken my shirt off made me a slut.

Officially, of course, the school condemned what happened. But there was also a kind of collective shrug. Jacob and I were both eighteen. We were two weeks away from graduating. The photos had been taken after school hours, off campus. They would have disciplined whoever defaced my locker, but nobody was talking. Maybe if I'd made more of a fuss about it—maybe if I showed school administrators the nasty messages I got after Jacob posted the photos—maybe then they would have done something. But I didn't want to show anyone. I just wanted it all to go away, and the best way to make it go away was to say nothing.

I'm still telling this wrong. You have to understand something. I grew up in Wellesley, surrounded by all these rich people, but I was never one of them. It's not like we were poor—we weren't—but my friends were *rich*. Haley's dad ran a hedge fund and had a collection of Rolexes; her mom headed up a wealthy arts organization that gave money to struggling artists. Tasha's dad was a partner at a law firm who was always traveling to London or Geneva; her mom was a biotech executive who wore the most amazing suits I'd ever seen.

They all knew that my dad was a professor and a sort-of famous author, and that my mom was an opera singer, even though she was never around to impress them. That had some cachet, especially with Haley's mom, but my artsy, educated parents could not make up for the fact that I didn't have the money to buy Birkin bags or take spontaneous weekend trips to Paris. And I definitely didn't have the resources to summer on Martha's Vineyard without their charity.

They always made me feel like a guest in their homes, but as a guest, I was easily uninvited.

The morning my dad left for the writers' colony, I pretended to sleep late, until there was barely enough time to say goodbye on the doorstep before he drove off in the rental car. Joan asked if I wanted breakfast, but I mumbled that I would shower first. The guest bathroom was painted buttercup yellow, and there was a skylight in the ceiling that let in the sun, but when I stepped under the hot spray, I closed my eyes so I could be in the dark.

I washed my hair with shampoo from the near-empty St. Ives bottle in the basket hanging from the showerhead. The sweet, buttery smell brought me back to previous visits here. Christmas with the whole family—Aunt Tammy and Uncle Brian and their twins, Luke and Noah, running up the stairs eager to open presents. Summer evenings with Dad and Joan on the deck, grilling tri-tip beneath the redwoods. And earlier, Grandpa greeting me with his giant swinging hugs.

I didn't want to miss them, and I didn't want to be here. I felt displaced and yet cornered.

I remembered Jacob's face afterward, so pleased with himself.

There was a weird, frantic fluttering in my chest.

I scrubbed the shampoo out of my hair, raking my nails across my scalp, the sudsy water running over my tightly closed eyes. The rich scent made me gag. I needed new shampoo.

The Safeway parking lot was laid out in diagonal rows that made it difficult to figure out how to approach the entrance. I ended up parking Joan's Honda out by the edge, facing Sir Francis Drake Boulevard. When I got out of the car, the dry summer heat radiated up from the asphalt with an almost physical force. I headed quickly for the store, plunging into the freezing air-conditioning.

I'd been to this Safeway on previous visits, and everything was the same as before, right down to the same eighties power ballads playing in the background. I was only here for shampoo, but I took my time getting to the toiletry aisle. I didn't have anything better to do. I was finally narrowing in on the shampoo section when my phone dinged. I pulled it out of my purse to find a text from Tasha.

Haven't heard from you in a while. You in Cali now? Everything OK?

I felt that panicky feeling in my chest again. I shoved my phone back into my purse.

After the slut situation, Tasha had been so supportive, reassuring me over and over that it wasn't my fault. But she still canceled our summer; she was still going to France. She told me it had nothing to do with what happened with me. She swore that her mom just wanted to take her to Paris for some mother-daughter time before college.

What would it be like to have a mother who wanted to do that?

I didn't know what to say to Tasha. I plucked a bottle of Pantene from the shelf and left without even smelling the other options.

At the checkout, only one cash register was open, and there was a line. I pulled a *Cosmopolitan* off the rack to distract myself. An article about sexual positions of the ancients featured a thin, white model draped in part of a toga, her lips painted bright red. She looked straight at the camera, just as I had.

"Excuse me, miss?" A woman in a Safeway vest was gesturing to me. "I'll take you over here."

I followed her to the next checkout lane and realized I was still carrying the magazine. She looked at me, clutching the shampoo and *Cosmopolitan.*

"Are you ready?" she asked a little impatiently. She had brownish-blond hair pulled back in a ponytail and a name tag that read LISA, MANAGER.

"Sorry," I said. I put the magazine on the conveyor belt along with the shampoo. I hadn't intended to buy it, but now it felt weird to put it back.

As Lisa rang up my purchases, the woman who did Joan's yard work showed up—it looked like she had come straight to my lane from the entrance—and said, "Lis, you ready?" She sort of did a double take when she saw me and said, "Oh, hey."

"Hi," I said to Steph.

Lisa shot Steph a puzzled look. "You know each other?"

Steph said, "I do her grandma's yard—you know, Joan West out in Woodacre."

"Oh." Lisa shrugged. "Do you want a bag?" she asked me. "It's ten cents."

"Um, that's okay," I said.

She handed me the shampoo, *Cosmo*, and a receipt.

"Thanks." I stepped out of the aisle and started to head toward the exit, but Steph was still there. "Nice to see you," I said. I didn't want to appear rude, but I didn't want to be in the Safeway anymore either.

"Yeah. Hey, hang on," Steph said. She glanced at Lisa. "Are you ready to go soon?"

"Maybe five, ten minutes," Lisa answered. "There's a backup. Cheryl didn't come in today."

"I'll meet you outside then." Steph looked at me. "You have five minutes?"

I hesitated, but I had all day. "Sure."

"I'll walk you out," Steph said.

We headed for the exit and I flipped my sunglasses back on. As we left the store, my phone chimed again. I ignored it and asked, "What's up?"

She gestured to a bench nearby in the shade of the entryway and we both sat down.

"I wanted to talk to you about your grandma," she said. "You're gonna be here all summer, right?"

"Unfortunately."

She grinned. "I got the impression this was a last-minute kind of thing."

"Yeah." I wondered what Joan had told her. Did Steph know why I was here? The idea of her knowing made me uncomfortable.

"I know your grandma's pretty healthy, especially for someone her age, but I worry about her, you know?" Steph said.

This surprised me. "I thought you just did her gardening."

"Yeah, I do that, but I help her out with other stuff sometimes. If she needs something fixed, she'll call me and I'll come climb a ladder to change a light bulb or whatever. And sometimes I help her move her canvases or set things up."

There was something in the tone of her voice that made me apprehensive. "Just tell me," I said. "Did something happen?"

She was turned toward me, right arm along the back of the bench, and now she crossed her left ankle over her right knee. She was wearing cargo shorts again, and her legs weren't shaved. For some reason, noticing that made me notice—really notice—the rest of her. Her hair was dark brown and cut very short on the sides, longer on top like a guy. She had little black gauges in her earlobes, and up along her right ear a line of silver studs. There was an easy boyishness to the way she moved. Yesterday I had thought she was cute but dismissed her because she was a girl. Today I just thought she was cute—exactly the way I might feel about any boy. It was confusing. I couldn't remember if I'd ever looked at another girl that way before.

"A couple months ago," she said, "I came over to help your grandma with her dishwasher. It's pretty old and sometimes it acts up. Anyway, I got there and she had totally forgotten she'd called me. I know that can happen when you get older, so I didn't think too much about it. But there have been other things—little things—but together they make me worry about her. Like, she told me she couldn't find Analemma's leash one day, which is weird because it's always on the hook by the front door. I was there that morning so I helped her look, but I only found it on accident. She'd put it in a kitchen drawer. For a while she was acting a little strange. Not only forgetful—sort of like she wasn't sure what was going on. She asked me when Matty was coming home for dinner a couple of months ago, when she knows he doesn't live here. She's better now, but I think it's a little dangerous for her out there all alone, you know?"

I realized that the tattoos on her arms were koi fish swimming in a yin-yang pattern. "She has a dog," I said. "She's not alone, exactly."

Steph gave me a strange look, as if I wasn't getting it but she didn't want to hurt my feelings. I flushed and glanced out at the Safeway parking lot. The cars were gleaming in the sun; it was getting hotter. This conversation with Steph about my grandmother was the least sexy topic I could imagine, but inside me I felt a tiny unfurling, as if a tender green shoot were turning toward the sun.

"Analemma is a great dog, but unfortunately she can't call 911," Steph said.

"You think she needs to call 911 a lot?" I said, suddenly worried.

"No, no," Steph assured me. "I just—it's that she's on her own, and she's—well, she's getting older."

I crossed my legs, and my right foot bobbed out of the shade into the sunlight. I was wearing flip-flops, and my purple toenail polish was chipped. I became aware that I was wearing stringy cutoffs and a faded blue tank top with tiny holes near the hem. And of course, even though I'd washed my hair, I'd pulled it back in a ponytail when it was still wet. I didn't look that great, and here was Steph looking at me and expecting me to be a responsible adult.

"I know," I said. I sat up, uncrossing my legs and tucking my feet beneath the bench so the chipped nail polish wasn't visible anymore. "I know she's getting older, but Joan's very independent." I saw Steph note my use of her first name. "I call her Joan. She's not really a 'grandma' type. So it's good she can ask you to come over and help her. I'm pretty impressed that she'll do even that."

"Did she tell you about her memory lapses?" Steph asked.

"No. But I'm her granddaughter. I don't think she would tell me."

"Well, now you know," Steph said gently.

"Yeah," I said. This was awkward. "Maybe I can talk to my dad about it."

"Okay. I hope it's all right that I brought this up—"

"Yo, Steph, what's taking so long?"

A woman was walking toward us from the parking lot. She was stocky, wearing a striped rugby shirt, knee-length baggy shorts, and sneakers. Her black hair was in a ponytail pulled through the back of a baseball cap.

Steph glanced up. "Lisa's running late."

The woman stopped a few feet away from us and flashed me a grin. "Hey," she said. "How do you know Steph?"

"This is Aria West," Steph said before I could answer. "She's Joan West's granddaughter."

"Oh, the artist lady," the woman said, nodding.

I was about to ask how she knew about my grandmother when Steph said, "Aria, this is Mel Lopez."

"Hi," I said.

"I hope Steph's not boring you with all her xeriscaping theories," Mel said. "She's a little obsessed."

I glanced at Steph, who cracked a tiny grin.

"No, she's not boring me," I said.

The Safeway doors whooshed open and Lisa emerged, looking a bit frazzled. She had taken off her Safeway vest and was pulling a pack of cigarettes out of her back pocket. As she lit up, Steph went over to her and rubbed a hand over her back. "You okay?" she asked.

Lisa frowned and nodded. "Just busy."

The way they stood together—Steph leaning in, Lisa letting her get that close—made me realize they were a couple. It jolted me a little, a tiny jab of disappointment.

Mel sat down next to me, taking Steph's place on the bench. "Hey, what are you doing Wednesday night?" Mel asked.

"Um, I don't know, why?"

"Steph's performing at the open mic at the Bolinas Café in Fairfax. You wanna come?"

"Mel, leave her alone," Steph said. "She doesn't want to come to some open mic night."

Mel looked at me almost slyly. "You sure?"

Lisa stood there smoking and staring at me, and then she slid her free hand into Steph's, their fingers lacing together.

"Where are you from?" Lisa asked.

"Massachusetts," I answered. "I'm visiting for the summer."

Lisa looked a little confused. "But originally, I mean?"

A prickle of irritation went through me. "I was born in Boston."

"We better get going," Steph said abruptly. "Thanks for talking, Aria."

"Sure," I said.

Lisa still looked confused, but she let Steph pull her toward the parking lot.

Mel stood up and asked, "So you want to come with us on Wednesday? Steph's got a new song."

"You don't have to come," Steph called back.

Mel waved off Steph's comment. "Come on, don't make me be the third wheel again. Only you can save me."

Mel was joking, but there was a wicked sparkle in her eyes, a challenge I didn't quite understand. I glanced at Steph, who looked a bit self-conscious.

"I don't know if I'll have a car," I hedged.

"We could pick you up," Mel said.

"Oh no," I said quickly. "I'm all the way out in—"

"Woodacre, yeah," Mel said. "It's not that far from Fairfax. I'll come get you. Steph has the address, right?"

"Um, yeah. But I don't want to make you—"

"Not a problem. What's your number?"

She already had her phone out. She was very pushy, and if a boy had been that pushy, I would've given him a fake number. But there was something flattering about Mel's interest, so I told her. I heard my phone ding after she texted me.

Lisa ground out her cigarette on the side of a nearby trash can and tossed the butt inside. "Mel, we gotta go," she said.

Mel gave me a quick grin. "Be ready at seven thirty on Wednesday."

As they walked out into the parking lot, Steph glanced back at me, mouthing the words *I'm sorry*. I wasn't sure if she was apologizing for Mel's pushiness or for Lisa's asking me where I was from originally, but I shook my head slightly. *It's okay,* I mouthed back.

Steph waved at me briefly before the three of them climbed into a dirty white VW Golf, and then I watched them leave. As soon as I saw the Golf turn onto the street, I got up and headed for Joan's car. I kept thinking about the twinge of disappointment I'd felt when I realized Steph and Lisa were together. When Lisa took Steph's hand, claiming her.

The house was too quiet when I got back from Safeway. Analemma didn't even bark when I opened the front door, but as I put away the shampoo and *Cosmopolitan*, I heard footsteps upstairs. I thought about how Steph had said she worried about my grandmother, all alone out here.

I went upstairs and knocked on the door that led to the master bedroom, which was connected to Grandpa's old office, where Joan now worked.

"Just a minute," she called.

I heard wheels rolling across the floor, and a swoosh as if a cloth had been tossed down. Then my grandmother opened the door.

I hadn't been up here in a long time, and I had a sudden memory of coming to see Grandpa on his hospital bed with the IV drip in his arm. But the hospital bed was long gone, and now only a queen-sized bed with a blue-patterned quilt faced the wall of windows. Grandpa and I used to climb through them onto the roof to gaze up at the stars. I remembered him pulling me up over the windowsill and outside, the ghost of his hand grasping mine.

I realized my grandmother was watching me. "Sorry to bother you," I said. "I didn't hear Analemma and wondered if you were home."

"My friend took her on a hike," she said. "Did you get what you needed at Safeway?"

"I ran into your gardener. Steph? And her friends Mel and Lisa." I wasn't sure if Joan knew Steph was gay, and for some reason I didn't want to say the word *girlfriend*.

"Oh, how's she doing?" Joan went through the connecting door into Grandpa's office, and I followed.

"She's fine." I definitely hadn't been in here since before Grandpa died, and I could barely remember it from back then. The room was long and narrow, with windows on three walls, and a counter had been built against the longest wall. I paused in the doorway and said, "They invited me to an open mic on Wednesday night in Fairfax. Apparently, Steph sings."

Joan looked surprised. "I had no idea. Well, you'll have to tell me all about it. Do you need to borrow my car?"

"No, they're going to pick me up." I wondered if I was supposed to run this kind of thing by Joan first. I'd stayed with her before, but never on my own, and never in this situation. "I mean, do you mind if I go?"

"Of course not. I don't expect you to stay in this house all summer." Joan sat down on a stool in front of the counter. Several rolling file cabinets were tucked beneath it, but a couple were pulled out, their drawers open to reveal hanging files. "But while you're here, maybe you could help me with something."

"Sure." I glanced at the far end of the room, where a lumpy structure on a wheeled cart was covered with a cloth. I thought Joan was going to uncover it to show me, but she gestured to a stack of folders on the counter.

"These are your grandfather's research notes from Boulder. Class lectures. Observations and research. Drafts of papers. Correspondence."

Grandpa had taught astronomy at the University of Colorado in Boulder in the seventies and early eighties, before moving to Berkeley in the mid-eighties.

"Why are you going through his notes?" I asked.

"It's part of the process. You're still planning to major in astronomy, right?"

"Yes. Well, I have to decide if I'm going to major in physics or EAPS—earth, atmospheric, and planetary sciences. MIT doesn't have a major in astronomy, technically."

She smiled. "You sound like him already. I'm hoping you can help me sort through his files."

"Of course. How do you want them sorted?"

"You have to be exact about it. I don't want class lectures mixed up with his research papers. These files look organized but they're all confused. He tended to throw all sorts of things into the nearest file even if it didn't belong there."

I picked up one of the folders and leaned against the counter while I opened it. It contained several pages of graphs with the axes labeled *wavelength* and *flux*. They depicted the spectra of stars. There was some handwritten math in the margins, and I felt a little shock as I recognized Grandpa's handwriting in the shapes of the numbers. He had held these pages just as I was holding them now.

"How do you know what pile this goes in?" I asked.

Joan pointed to the tab of the folder, which was labeled IRTF. "I think that's for Infrared Telescope Facility. That's in Hawaii. He did some observations there in the eighties. It goes in the research pile. You'll have to look through everything in that folder, though. There may be some letters in there as well, and I don't want those mixed in with the research notes."

"What are you doing with all these papers once you've sorted them?"

"Something new," Joan said. "You can take the files downstairs and sort them there."

I looked up, and across from me the wall was covered with

black-and-white photos. I recognized some of the people in them. "Is that Grandpa? And you?"

"Yes."

I went to get a closer look. They were a lot younger in these pictures. Grandpa looked even younger than my dad, and Joan's hair was in a sixties-style flip in a few.

"Did you take all these?" I asked.

"No, but I took most of them." She came to stand beside me. "That's your grandpa in college, around when we first met. That's just a snapshot. I didn't really take up photography until after your dad and Tammy were born." She moved to a section of the wall by the door and pointed to a photo of Grandpa in which he was partially framed by an open doorway. "This is Russ in Boulder, at his office. 1972. One of the first pictures I made with my Rolleiflex."

This photo did look different from the earlier ones. It was somehow both more composed and more spontaneous. I realized the photos must be in chronological order, because my grandparents got younger as I moved to the left. I stopped at a picture of a nude woman lying on the floor, her body covered in streaks of dark paint. I looked closer; her face looked familiar.

"That's me in the sixties," Joan said. "I was living in New York then, and one of my friends recruited me to help with a performance art piece. He had me cover myself in paint and roll around on a canvas." Joan shrugged. "It was pretty derivative, but the photos were interesting. That's probably when I first became interested in photography." She gave me a sly look. "My parents were scandalized. They thought I went to art school to paint nice little pictures of fruit."

I couldn't imagine her painting nice pictures of fruit, but seeing her in this nude photo—even if it was art—was just as weird. She saw the expression on my face and laughed.

"I was only involved in those performances a few times. Then

I got married to Russ and we moved to Cornell—he had a postdoc there for a few years." She went to a photo of herself and Grandpa standing on a bridge, his arm around her. In the picture she had one hand extended as if to direct whoever the photographer was, and now she reached out and touched her image with a fingertip. "This is from Cornell. I was painting abstracts then, but once I had your dad and Tammy, I didn't have enough time for that. I could take pictures, though, and develop them when the kids were asleep. By the time they were old enough that I could get back to painting, the art world had changed. I changed." She went back to the stool and sat down again. She seemed a little tired. "Everything changes. That's unavoidable. I know you don't like the way your summer plans changed—"

"It's fine," I said quickly, but she held up her hand.

"Hang on. I'm only going to bring this up once. I'm not sure I agree with your parents' decision to send you here for the summer, but I'm not your parents. I know you'd rather be with your friends than with me."

"That's not true," I said unconvincingly.

"I know it doesn't mean you don't love me," Joan said dryly. "But I'm your grandmother, and even though I'm probably the hippest, coolest grandmother there is, I know if I were eighteen years old I would not want to spend my summer being chaperoned by an old lady."

Her matter-of-fact tone made me ashamed. "I'm sorry," I said. "I've been a jerk about being here."

"You don't need to apologize to me. I understand. But you're here now. I know this isn't the summer you planned for, but I for one am glad to have the company."

She spoke lightly, but it reminded me of my conversation with Steph. "You know," I said, "I was wondering . . ." I trailed off, unsure of how to proceed. I felt as if I were pretending to be a grown-up.

"You can ask me anything," she said.

"Um, Steph—when I saw her at Safeway—she said she was worried about you. That you've been having some trouble with your memory?"

She was clearly surprised. "Oh. Sometimes I forget things, that's all. I'm getting older. It was thoughtful of her to talk to you about it, but it's not a big deal."

"Are you sure?"

"Of course. You don't need to worry about me."

"Okay," I said. The silence between us was a little awkward, and I wondered if I had made a misstep by bringing up Steph's concern. "So, you want me to take the files downstairs?" I said.

"That would be great. Let me find a box for you to use."

I went to the filing cabinet and pulled out the rest of the folders. At the back of the drawer, I found a bunch of flat rectangular boxes, each with a photo of Grandpa on the front. He was about my dad's age or maybe a little older, wearing a blue shirt and a wide paisley tie. Each box contained a videotape titled *Understanding Astronomy*.

"What are these?" I asked.

Joan came over to take a look. "Oh, Russ did a series of lectures in the nineties for that company that sells them." She picked up one of the tapes. "Yes. Lifelong Learning. They paid him pretty well, I remember now. It's basically the survey course he taught at Berkeley."

I pulled out a bunch of the tapes and looked at them. Each tape contained four lectures, and there were at least a dozen tapes. "That's a lot of lectures."

"He was such a good teacher. He loved his research, but I think he loved teaching even more."

"Can I watch them?" I asked.

"Of course. I think there's an old TV/VCR out in the studio." She handed me an empty cardboard box. "You can put the files in here."

"Thanks." I started to pack up the files and videotapes. "So, what's under the sheet?" I asked, trying to sound casual as I glanced over at the covered structure.

"It's in progress."

"You said you've never done anything like it before?"

"That's right."

"So, it's not a painting or photography? Or that performance art thing where you rolled around on a canvas?"

Joan laughed. "No. It's none of those things, exactly. I'll tell you when it's ready."

I lugged the box of files and videotapes out back to Joan's old studio. The side that faced the house looked like a gardening shed, with stained-wood siding and a white door with an inset window. The window was dark, and as I reached out to turn the handle I felt an uncanny moment of premonition, as if I were about to open a box of wonders. And then I felt a little silly—I'd been inside before—and I opened the door.

The smell of old paint struck my nose immediately, the scent of artwork long finished, and I wondered how long it had been since Joan used the studio. It was dark inside because the exterior storm shutters had been closed over the windows, so I turned on the overhead track lights. Footprints crossed the dusty floor to a high work-table in the middle of the room. A stool had been pushed beneath, and I remembered Dad had worked in here a few days ago. A counter with cabinets beneath was built along the wall where the door was located, and to my left was a deep stainless-steel sink, splattered with paint.

The opposite wall was floor-to-ceiling windows, currently covered by the storm shutters. I set the box down on the worktable and went back outside to open them. When I returned, the studio looked much more spacious. The ceiling angled up from the wall where the door was, and the windows opened directly onto the view of oak trees and hills and big blue sky. Along one of the short walls was a cabinet for supplies, and on the floor between the cabinet and the counter was a boxy old TV. It was pretty small, a little more than one square foot all around, and it had a slot in the front that must be where a videotape could be inserted.

I squatted down to pick up the TV—it was heavier than I anticipated—and set it on the counter, plugging it in. The screen fuzzed to life with a loud staticky noise. I popped in the first tape. The screen went blue, then the logo for the Lifelong Learning Company faded in, followed by an introduction about the class and the professor, Dr. Russell Harper West. Finally, there he was: Grandpa. Smiling his goofy smile.

"Welcome to *Understanding Astronomy*," he said.

It was startling to hear his voice out loud. He sounded and looked younger on the video than when I had known him. I picked up the box and looked for a date: 1993. I hadn't even been born yet.

"If you've never taken an introduction to astronomy class," Grandpa said, "some of the phenomena in our universe may seem mysterious and inexplicable, but soon you'll learn the answers to some of your most basic questions. Why do rainbows look the way they do? Why does the sunrise or sunset turn the sky red? The answers to these questions are actually easily understandable, and I hope they will serve as an appetizer—as an inspiration to you—to seek out even more knowledge."

I pulled the stool across the dusty floor so I could sit in front of the TV. At first it was surreal to see Grandpa there in living motion, but after a while the strangeness wore off, and Grandpa ceased to be my grandfather and became Dr. Russell West, professor of astronomy.

I had never thought of him as his own person before, separate from his role as my grandfather. I kept watching all the way through the first lecture, and let the tape roll on to the second.

I could have brought the TV into the house, but I liked being out in the studio. It just needed a little sprucing up. I found some cleaning supplies in the basement and swept the floor and wiped all the dusty surfaces, even polishing the chrome on the sink. I found a camping chair down there, too, and brought it out to the studio so I wouldn't have to perch on the stool. There was an overturned bucket that I used as an end table for my glass of iced tea, and a plastic crate that I used as a footrest. I didn't forget about the files Joan had asked me to sort. I laid them out on the worktable and did them a folder or two at a time, while I took breaks between lectures.

There was something very soothing about being out in the studio by myself, with Grandpa on the old TV. Sometimes when I think back on that summer, this is what I choose to come back to. If I blur the edges of my memory, the feeling comes back to me. A warm, soft quiet; the certainty of science in my grandfather's voice. The scent of dry grasses and wildflowers and oak trees coming through the big windows. The light, steady and golden all afternoon, until it slanted into bluer and bluer shades toward night. It was a pocket of calm in which Jacob had never happened, my friends and I were okay, and all I had to do was sort the files and listen to Grandpa tell me about the wave-particle duality of light.

O n Wednesday, Steph, Mel, and Lisa were late, so I had plenty of time to second-guess why I was going out with them. I didn't know them at all, and although I'd never gone to an open mic and had little idea what it would be like, I was somehow sure it would mean listening to terrible amateur singers, like *American Idol* auditions in person. If Tasha or Haley had asked me why I agreed to go, I would have lied and told them I had nothing better to do.

While I waited for Steph and the others to arrive, I worried about my outfit, scrutinizing my reflection in the bathroom mirror. I'd put on rolled-up jean shorts and a slouchy white blouse, but I wasn't sure if it was right for an open mic in Fairfax. I thought about wearing something else, but my wardrobe choices were limited, and then Analemma started to bark. I grabbed my purse and went down to the front door, which Joan was already opening. Analemma plunged outside and I heard Steph greeting her.

"You never told me you sing," Joan was saying.

I came outside to see Steph give Joan a slightly embarrassed smile. "It just never came up, I guess."

"Sometime you'll have to sing for me," Joan said.

Steph seemed even more embarrassed now. "Sure, yeah." She straightened up and said to me, "Sorry we're late."

"No worries," I said. "Bye, Joan."

"Have a good time," she replied.

"Bye," Steph said.

Joan called Analemma back inside, and Steph and I started down the path toward the street. She was wearing faded jeans and a gray T-shirt printed with a black tattoo-like illustration of a bird that wrapped around her shoulder. She looked so much like a boy—a cute boy. I wondered what Haley and Tasha would think of her.

"We're going out to eat after," Steph said. "Probably somewhere in Fairfax. That okay with you?"

"Sure."

Just outside the green gate, the white Golf was parked on the side of the road, the engine still running, and I saw Lisa in the driver's seat. The back door popped open as I approached.

"Hel*lo*," Mel said.

I climbed in as Steph took the passenger seat. My feet bumped into a giant purse and an empty soda can.

"Sorry about that; you can move it out of your way," Lisa said, turning down the stereo. I didn't recognize the music; it was sort of country, sung by a woman with a raspy voice.

"That's okay." I nudged the bag over and pulled the door closed.

As Lisa began to turn the car around on the narrow road, a phone chimed. "That's mine," Lisa said. "Can someone get my phone out of my bag?"

"Here," I said, picking up the bulging bag and gingerly stuffing it through the gap between the two front seats.

"Who is it?" Mel asked. "Is Joey bailing?"

"Actually, yeah," Steph said.

"I knew it," Mel said.

"I told her it was important to you," Lisa said. "I'm sorry, baby."

"She's bailing because there's something happening in the Castro," Steph said. "There's a street party because of the decision."

"Aw, that's sweet," Lisa murmured.

Steph turned toward her. "Do you want to go?"

"We have your open mic, baby. I don't want you to miss it." Lisa put her hand on Steph's thigh.

I looked at Mel and asked, "What happened? What decision?"

"The Supreme Court overturned Proposition Eight," Mel said. "Gay marriage is legal in California now."

I didn't know much about gay marriage, but I remembered when it had been legalized in Massachusetts because my dad and I had gone to a lesbian wedding in Cape Cod. They were grad-school friends of my dad's, and it was the first wedding I'd ever attended. I was nine years old. Both brides wore long white gowns, and when they kissed at the end of the ceremony, it was like seeing one woman reflected in a mirror.

"That's great news," I said now.

Mel wrinkled her nose. "Marriage is a tool of the patriarchy and gays getting married just buys into the system."

I had no idea what to say to that.

"Tell us how you really feel," Steph joked.

"Just because you hate marriage doesn't mean everybody does," Lisa said.

"I don't hate marriage," Mel said. "I just think it's not for everyone."

Mel's phone chimed and she pulled it out of her shorts pocket. I realized the tattoos on her forearms weren't flowers; they looked more like cabbages.

"Roxy says hi," Mel said as she typed a text message.

"You two talking again?" Steph asked.

"Yeah." Mel glanced at me. "Roxy's my ex."

"Oh," I said. I had assumed Mel was gay, but it was still a surprise to get this confirmation so directly. After Mel put away her phone, I pointed to her tattoos and asked, "Are those cabbages?"

Mel grinned and stretched her arms out to show me. "Yeah. Some cabbages, and also you see carrots here underneath? They're not finished yet. I still have to add chiles and tomatillos, some tomatoes, too. All my favorite vegetables. Doing the red stuff will be another pass."

"Why vegetables?"

"I'm training to be a chef. I work at Rosa Masala in San Rafael. Do you know it?"

"No, but I don't know that many places around here."

"It's a Mexican-Indian fusion restaurant. Rosa, the owner, is half Mexican and half Indian. I'm a prep cook now but I plan to open my own restaurant someday."

"That's cool."

"You have any tats?"

"No."

"They'd look good on you. Flowers, maybe." Mel ran a finger lightly up my arm and shoulder. "Some peonies right here."

I thought she was flirting with me, and it felt kind of nice.

The Bolinas Café was a little more than half full when we arrived. There was a low stage on one side of the room, a counter at the back where food could be ordered, and about a dozen square tables throughout. The crowd was more mixed in age than I expected, ranging from a couple of kids who had come with their parents all the way to a few gray-haired hippies. The place smelled like coffee laced with onion bagels, and the front windows were open to the darkening evening while the ceiling fans whirred overhead.

"I'm gonna go sign up," Steph said as we entered, and she edged around me, the guitar case on her back bumping against my arm.

"Let's get that table by the window," Mel said. Lisa and I

followed, but the table only had two chairs. Lisa quickly dropped her giant purse on one of them while Mel went to take two more from another table.

"I'm getting a coffee," Lisa said, pulling her wallet out of her purse. "You guys want anything?"

Mel dug a billfold from her pocket and fished out a five. "Get me a mocha?"

Lisa glanced at me questioningly, but I shook my head. "I don't know yet. You go ahead." I picked up the laminated menu on the table and looked at the beverages. There were a zillion kinds of tea in addition to coffee, each with their country of origin listed.

Mel took a seat by the window, so I sat down beside her, across from Lisa's purse. "Have you been here before?" I asked.

"No, but Steph has played here a couple times. She didn't tell us, though. She said it was for practice."

"So is this new for her? Performing in public, I mean."

"No, she used to be in a band with Roxy. That's how I met Roxy actually. But Steph's not in the band anymore." Mel straightened up then and waved at someone behind me. "Steph! Over here!"

I turned to see Steph weaving her way through the tables toward us.

"Did you get a slot?" Mel asked.

Steph placed her guitar case on the floor, partly beneath the table. "Yeah, but I'm going next to last. Where's Lis?"

"She went to get coffee," Mel said.

"I'm gonna get a water. Do you want anything?" Steph looked at me and Mel.

"Lisa got me," Mel said.

"Sure, a chai?" I said. I opened my purse to pull out some money but Steph waved it off.

"I'll get it. Be right back."

Steph went to stand in line, and I put away my wallet. I saw Mel smirking at me.

"What?" I said.

"Nothing," Mel said.

The look on her face told me she was holding something back, but before I could ask, a white woman in a shapeless linen dress and Birkenstocks stepped onstage and tapped the mic. "Good evening, Bolinas Café!" A spotlight snapped on, slightly delayed, lighting up her curly gray hair.

A half-hearted round of applause greeted her.

"We're going to need more enthusiasm than that," she scolded us. "Let's try that again. Good evening, Bolinas Café!"

I clapped this time, and Mel whistled.

"That's better! I'm Linda Goode, your open mic host, and we've got an amazing lineup for you tonight! First up, and making her Bolinas Café Open Mic debut, is Fairfax's own Lexie Anderson. Lexie, come on down!"

A woman with bright blue hair made her way through the café, holding a banjo. Lisa rejoined us and handed Mel her mocha as Lexie stepped into the spotlight.

"Hello, Fairfax!" Lexie Anderson said, smiling. "I've got a couple of bluegrass songs for you tonight. The first is called 'Edge of the River.'"

She launched into a lively number on the banjo and then began to sing in a bright, sweet voice. She was good, and it surprised me. Now I wasn't sure why I'd been certain the open mic would be terrible. Mel seemed a little surprised, too. When she caught me looking at her, she winked, which made me smile.

As Lexie finished her second song, Steph returned with her bottle of water and my chai. "Thanks," I said. As I took the large white mug, Lisa shot me a surreptitious look. I blew on the foamy top before I took a sip, and out of the corner of my eye I saw Steph lean back in her chair and put her arm around Lisa's shoulders. She seemed to relax a bit.

There were five more performances before Steph. They were all decent, and a couple were really great. One duo—a singer in a green velvet dress, accompanied by another woman playing a fiddle—were so good they got an encore. Across the table, Lisa leaned over to Steph and whispered something in her ear. Steph had been watching the duo onstage, but now she cast her eyes down and looked a little nervous. I wondered if she had stage fright.

My mother never seemed to be afflicted by it. She relished performing live, and she always seemed to be in control of her performance; every last gesture was choreographed. Some critics called her too calculating, a little false. She told me they didn't understand. She wasn't false; she was larger than life. That was the point, she said, of opera.

Applause rippled through the café, and Steph leaned down to unlatch her guitar case. Her eyelashes were dark against the pale skin of her cheek. And then Linda Goode called her name, and Steph got up, throwing the strap of her guitar over her left shoulder. The café had filled over the last hour, and it took Steph a minute to make her way through the crowd. By now night had fallen completely, and the overhead lights had been dimmed, leaving only a few pools of brightness over the back counter and on the stage. Steph stepped into the spotlight and smiled.

"Hi, Fairfax," she said, pretty low-key. "I'm Steph Nichols."

Lisa whistled, and there was a smattering of applause from the audience. I joined in while Steph strummed a couple of chords on her guitar. The movement of her hand and forearm caused the koi tattoo to wriggle as if it were alive. She began to pluck out a wistful melody, and then, without further introduction, she leaned into the microphone and started to sing.

Her voice was soft and edged with roughness at the same time. The song she sang was about two kids who picked wild blackberries together during the height of summer, but as they grew up, their friendship changed.

"You never said you loved me
But I know you well enough to know
You don't have to say it for me to hear it
I can hear you even so."

Longing bloomed inside me, a sweet ache that I was embarrassed to feel. I didn't know Steph at all. I had never been attracted to girls before. And yet here was this girl—this very confusing human being—and here was my body responding to her. A heated flush across my skin; my pulse leaping. Her voice was like a hook in me. I felt as if everyone near me must be able to tell.

I shrank back in my chair and forced myself to look away from the stage. I made the mistake of glancing across the table at Lisa, and of course Lisa was gazing at Steph with a single-minded focus, as if Steph were the answer to every question. There was a great intimacy in her expression, and my embarrassment at my own reaction changed to embarrassment at witnessing Lisa's. I hastily looked down at the table and saw my mug of chai. I picked it up and took another sip, but it was cold by now, and the bittersweet dregs were gritty on my tongue.

After the open mic ended, Lisa was exultant. "You did so good," she gushed, pulling Steph close to kiss her. Steph seemed a little self-conscious, and I wondered if it was Lisa's praise or the public kiss that made her face pink.

Everyone was getting up now, either going to the counter to buy another drink or heading out to another show.

"Let's go eat," Mel said, coming around to slap Steph on the shoulder. "That was great. I didn't know you'd finished that song."

"Yeah, just last week. I think it works."

A girl came up to Steph as we headed out of the café, touching her arm. "Hey, Steph Nichols," she called. "I loved your set."

We all turned to look at her. She was pretty, with honey-blond hair in a long ponytail pulled over one shoulder, wearing a pink-and-yellow-flowered sundress.

"Thanks," Steph said.

"I'd love to talk to you about your songwriting," she said, smiling, and I realized she was hitting on Steph.

"I'd love to, but I can't stay," Steph said, moving away from the girl. "My girlfriend and I are heading out."

The girl's gaze traveled over Mel, me, and Lisa, dismissing Mel and then hesitating between me and Lisa. "Oh." She twined her fingers through the end of her ponytail and smiled again, equal parts carefree and calculated. "Well, if you ever change your mind, I come here a lot."

Steph looked uncomfortable. "Good luck with your songwriting," she said politely, and we continued toward the door.

As we exited the café, I heard Lisa say, "I knew it."

"You don't need to worry," Steph said.

"I'm not worried," Lisa said, sounding testy. "I just need a drink."

"Lis—"

Lisa started to walk away, and a frustrated expression flashed across Steph's face. She hurried to catch up with her, grabbing Lisa's hand. I saw Lisa stiffen slightly—almost as if she wanted to pull away—but then she relented, and Mel and I followed the two of them away from the café.

At the Fairfax Grille, we were seated at a table tucked in the back corner of the busy dining room. As I looked at the menu, I realized I'd been here before with my grandparents. There were a bunch of burgers named for places in California: the San Francisco (blue cheese and caramelized onions), the Marin (avocado and microgreens), the San Rafael (pepper jack and salsa), and the Fairfax (a black bean and brown rice veggie burger).

"Where's the server?" Lisa asked. "I'm going to the bar. Can you order me a medium cheddar burger when they get here?"

"Sure," Steph said.

"Will you get me a beer?" Mel asked.

"*I'm* not the server," Lisa said. "Come get your own."

Mel grumbled but got up to follow her. She glanced at me and Steph and asked, "You two want anything from the bar?"

Steph shook her head. "I'm driving."

"No thanks," I said. I wasn't sure if Mel knew how old I was. I wondered whether I should tell her, but that seemed so childish, like a three-year-old announcing their age.

"Will you get me the San Francisco burger?" Mel said over her shoulder.

"Yep," Steph said. Then she looked at me. "So what did you think of the open mic?"

"I liked it," I said. "I've never been to one before, so I didn't know what to expect, but it was really great. I liked your song. You wrote it, right?"

She smiled at me, and the corners of her eyes crinkled. "Yeah, I wrote it."

"Was it autobiographical?" I immediately wanted to take it back—Dad was always irritated when people asked him if his books were autobiographical.

Steph laughed shortly, as if she'd gotten that question before.

"Sorry, I—"

She shook her head. "It's okay. Maybe some of it. But by the time I've really worked on a song, whatever's true to my own life is mostly gone. The song isn't about me, even if it started out that way. Besides, I think it would be hard to perform them in public if they were really about me. It would feel too confessional. But I also feel like all songs should feel a little autobiographical, except not only for the singer—for the listener, too. They should connect with it on a personal level, as if it happened to them." She suddenly looked self-conscious. "Sorry, I get a little intense when I talk about this stuff."

"No, I love hearing about it," I said.

Steph seemed pleased. "I want to write songs that feel universal, you know? Specific, but universal. That's why there's no gender in the lyrics."

"Oh, I didn't realize that."

"A lot of songs are like that. They apply to everyone. You know, love is love."

The way she said it made me wonder if she was being sarcastic. There was a moment of silence between us, and it felt unexpectedly intimate. Although we were in a restaurant with plenty of other people around, it suddenly felt as if we were alone. Her eyes were brown with flecks of green in them.

I took a breath. "Mel told me you used to be in a band?"

"Yeah."

"What made you decide to . . . go solo?"

Steph glanced over at the bar, where Lisa and Mel were still waiting for their drinks. "It just wasn't working out. The other band members were in San Francisco, and I was up here, and there was just too much driving involved. I couldn't fit it around my job and stuff. I'm trying the solo thing to see if it works better."

Her answer sounded mechanical, like a story she was telling her-self rather than the truth. "How do you think it's going so far?" I asked.

She fidgeted with her napkin-wrapped flatware. "I don't know. I've only done a couple open mics."

"I'd love to hear more of your stuff."

"Yeah?" Steph didn't seem to believe me.

"Absolutely. You're really talented."

She smiled almost shyly, and a buzz went through me.

"Thanks," she said. "It's just hard to find the time to focus on my music."

"You have to make the music your priority, or you won't make it." I spoke before I knew what I was saying, and as soon as the words came out of my mouth, I froze. My mom had said that to me. I was visiting her in New York, and we'd had a fight. I was suddenly back in my mom's concrete-and-stainless-steel kitchen with the crushing realization that I was not her priority.

"Priorities can be complicated," Steph was saying.

I blinked. She was picking at the edge of the menu, a slight furrow developing on her forehead.

And then the server plunked down two glasses of ice water on the table between us. "Sorry about the wait," she said. "Is it just the two of you?"

The sounds of the restaurant seemed to swell in my ears. I had almost forgotten what we were here for.

"There's four of us," Steph was saying. "They're at the bar, but I know what they want." Steph gave her Lisa's and Mel's orders, then asked for a Marin burger and Diet Coke for herself.

When it was my turn, I realized I hadn't decided what to get, so I said, "I'll have the same."

After the server left, I looked at the bar, where Mel and Lisa were partially hidden behind a group of guys in Giants shirts. "How did you and Lisa meet?" I asked.

"Mel and I snuck into a gay bar during senior year of high school," Steph said. "It was our first gay bar. Lisa was playing pool with some other women. When their game finished, Lisa challenged me and then she beat me." She seemed amused by the memory. "She wanted me to buy her a drink because I lost, but I wasn't sure if my fake ID would work on the bartender, so I asked if she wanted to get pizza instead. I thought she'd turn me down, but she didn't, and the rest is history."

I knew I was supposed to think the story was cute, but instead it disappointed me. "So you've been together for what, a few years?"

"Three and a half years. What about you? You have a boyfriend?"

Before I could answer, Lisa and Mel returned.

"Did you order?" Lisa asked, pulling out her chair.

"Yeah," Steph said. "Just now."

"I'm starving," Mel said, and sat down with her beer.

"Baby, you have to see this," Lisa said, holding her phone out to Steph. "Look what Joey sent me. There's a street party in the Castro right now to celebrate the decision."

She handed her phone to Steph, and I could hear the tinny sound of dance music and cheering.

"Wow, that's a lot of people." Steph turned the phone around to show me and Mel.

I leaned forward to look at the video. Thousands of people were packed onto a long street that rose up a hill in the distance, many waving flags with yellow equal signs. Their bodies moved like waves as dance music blared, and then the camera jerked upward and showed a red neon sign that read CASTRO before the video abruptly ended.

"Looks like Pink Saturday," Mel said.

"Without the straight people," Lisa said.

Steph gave the phone back to Lisa. "Sorry we couldn't go down there tonight."

"No, I'm glad I saw your show," Lisa said. "You were so good." She pulled Steph to her and smacked a big kiss on her lips, and then turned to Mel with a grin. "Wasn't she great?"

Mel nodded. "You been holding out on us. Was that a new song? You need to play your own show sometime. We could get people there."

"I don't have enough songs yet." Steph glanced at me. "I'm still working on a few before I can do a solo show."

"Maybe you can rework some of the songs you wrote for Madchen," Mel said. "You should talk to Roxy about it on Saturday."

"You made plans with her?" Steph asked, surprised.

"Not *plans* plans, but it's Dyke March, so she'll be there." Mel turned to me. "What about you? What are you doing Saturday?"

"Um . . . not sure," I said.

"You should come," Mel said.

Lisa began to smirk.

"Come to what?" I was confused.

Mel grinned. "The Dyke March."

"Uh, I'm not . . ."

"It's a party," Mel said. "In Dolores Park in San Francisco. It's free. All our friends will be there."

"Mel," Steph said, "she doesn't know our friends." Steph gave me a look like, *You don't have to come.*

"You're right," Mel said, and then she turned to me. "Let me tell you about our friends. There's Roxy, my ex, and probably the rest of the band will be there, too. The band is called Madchen. They're all great. And Joey, Lisa's best friend, who's a real sweetie. A thousand—no, ten thousand—queer women, all of them gorgeous, hanging out at the park all afternoon. Then we march through the streets of San Francisco from the Mission to the Castro, for Pink Saturday. It's a street party, like tonight on Lisa's phone, but bigger. But no pressure—you can think about it and just let me know if you want to go. I'll text you."

It was nice to have someone be clearly interested in my company. "Okay," I said. "I'll think about it."

Finally the burgers came. As I picked mine up, warm juice oozed down the side of my hand, and the avocado was cool and creamy against the grilled edges of the beef. I remembered I had ordered the same burger as Steph, and when I looked across the table at her, she raised hers in a silent toast.

Hazel, I thought. The color of her eyes is hazel.

"B e careful," Joan called. "I don't remember the last time I went back there."

"I'll be fine," I said, and pulled the dangling string to turn on the overhead bulb.

A harsh white light washed over the back basement. The hill sloped inside the house here, held back by a knee-high brick wall. Cardboard boxes were lined up on top of the wall, and behind the boxes lay a musty darkness I wasn't eager to explore. Overhead, insulation erupted from plastic sheeting in dirty pink clumps. The room smelled of dirt and disintegrating cardboard and something disturbingly organic. I hoped to find what I was looking for quickly.

Joan was behind me in the storage room, which opened into the civilized part of the basement, including the laundry room and an old darkroom. She was currently searching through boxes looking for the last of Grandpa's files from his time at the University of Colorado. She had asked me to help look in the back basement.

So far I'd found dusty boxes of children's clothes, old costumes, and books. I pulled out a dog-eared copy of *The History of Sexuality* by Michel Foucault and saw my dad's handwriting in the margins. I pulled out a few more: *Orientalism; Distinction; Being and Time; Gender Trouble.* At the bottom of the box, there were several volumes of poetry. Emily Dickinson, Walt Whitman, Allen Ginsberg,

Langston Hughes, Adrienne Rich. A slip of paper poked out of the Rich volume. It looked like a photo, and I tugged it out to see a photo-booth strip of two people laughing at the camera.

They were my parents. My mom looked barely older than me, and there was kind of a baby softness to my dad's face. They both looked so happy to be pressed together in that photo booth, my dad's arms encircling my mom as she leaned against him, her eyes bright.

My phone vibrated in my pocket. I slid the photo strip back into the Adrienne Rich book, feeling as if I had glimpsed another world. I took out my phone to find a text from Mel.

Checking if you wanna do dyke march Sat? Still planning but we'll probably leave together from my place in San Rafael. Hope you can make it

I wasn't sure what to say. I looked down at the box of my dad's books again, wondering what else was hidden in them. That was when I saw the rectangular black case tucked behind the box. There was something familiar about it, and as soon as I pulled it out, I realized it was my old telescope.

When I was ten years old, Grandpa had given it to me for Christmas. It came unassembled, but he told me I could put it together myself to build the same kind of telescope Galileo had used. Grandpa had ended up helping me, but afterward I had taken it apart and put it back together several times. I'd brought it to Woodacre when we visited in the summer, and he and I would go up to the roof at night to look at the moon and some of the planets. I must have left it here.

A big crash sounded from behind me, and I straightened up. "Joan, are you okay?" I called.

I went back to the storage room and looked through the

doorway. The room wasn't very large, and boxes had been stacked precariously high along one of the walls. One of the boxes must have fallen, because it lay smashed open on the floor. Books and papers were spilling out, and Joan was using her foot to nudge them together.

"I'm fine," Joan said. "This box broke. Can you help me?"

"Sure." I started to round up the items that had skidded across the floor. One of them was a reddish-brown faux-leather photo album. It had rigid pages where photos were stuck beneath sticky plastic film. I glimpsed old pictures of my grandparents, and I brought it over to Joan. "Look at these," I said.

Joan set the album on top of a stack of boxes and opened it. "I'd forgotten about these," she said. The first page had a couple of snapshots of Grandpa as a young man, dressed in a short-sleeved Hawaiian shirt and a pair of shorts, standing on a beach with a little boy.

"Is that my dad?" I asked.

"Yes. These are from our trip to Hawaii." Joan pointed to an image of herself in a flowered dress, the photo faded with age. "I was pregnant with Tammy then but I didn't know yet."

She flipped through several pages, past photos of my dad in the ocean with Grandpa or building sandcastles with Joan.

"Dad looks just like Grandpa did back then," I said.

"He does," she agreed. She turned another page and paused on a picture of four men wearing fur-lined parkas on a snow-covered mountainside. "Here's Russ and Peter and—I can't remember their names—Joseph, I think?"

"Where is this?"

"Still Hawaii. They're up on the mountain, Mauna Kea. I remember that day. Your grandpa knew some of the people who were working on building the observatories there. They drove us up to the site.

It was so cold, and coming up from the beach, it felt like we'd traveled to another world."

On the next page was a small square photo of the mountaintop, surrounded by clouds. "That looks like something from Instagram," I said, leaning over to get a closer look. The colors were faded, but the perspective was dramatic—as if the photographer had been hovering above the earth and looking out on a sea of roiling mist.

"I took that one with your grandpa's Instamatic," Joan said. "That was a kind of camera. Everybody had them." She closed the photo album and surveyed the mess on the floor. She picked up some of the papers and shuffled through them. "I think this is what I was looking for. It's not exactly what I remembered, but my memory's not what it used to be. Will you help me take these things upstairs?"

As we gathered up the box's contents, I thought about Mel's text. "I was wondering," I said, "are you using your car on Saturday?"

"I don't have any plans right now," my grandmother said. "Do you need it?"

"I was thinking of going to San Francisco."

"You're welcome to use the car."

"Thanks."

I picked up the box to carry it upstairs, and Joan followed with the photo album. In the living room, Analemma raised her head from where she'd been napping in the corner of the sofa, her tail thumping against the cushions.

"I need to take her for a walk," Joan said. "Do you want to come? We can go for a hike in the hills."

"Sure. Give me five minutes? I have to close up the back basement."

"Take your time."

I went downstairs again, taking out my phone on the way. I texted to Mel: *I'd love to come, thanks*

In the back room, I started to put Dad's books away and spotted my old telescope on the floor beside the Adrienne Rich book. I decided to take the telescope and the book upstairs with me. As I closed the basement door, my phone vibrated with Mel's response: a thumbs-up.

Mel lived in a little white stucco house on a residential street in San Rafael. There was a shiny black Jeep in the driveway, so I parked Joan's Honda on the side of the road just past the address.

Before I got out, I checked my makeup in the mirror on the back of the sun visor. I'd gone for a beachy, sun-kissed look with a glossy lip, and I wondered if my makeup was all wrong—and my outfit, too. White shorts, a loose teal blouse, wedge-heeled sandals, dangling silver earrings. I had bought this outfit for Martha's Vineyard, and after that got canceled I packed it to bring to California. This was my first opportunity to wear it, but I was suddenly sure it was totally wrong for a Dyke March.

I had tried to arrive a few minutes late so I wouldn't be the first, but I didn't see Lisa's white Golf on the street. Maybe Steph drove the Jeep. I checked the address Mel had sent me for the hundredth time, then forced myself to get out of the car. Halfway up the path to the house's front steps, I almost turned around. I could go back to Joan's and tell her I was feeling sick. I could text Mel an apology, say my grandmother needed her car unexpectedly. I still had my phone in my hand and I even unlocked it, my thumb poised over the text messages icon, when I heard a car come down the street. I turned to see Lisa's car pulling over. I was both disappointed and relieved.

Steph climbed out of the passenger seat, wearing ripped jeans and Vans and a black T-shirt. She saw me right away and waved before going to open the trunk. Lisa got out a second later, dressed in cutoff jean shorts, purple Converse high-tops, and a white ribbed tank top that was kind of see-through. Beneath it she wore a rainbow bikini top that tied around her neck. She had gotten her hair done; now it was blonder and sleeker, pushed back behind her sunglasses, and she looked good.

She gave me a once-over and said, "Your shoes are gonna kill you."

"They're pretty comfy," I said. "I like your rainbow bikini."

Lisa seemed a little surprised. "Thanks." She pulled a tiny messenger bag over her head, and the strap fell between her breasts. I felt uncomfortable noticing, so I looked at Steph, who was pulling a backpack out of the trunk.

"What did you bring?" I asked. "Was I supposed to bring something?"

"It's a blanket and some stuff for the park. You didn't need to bring anything." She shut the trunk, and she and Lisa headed toward me.

I waited for them to catch up, and then we all went up the stairs to the front door. I got to the top first and pressed the buzzer. It didn't take long for Mel to open the door, her face breaking into a broad grin. "Welcome! You're all here! Awesome, come on in. I'm almost ready."

The front door opened into the living room, which was sparsely furnished, as if Mel had just moved in. Lisa plopped herself down on the squishy-looking beige sofa and started scrolling through her phone, while Steph asked, "Is Dani coming with us?"

"Nah, Dani went down already," Mel said, going into the next room. "We might run into her."

Steph followed Mel, and I followed Steph through the doorway into the kitchen. This room was the opposite of the living room. Where the former had felt barely inhabited, this one was lived in. Three of the walls were painted butter yellow and covered with photos of fruits and vegetables; the fourth, which contained the window, was turquoise blue. A narrow table beneath the window held a long planter full of herbs. Pots and strainers hung from a rack over a mini island, and built-in shelves were packed with cookbooks that were bristling with Post-it notes.

Mel was putting a few things into a backpack and asked, "You want some water before we go?"

"No thanks," I said. "This kitchen is great."

"Yeah, I love it. It's why I rented the place. Also Dani never uses it—she's my roommate—so I get it all to myself." Mel zipped up her backpack. "All right. You need the bathroom before we head out? There will only be porta potties down there."

"I'll use it," Lisa said from the living room. I heard her footsteps crossing the wooden floors, and then a door closed.

Mel was wearing long, baggy blue shorts and a short-sleeved yellow button-down printed with pineapples. "I'm glad you decided to come," she said to me.

"I hope I don't embarrass you with my straight ignorance," I joked.

Mel smiled at me. "We all gotta start somewhere."

She shared a look I didn't quite understand with Steph, whose mouth twitched into a sort of smile.

Mel drove the black Jeep, and I sat up front with her while Steph and Lisa took the back. Mel played Rihanna and Icona Pop on the drive down to San Francisco, and as we crossed the Golden Gate

Bridge I gazed out at the glittering Pacific and remembered driving the other way with my dad only a week ago. Time felt both stretched and compressed in that instant, and then Mel hit repeat on "I Love It," and it was impossible to not be there in the Jeep at that moment, screaming the chorus with these three women I hadn't even known seven days ago.

San Francisco was all sunshine and steep hills. When the Jeep careened up and over Divisadero, Lisa let out a whoop. I thought I knew the city from previous visits with my dad and grandparents, but as Mel maneuvered her way across Market Street, which was hung with dozens of Pride flags, I realized I only knew a small slice of it. We were heading for the Mission District, and I didn't think I'd ever been in that part of San Francisco before. The streets were unexpectedly flat, with long blocks that reminded me of New York, but the buildings were mostly three or four stories with bay windows jutting out over the sidewalks. They were painted pastel shades of blue and yellow and pink, all of them slightly grimy and a little worn. On the ground floors were taquerias and vegetable markets, bars and bookstores, their doors open to the sunny day.

The parking garage was accessed down an alley behind a Pakistani restaurant, and Mel drove up a very steep, dark driveway to the rooftop, where she tucked the Jeep into a cramped corner parking space. Outside, the air smelled of asphalt and gasoline, and behind that came the scent of curry.

"We should pick up some drinks," Lisa said, flipping down her sunglasses. "It's such a nice day."

"We got lucky," Mel said.

"God loves Pride," Steph said, and they all laughed. I joined in a little late.

On the way to the park, we stopped at a corner store where Lisa and Mel bought beer and I got a bottle of water. After I paid, I went outside to wait for them, standing in the tiny bit of shade next to the building. A bunch of posters had been pasted to the wall there: salsa night at El Rio; Frameline: San Francisco International LGBTQ Film Festival; Fresh Meat Productions, with a photo of two Black male dancers, arms entwined. One poster featured an arresting photo of a young Asian woman sitting on the floor next to a large blue-and-white abstract painting. The woman was wearing paint-splattered pants, a frumpy blue sweater, and a slightly sly smile. It made me wonder who had photographed her. The poster advertised a movie called *The Worlds of Bernice Bing*, which was the closing night film for the Queer Women of Color Media Arts Project Film Festival. There was a small tagline at the bottom of the poster: "A documentary illuminating the visionary Chinese American lesbian artist Bernice Bing."

I was a little disappointed to find that the date of the screening had already passed. I took out my phone and snapped a photo of the poster, and just as I finished taking the picture, Steph came out of the corner store.

"They're almost done," she said, cracking open a bottle of water.

"No worries. Hey, have you ever gone to this film festival?"

Steph came over to look at the Bernice Bing poster. "No. She looks interesting, though." She studied the photo a beat longer and added, "I like her painting. I'm assuming that's her painting, anyway."

"Yeah. I like it, too."

"I'm not saying I understand it, but I like it."

"Joan says abstract art is supposed to make you feel things."

"What does this make you feel?"

I looked more closely at the painting behind Bernice, with her enigmatic smile. "Expansive. It makes me think of space. No, planets. Look at that orangey spot. It's like that storm on Jupiter, the one that looks like an eye."

"Hmm, I can see it," Steph said. "If you look at Bernice, too—her eyes and the eye behind her. It's like she's looking at you through her painting."

I felt a warm rush go through me. "Yes! I love that. And don't you think—well, she's looking at the photographer, who's looking at her, and there's her painting looking at us. I feel like there's a lot going on here."

Then we looked at each other, and there was a kind of understanding between us, as if we were seeing the same thing at the same moment, and it was a little surprising to both of us. I saw her mouth open slightly as if she was about to speak, but then behind her the door of the corner store opened and Lisa and Mel came out, carrying their purchases in brown paper bags.

Steph and I turned away from each other and toward Lisa and Mel. I was glad I'd taken the picture of the poster, because later I knew it would bring me back to this moment.

We walked down the broad, palm-tree-shaded sidewalks of Dolores Street toward the park. The rhythmic thump of dance music floated through the air. When 17th Street came into view, I saw dozens of motorcycles lined up all in a row. Leaning against or sitting astride them were women in leather chaps, in pink feather boas, in bikini tops.

Mel must have seen the surprise on my face because she explained, "Dykes on Bikes. They start the march."

Across the street was a row of tennis courts, and then a bank of porta potties, and beyond them, Dolores Park rose up a big hill that was completely covered with people. I had never seen a crowd like this before, with women of all ages and races and sizes, wearing all kinds of outfits in every color, from head-to-toe rainbow gear to jeans and T-shirts, many with tattoos up and down arms and legs and upper backs exposed to the sun. I was sure now that my outfit was exceptionally straight.

Up ahead, a crowd was gathering at a little plaza where steps led into the park. Everyone was watching an Asian couple standing together on the steps. One woman was wearing a black satin corset and pink ruffled hot pants, fishnets and shiny Doc Martens. The other woman's outfit could not compare; it was just shorts and a button-down shirt, but she did have on a fun newsboy cap. Now she knelt down on one knee and reached in her pocket, and although I couldn't see what she was holding up, the gasp from everyone watching made it obvious that it was a ring. The woman must have accepted the proposal, because now the kneeling girl got up and they were kissing, and the entire circle gathered around them was cheering.

"That's so sweet," Lisa said. She was clinging to Steph's arm, and Steph leaned in and kissed her. She was tender, gentle.

I looked away, toward Mel, who was texting on her phone and paying no attention to the proposal or Steph and Lisa.

"Finally!" Mel said. "Roxy's on the hill behind the playground. Come on."

Roxy Berlin was a tall white woman with a Bettie Page haircut and bright red lips, dressed in cutoffs and a ripped black crop top that revealed a tattoo of twined red roses inked along the side of her torso. She was what my mom would call "big-boned," but to me she looked like all she needed was Thor's hammer to become a superhero. She was also wearing steel-toed boots with metal buckles and had a brassy magnetism that was apparent even from a distance. She greeted Mel with a kiss that left a red lipstick print on her cheek; she squeezed Steph while thumping her on the back with a ringed hand; and she kept her distance from Lisa, leaving a triangle of space between their bodies when they hugged.

Mel introduced me to Roxy, who offered me beer from a big blue cooler and told me to make myself at home. She and her friends had claimed a prime spot beneath a tree at the top edge of the park, where they'd spread a couple of fleece blankets over the ground. From up here, we had a good view of everything: the bowl of the park crowded with people; the palm trees lining Dolores Street; and the skyline of downtown San Francisco in the distance. Down the hill and past the playground was a stage, where a DJ was playing dance music that reverberated up the slope toward us. In front of the stage was a roped-off area for people to sit in lawn chairs or wheelchairs, and all over the park people were dancing and drinking and shouting and laughing. It was so different from the beach parties at Haley's parents' house on Martha's Vineyard, which I remembered in palettes of sand and dun and white linen. Here, Dolores Park was a riot of color: electric blue hair and red vinyl hot pants, hot pink feathers and rainbow face paint.

I grabbed a can of PBR from the cooler and took a seat on the corner of the blanket next to Mel. She introduced me to the other Madchen band members, Talia Dutton and Jasmine Harris, before she spotted someone selling tamales and went over to buy some. Then I tried to not look like I was listening in on everyone else's conversations. Talia, the drummer, was half Filipina and had dyed the ends of her dark hair hot pink. Jasmine, who played keyboards, was Black and had a shaved head and a lip ring. Talia's boyfriend,

Gabe, was trans, and he was also a sound engineer who was helping the band record a new demo—this time without Steph.

"We miss you," Roxy said to Steph. After Mel left, she had scooted into Mel's seat between me and Steph. "Gabe keeps telling me we need a new guitarist but I can't find anyone who gels with us like you. We've tried out a few people but nobody seems to work."

"What are you going to do about the demo?" Steph asked.

"We might hire someone," Roxy said. "We haven't decided yet. Mel told me you did an open mic last week. How'd it go?"

"I guess it went fine. I miss you guys, too."

"You can always come back."

"Don't tempt me."

"I'm all about tempting you." Roxy glanced around. "Wait, Lisa's not here, right?"

Lisa had passed out pot brownies when we first arrived and then gone off to find her friend Joey.

Steph shook her head slightly. "Come on."

"Sorry, babe. You know what I mean."

"We're trying."

"I know, I know!" Roxy raised her hands in surrender. "I'm sorry, I take it back. Just listen. We got into QMF. It's one day in August. You could join us."

Steph didn't answer for a bit. Roxy simply sat beside her as they both looked out at the park. The sounds washed over us: laughter; the roar of conversation; motorcycle engines gunning.

"I'll think about it," Steph finally said.

"Okay," Roxy said, all low-key. "It's August third in Golden Gate Park." Then she checked her phone and said, "Mel's texting me. I'll be back."

After Roxy left, I asked, "What's QMF?"

"The Golden Gate Queer Music Fest," Steph answered.

"You should do it."

She took a sip of her beer. "I should, huh?"

"It sounds like you want to."

"I want a lot of things. That doesn't mean I get them."

The Dyke March was a raucous but slow-moving tide of people waving rainbow flags and carrying protest signs and banging bongos. At first I felt like an interloper, but after a couple of blocks, I realized there was so much going on, nobody was paying any attention to me. Above us, people leaned out their bay windows, unfurling sheets painted with GO DYKES or HAPPY PRIDE!!! Some of the women in my vicinity were marching topless; one had written LOVE IS LOVE across her chest in rainbow letters. The smell of grilled meat wafted out of taquerias; the funk of weed floated on the air; and the sound of drums and dance music was a moving soundtrack around us. I was a shell buoyed by a wave in an ocean I'd never known to exist.

We parted from Roxy and her friends at the end of the march in the Castro, where Pink Saturday was already a massive street party hemmed in by metal barricades and police officers. Roxy, Talia, Jasmine, and Gabe were headed to a club where they were playing, and Mel and Lisa both had crack-of-dawn shifts at work in the morning. Everybody said their goodbyes in the middle of the street, and then we walked back to the parking garage, stopping at a taqueria on the way to inhale tacos al pastor doused with green salsa from a sticky squeeze bottle.

By the time we got to the Jeep, I was tired and full, the way you feel after spending a day in the sun with friends. It surprised me to feel that way; it surprised me that climbing into Mel's Jeep and smelling its leather interior already felt familiar.

Mel put on Frank Ocean as we drove back to Marin. As we crossed the Golden Gate Bridge, I twisted around to look back at the city lights glimmering in the darkening night, and Steph smiled at me from the back seat. Lisa had fallen asleep, her head on her shoulder. I smiled back and felt as if I had passed some kind of test.

Outside Mel's place we climbed out into full night. The streetlight at the end of the driveway cast harsh shadows. Lisa was still half asleep as Steph bundled her into their car. Before I left I said to Mel, "Thanks for inviting me today. I had a really good time."

"I'm glad," Mel said. "And you're invited to this summer. Period, okay?"

I smiled. "That's really nice of you, but you don't have to baby-sit me."

Steph and Lisa's car turned on, and Mel and I waved to them as they drove off.

Mel said, "You must be bored out of your mind over at your grandma's."

"It's not that bad. I'm helping her with a project, but I do miss my friends. We had big plans for the summer."

"Like what?"

"Parties on Martha's Vineyard. Lobster rolls and beach parties. Cute boys." I laughed; it sounded like a foreign country.

"All the cute boys I know are gay. Maybe you should branch out a little."

"Got any suggestions?" I said, without thinking.

Mel stepped a little closer and I saw her smile change, making the tiny switch from friendly to flirtatious. "You want a suggestion?"

I heard the unmistakable invitation in her voice, and for a moment,

I was tempted. Only half of her face was lit by the streetlamp, turning her into dramatic color and shadow. The edge of her jaw was golden, the curve of her mouth was soft and full, and the tiny hoop earring that hung from her right ear glinted.

"I thought your heart belonged to Roxy," I teased her.

Mel grinned. "Roxy and I have a long history, that's true. She's poly. I wasn't ready for that when we were first dating. I guess I've . . . matured since then."

"Polly?"

"Polyamorous," Mel explained. "Nonmonogamous."

"Oh." I had never heard of it, but the tone in Mel's voice didn't make me feel ignorant. It made me feel like she was inviting me into a private club. "Are you poly also?" I asked.

"Yeah," she said. It sounded like a relief to her.

Later on, I wondered what would have happened if I'd given Mel a chance. It would have been a lot simpler, because Mel was fun to be around, and she was kind, and she was available.

In that moment, though, standing in Mel's driveway, I thought: *I wish I was attracted to you, but I'm not.* And once that thought came into my head, there was no erasing it.

I said apologetically, "I should get home."

The flirtation vanished from Mel's face, and if she was disappointed, she didn't show it. "You didn't drink too much, right? You're okay to drive?"

"Yeah, I'm fine."

"You know, you should give me a call if you ever want to talk about . . . anything." Mel sounded oddly serious.

"That's really nice of you. Thanks."

"Drive safe," she said, and she pulled me into a goodbye hug.

On the drive back to Woodacre, I thought about what Mel had

said to me. I was pretty sure she meant I should call her if I wanted to talk about gay stuff. Or was it queer stuff? I had no idea what the proper words were. I only knew what it was beginning to feel like in my body. An edgy, slightly queasy feeling; anticipation mixed with seasickness. It was that Frank Ocean song, "Thinkin Bout You," playing on a loop.

On Sunday morning I woke up remembering the day before, and I picked up my phone to scroll through my photos. A selfie with Mel on Market Street right before we left, the Castro behind us. A truck with go-go dancers that had driven past us during the march. A shot of Dolores Park filled to the brim with people and color and palm trees. And the picture of the movie poster I'd seen outside the corner store. There was Bernice Bing seated on the floor beside her big blue painting, looking straight at me like a challenge. I hadn't taken any photos of Steph, but I could feel her standing beside me.

I opened Chrome and googled Bernice Bing. There were links to the documentary, but there were also links to the Queer Cultural Center, which had hosted a retrospective of her work in 1999, the year after she died. Her bio was sparse, but dramatic. She had been born in San Francisco in 1936 but lost both her parents as a child, and was raised by foster families. She'd gone to art school here and started exhibiting paintings in the 1950s at the height of the Beat era. She had been out as a lesbian and accepted by the art community, but the bio didn't mention her having a surviving partner.

The Queer Cultural Center website included small photos of her paintings; the images were so tiny on my phone I pulled out my laptop so I could enlarge them. Bernice Bing used giant sweeps of color in some; in others she painted with strokes that looked like Chinese calligraphy. I lingered on one painting in particular. The top third looked like water with a mountain emerging from it; the bottom two-thirds was dark, with a swirling mass of blue and white on the right. I wanted to know what the swirling mass of color meant to Bernice. I studied her photo in the documentary poster, but she eluded me.

I took my computer with me into the kitchen, where Joan was at the table drinking coffee and reading the Sunday *Chronicle*. I set my laptop down beside the discarded Arts section.

"Good morning," she said. "You slept in. How was yesterday?"

"It was interesting," I said, taking out milk and cereal.

"Is that the word you use when you don't really enjoy something?"

I could hear the smile in Joan's voice. "No, I had fun. I just didn't know anyone very well, so the whole day was meeting new people." I poured myself a cup of coffee and brought my breakfast to the table, where I sat down. "Have you heard of Bernice Bing?"

She considered the name for a moment. "I don't know. Who is she?"

I turned my laptop around to face her, showing her the bio. "She was an artist here in San Francisco. She's dead now."

Joan skimmed the bio. "She had a show at SomArts, and I taught there around the same time. I might have met her, but I'm not sure." She began to click through the pictures. "Her work feels familiar to me somehow."

"I thought some of your early paintings looked like these," I said.

Her eyebrows rose a little but she nodded. "Abstract Expressionism. It was hard to escape in the fifties and sixties. You know, Jackson Pollock and Mark Rothko. Most of the famous Ab-Ex artists were men, but that's because back then it was still acceptable to say that women couldn't be painters."

"But you were painting," I said. "And Bernice Bing."

"Oh, sure. Women were painting—including Jackson Pollock's wife, Lee Krasner. But we haven't always been seen. I think that's changing now." She turned the laptop back to face me. "But tell me why you're looking up Bernice Bing. What led you to her?"

"I saw this poster yesterday." I showed her the photo on my phone. "I thought it was interesting. I mean, I wanted to know more."

She zoomed in on the photo. I wondered if she was reading the tagline about Bernice Bing as a visionary Asian American lesbian artist. I wondered if she would say the word *lesbian* out loud. I wanted her to.

But she gave me back my phone and said evenly, as if nothing were out of the ordinary at all, "That's where it all begins. Wanting to know more. You should keep looking."

That afternoon I went back to the studio, taking my old telescope with me. I opened all the windows and put one of Grandpa's astronomy tapes on the TV, listening to him talk about sunsets while I opened the telescope case. The last time I used the telescope I must have taken it apart, because it was completely disassembled. I laid out several halves that would snap together to form the long barrel of the telescope, multiple O rings that would clamp it together, the focuser tube halves and several lenses that were smudged with fingerprints and needed to be cleaned.

"What color is the sun?" Grandpa was saying. "Contrary to popular childhood crayon colors, it's not yellow or orange. The sun is white, which you can see if you observe it from space. Or, if you're not in space, at noon when it's highest in the sky."

I found a folded-up printout at the bottom of the telescope box that contained the assembly instructions. I smoothed it out on the worktable and started to sort the pieces.

"When the sun sets or rises, though, it appears to be yellow, orange, or even red. Why? This is due to the scattering away of light particles by the atmosphere."

Grandpa pulled up a slide that illustrated light scattering. It showed a series of suns—a white disc overhead at noon, descending through shades of darkening yellow-orange to an orange-red disc at sunset, low over the horizon. A beam of light emanated from each sun, and as it struck the atmosphere, which was symbolized by a fuzzy white line, particles of light were reflected in all directions. The light particles looked like squiggly arrows colored blue or violet or green, to illustrate the color of the light that was scattering.

"At sunset, when the sun is low, the light has to travel farther through the atmosphere than it does at noon, when the sun shines straight at us. That means more of the blue and green light is scattered away, leaving predominantly yellows and oranges. That's why the sun appears redder at sunset. Remember, it's not *actually* red. It's the scattering of light that makes it seem that way to our eyes."

I finished laying out the telescope parts, and as I compared them with the guide in the instructions, I realized something was wrong. The objective lens—the one that went at the far end of the telescope—was missing. I looked inside the case, but it was empty. Without the lens, the telescope wouldn't work.

I sat down in the camping chair, disappointed, and looked back at the TV. Grandpa had moved on to discussing how mirages worked to bend light, creating illusions like the vision of shimmering water over a desert. He smiled almost conspiratorially at the camera. "This is what is so amazing about science. It can show you what is really happening. You may think you see something, but in fact it's something else."

My phone rang, the sound cutting through the still air. I immediately hoped it was Steph, but just as quickly knew it couldn't be. She didn't have my number.

I picked up my phone from the table and read *International Caller*. There was only one person I knew who would have that ID. She was in Munich for an opera festival. I wondered what finally made her call me. I paused the video and answered the phone.

"Hi, Mom," I said.

"Aria, how are you?" she said. My mom had a slight Chinese accent when she spoke English. She spoke French and German, too, but I wasn't sure if the accent carried over to those languages.

"Fine." I waited for her to acknowledge the rocky way we had left things.

I heard the clink of porcelain against a table on her end of the phone, and I realized it was after midnight where she was. If she had just returned from the opera house, she would be drinking an herbal tea for her throat. This was when she usually called me, and as if everything were completely normal, she asked, "How is your summer going?"

With a sinking feeling, I realized she wasn't going to acknowledge anything. "Fine," I repeated.

"What are you occupying yourself with? I hope you're taking advantage of this time to prepare yourself for college. MIT's going to be a lot harder than high school."

She had never been enthusiastic about my love for astronomy, although as a good Chinese mother she couldn't exactly tell me not to pursue science. Instead she often implied that I wasn't entirely cut out for it, or that my interest in it would die after high school. I generally avoided thinking about my relationship with her, but even I was aware that that was one of the main reasons I applied to MIT—to prove her wrong.

"I'm taking an astronomy course on video," I said stiffly. Grandpa was frozen on-screen in mid-gesticulation, his face distorted into a look of surprise.

"You are?"

"Yeah. Grandpa recorded one of his classes on video and I'm watching it."

"Oh. Well, that's lucky for you. You can get a jump start on the fall."

"I'm just watching it for fun."

There was a beat of silence, and then Mom said, "Your grandpa wasn't the only scientist in the family, you know. One of my cousins or aunts—I don't know the exact relation—she was an engineer, I think. She worked at that place in Los Angeles. The one that builds rockets. You know the one? Your father's sister works there."

"The Jet Propulsion Lab."

"Yes, that's it."

"You never told me that before."

"I forgot. I think it was my cousin Eddie's sister who worked there. Eddie just sent me a video of his grandson. He won a piano competition."

I wondered if this was the cousin Dad had mentioned, but I didn't ask for more details. In my experience, it was best if I said as little as possible on the phone with her, because that made her get to the point faster, and she always had a point.

"Listen, I have good news. I'm flying out to Hong Kong in a few weeks and I have a brief layover in San Francisco, so I can see you."

My gut clenched. "Oh. Really?"

"It's less than twenty-four hours, but there's time for me to meet you for lunch at the hotel." Her voice lowered, as if she were getting serious. "Aria, I'm sorry I've been in Europe for so much of this year. I wish I could've been with you. You're becoming a young woman and you need your mother's guidance more than ever."

I said in a tight voice, "I'm fine, Mom."

"You need to take a step back and think about who you've been spending your time with."

"I'm not spending my summer with anyone now," I snapped.

"You need the time to yourself," Mom said, her tone hardening. "And we need to talk. In person, not over the phone. I need to look in your face and see what kind of a girl you've become. I wouldn't raise my daughter to—to expose herself like that."

As if I'd done it on purpose.

"Why did you do it?" she asked.

"We are not getting into this again," I said.

To my surprise, she didn't argue with me. She sighed, her breath sending a rush of static over the international connection. "I blame myself. It's all my fault. I should have been there for you, and I'm going to change things."

She sounded so melodramatic, and yet I couldn't help but feel a twinge of hope. I wanted to believe her.

"I know we don't get along all the time, but we need to talk," she said. "I'll be in San Francisco on July twenty-fifth. Would you come and have lunch with me?"

She made it sound like I had a choice, but I could never have said no. "Okay," I agreed.

"Good," she said, sounding relieved. "I can't wait to see you, darling. I'll have Jeri email you with the details." Jeri was her assistant who booked all her travel. I'd gotten a lot of emails from Jeri over the years. "I should go now. I need to get my beauty sleep. I'll see you in San Francisco."

On Monday I accompanied Joan to Spirit Rock, a nearby Buddhist retreat center, for their weekly meditation night. She had been a regular for a while, but I'd never gone with her until now. She wore cloisonné earrings in the shape of flying birds, and they glowed turquoise and emerald green and pink in the golden evening light as we walked from the parking lot to the community hall. It looked like a giant double-wide trailer, and when we entered the meditation room, the floor creaked and swayed, as if it wasn't quite fixed to the ground.

Joan seemed to know a lot of people, and she introduced me to some of them before the meditation began. They greeted her with hugs and smiles, asking about her art and whether she was going to teach another class. Most were middle-aged or older white women, and I was probably the youngest person in the room. I remember thinking that Joan was different here, but I couldn't put my finger on why.

The teacher, who sat cross-legged on a low platform in front of the altar, was a wiry, balding white man with a bushy gray mustache. About a dozen people sat on cushions on the floor facing the altar, but we sat in the uncomfortable folding chairs lined up in rows. I struggled to stay awake during the half-hour meditation session, but eventually a bell rang to indicate the end, and everyone shifted and stretched, making the plastic chairs squeak. And then the teacher began to speak.

"A little over a week ago we marked the summer solstice—the longest day of the year. I was in London at a conference then, and everywhere on the news were pictures of people at Stonehenge celebrating the solstice. Stonehenge, of course, was built to align with the movement of the sun. On the solstice, people are allowed to walk into the actual ring of stones that makes up Stonehenge, and if you're standing there—in the middle of the stone circle—at dawn on the summer solstice, you'll see the sun rising just to the left of what they call the Heel Stone. Apparently there used to be another stone beside the Heel Stone that would have actually framed the sunrise, but it's gone now. Stones, of course, seem immovable. Permanent. But even stones fall down. And yet we don't stop putting them up, do we?"

A low ripple of laughter went through the room.

"I don't know how many of you have seen Nancy Holt's monumental work of land art called *Sun Tunnels*," he continued. "It's in Utah. There are photographs, but to get the full effect you have to be there in person. It's a series of massive concrete tubes that are positioned to line up with the sun at the summer and winter solstices. Sound familiar? When I was a child, I thought erroneously that we were closer to the sun during the summer, and closest at the summer solstice. Of course I learned later on that the seasons have nothing to do with how close or far the earth is from the sun. It's the tilt of the earth's axis, instead, that marks the seasons. At this time of year, the northern hemisphere is most tilted toward the sun, making it warmer in our neck of the woods. Paradoxically, the earth is actually closest to the sun during our winter. I think this goes to show that what seems to be true may not be true."

The teacher gave us all a tiny, ironic smile.

"What seems to be fixed—Stonehenge, even—is not fixed. This

brings us back to the core teaching of the Buddha. Impermanence. Nothing is permanent. Everything changes."

He paused, and the entire room seemed to exhale.

"Flowers bloom and die. Stones rise up and are slowly weathered away. People change, too, obviously. We change continuously. We age. Our hair grows. We even shed our skin. This can seem frightening or overwhelming, and I think maybe that's why we build structures like Stonehenge, or make art like the *Sun Tunnels*. The stones frame this constant change with the illusion of permanence, and for a moment—while we are watching the sun framed by the stones—for a fleeting second the world seems stable. Beautiful and miraculous. But you know what makes it a miracle? The fact that we are present in that moment, experiencing it fully, before it inevitably changes."

A shiver went across my skin. I curled my fingers around the edge of the plastic chair and hung on to it, but beneath me I imagined I could feel the floor swaying as it had when we'd entered.

After the talk ended, everyone went to the lobby to make themselves paper cups of tea, which they took out onto the steps and into the soft dark night. I remember the whisper of the breeze on my skin, the smell of mulch and mint tea, and the way light from the community building's doorway spilled in a yellow rectangle onto the ground. It glinted on Joan's wedding ring, which she still wore, as she raised her cup of tea to her mouth. There was something about the angle of shadows across her face or the way she lifted her arm that made her look younger to me, as if time had slipped backward and she was drinking tea somewhere else. In her studio, maybe, but not the one in Woodacre; somewhere I'd never been, and she was studying a painting in progress and asking herself if it was finished yet, or if there was more waiting to emerge from the canvas.

Someone was asking Joan whether her next gallery show would take place before the end of the year, which surprised me. I hadn't known she was even thinking of doing another show. Of course she'd exhibited before and was represented by a gallery in San Francisco, but since Grandpa had died, she hadn't shown any new work. I realized, with a little shock of dismay, that even though I knew Joan *was* an artist I had ceased to think of her as *being* one.

That's what made her look different to me that night. She was Joan West again, and it was only in seeing the artist return that I recognized that part of her had been muted for years. It became clear to me in an instant how incredibly life-altering Grandpa's death had been for her. How it had overturned so much of who she was, or at least called it into question. Was this why she had begun coming regularly to Spirit Rock? I had never thought of my grandparents as religious, though Grandpa's funeral had been at a church. I remembered, suddenly, a Buddha statue in their small Berkeley backyard, overhung with dripping green leaves after a rainstorm.

And now she was here, in this community who knew her better than I did. I felt uncomfortable and thrilled by this revelation all at once, as if I'd discovered a stranger inside someone I loved.

That summer, when Joan was working in Grandpa's old office, I spent most of my time in Joan's old studio, watching Grandpa's lectures while I sorted through his files. Sometimes I took Analemma on hikes nearby, and on the way to the trailhead I passed houses that still had their signs up for marriage equality. I hadn't noticed them before, but now I seemed to see them everywhere. A VOTE NO ON PROP 8 bumper sticker peeling from the back of a Prius; a rainbow flag flying from a wooden front gate.

When I returned, I'd take a glass of ice water out to the deck, where I'd scroll through my phone waiting for a text that didn't come. I began to think that maybe my friendship with Mel, and by extension Steph, was over. *You're invited to this summer, period*, Mel had said. But I was convinced there was a loophole. Sometimes friendships didn't get off the ground, even if they had a promising start.

One afternoon I finally brought the Adrienne Rich book outside with me. It had been lying on the nightstand by my bed ever since I found it in the basement, one corner of the photo-booth strip peeking out from the top. I sat down on the lounger in the shade and pulled out the pictures of my parents. I expected it would hurt to see them like that, so young and happy, but the twinge I felt soon dissipated, and then I was studying the images as if they were celebrities or criminals. It didn't seem possible that I was related to these two people.

They had lived in a world I didn't know, and it unsettled me, making me think about branching universes and whether there was another one where they had stayed together. What kind of person would I be if I had grown up in that world?

I carefully tucked the photo into the rear of the book, hiding my parents' faces from view. And then, because I didn't know what to do with the strange uneasiness inside me, I started to flip through the poems. In the titular poem, "Diving into the Wreck," the narrator puts on scuba gear and dives into the ocean to explore a shipwreck. I saw the ocean that Rich described, colors shading from blue to green to black as the diver descended. I saw the diver with her oxygen tank strapped to her back, poking through the ruins of something that had once been beautiful, taking photographs to record it. I saw the body of the diver morphing, female to male, male to female, the shape of her/him outlined by the shifting light.

I thought of the Bernice Bing painting with the swirl of color surrounded by darkness, and in my mind her painting became inextricably linked to the poem. I saw the diver swimming closer to that swirl, that vortex, her hands parting the waves, her flippered feet kicking through the water. I saw her reaching for it as if it were a treasure long lost to the deep. But it was unreachable. The diver's map was wrong. She kept swimming the wrong way, and the current would push her back over and over again, like the waves in the ocean pushing a frond of seaweed out and out. I was captivated by that imagined image: the diver hanging in mid-water as if suspended between past and future, as if trying to make a choice.

I must have dozed off, because when my phone rang I was so startled that I jerked, and the phone tumbled out of my pocket and fell onto the deck. My heart was thudding in my chest as I reached for it, hoping that the screen hadn't broken, and I was so startled to see Tasha's name come up that I didn't hesitate. I answered her call.

"Aria?" Tasha's voice sounded so familiar to me, and yet it hurt to hear it.

"Hey." I blinked. I felt like I was the diver, pushing against the current to reach the surface.

"You didn't answer any of my texts. What's going on? Are you okay?"

I sat up and swung my legs over the side of the lounge. *Diving into the Wreck* slid from my lap onto the deck. The photo strip slid partway out, and I nudged it back in with my toe. "Sorry. The reception isn't so good out here. I must not have gotten them."

"Oh."

There was a beat, two beats of silence. I knew she knew I was lying. "How was Thailand?" I asked.

"It was amazing. We stayed in this gorgeous little village on the ocean, and the food was like—I've never had Thai food like this."

Tasha went on, gushing about her two-week internship, while I barely listened. My stomach was churning in a weird way, and nothing Tasha said seemed relevant to what was happening now, to me. It had only been a few weeks since high school graduation, but it already felt like a year ago.

"I'll send you some pictures," she was saying. "You have to see how beautiful it was."

"Wait—where you are now?" I asked, suddenly checking in. "Aren't you supposed to be in Paris?"

She paused. "I'm back for a week. We're on the Vineyard for the Fourth, but we're leaving on Saturday for France." She paused again, then said, "I wish you were here. I really do. I'm sorry it didn't work out this summer."

The churning in my stomach seemed to increase. "Have you seen Haley?" I asked. Unlike Tasha, Haley hadn't contacted me since graduation, and I hadn't contacted her. It was as if we had mutually agreed to the silent treatment so we could avoid being awkward together.

"Not yet," Tasha said. "It won't be the same without you."

The only responses I could think of were mean, so I said nothing and stared down at the deck. The sun was burning bright against the brown cover of *Diving into the Wreck*. I began to imagine it burning so hot it would singe a hole through the cover.

Finally, Tasha asked, "So, what have you been up to?"

Steph and the open mic and the Dyke March and that conversation with Mel on Saturday night under the streetlight. Tasha had been one of my best friends for so long, it still felt natural to spill it out to her, but I caught myself in time. I felt superstitious about it, as if any tenuous friendship I'd begun with Steph and Mel would definitely vanish if I talked about it.

"Nothing much," I said instead, and then I fed her the same line I'd given my mom. "I'm taking an astronomy class on video."

"You're such a nerd," Tasha said, but fondly.

"So are you," I countered, and a little bit of warmth seeped into my voice.

Tasha sighed. "I miss you. I don't want what happened with Jacob to screw up our friendship."

My eyes grew hot, and I closed them for a moment. I had tried to convince myself I didn't care that much, but I missed Tasha, too. As soon as I admitted that to myself, I felt something release inside me. "I don't want that either," I said.

"Then answer my texts next time!" Tasha said, but she sounded relieved.

I choked on a laugh. "Are you going to text me from France?"

"Yes. Absolutely. And next time you can come to France, too."

"I don't speak French."

"Well, I do so I'll translate."

"Okay, when's next time?"

"Let's go over Christmas. Christmas in Paris!"

I knew that she wasn't being serious, but I played along. "I want to stay at a five-star hotel," I told her.

"Obviously. We'll get room service. *Champagne*," she said in her excellent French accent. "It'll be amazing."

"*Fantastique*," I said in my bad French accent.

"Oh, hey—I meant to tell you—I saw that boy Nathan at Mad Martha's ice cream. Remember him?"

The change of subject took me by surprise. "Nathan? Yeah, I remember."

"He *definitely* remembers you," Tasha said suggestively.

I wasn't sure how to respond. "What do you mean?"

"I think he had it bad for you. He even seemed to be *pining* a little. And he definitely has gotten cuter."

I knew I was supposed to be flattered by this, but I just felt uncomfortable. "Really?" I said, trying to pretend like I was interested.

"Oh yeah. If I see him again, I'll take a picture."

"You don't have to."

"Oh, I know," Tasha said, laughing. "Take it as a favor from me. Listen, I have to go, but I'm so glad we finally talked. Let's keep it up, okay?"

"Okay. Have fun in France."

"I'll text you. You better answer."

On the Fourth of July, there was a parade in Woodacre. Joan and I brought camping chairs down to Railroad Avenue, where her friend Tony Merritt had wheeled a big cooler full of water and Popsicles. Because the parade ended at a horse-boarding ranch, kids riding horses made up a big portion of the spectacle. There were also tractors bearing American flags, a giant papier-mâché unicorn pulled on a trailer, and a truck hung with Pride flags. In the truck bed, a bunch of people dressed in rainbow gear were waving and tossing candy out to the kids. They wore sashes that declared LOVE IS LOVE and JUST GAY MARRIED!

After the parade, there was a flea market with vendors and food stands at the ranch, and Joan and I wandered through the stalls looking at carved wooden mobiles of flying pigs, or Tibetan singing bowls on bright silk cushions, or collections of Grateful Dead memorabilia. Tasha had been texting me photos from the Edgartown Fourth of July parade—which, like every New England event, had people dressed up in colonial costumes carrying fake muskets—so I sent her photos of a flying pig mobile and a selfie in front of the papier-mâché unicorn.

Tasha texted: *What is that doing in a 4th of July parade?!*

I replied: *It's Marin*

That night we went to a barbecue at Tony Merritt's place. It was about a fifteen-minute walk from Joan's house. Tony was a carpenter and had a workshop on his property, and Joan told me he had done the built-ins in Grandpa's office as well as her art studio. We brought Analemma with us because she was friends with Tony's dog, Goldie, a pit bull–yellow lab mix with the sweetest eyes and extremely bad breath, and I realized Tony was the person who sometimes walked Ana. There were many people at the barbecue I didn't know, but some of them knew who I was because Joan had told them about me. There was a lot of "Congratulations on MIT!" and "Sounds like you're following in your grandpa's footsteps!"

Tony grilled tri-tip and sweet corn over wood in a big firepit, and veggie burgers on a gas grill. We had brought a tangy coleslaw, and others contributed food as well: slices of heirloom tomato drizzled in balsamic vinegar; peppery arugula salad with coins of bright white-and-pink radish; big wedges of dripping watermelon. As darkness fell, kids began to light sparklers that sizzled and spit. Through it all, I noticed Tony always kept an eye on Joan. He made her a special mojito with mint grown in his garden. He brought her a new napkin when she dropped hers on the ground. He served her slices of rare tri-tip first, with a flourish.

Tony was a white guy with salt-and-pepper hair in his late fifties or early sixties, probably younger than Joan by at least ten years. But I could tell she liked his attention. She let him wait on her in a way that showed she enjoyed it. I thought she might have taken extra care with her appearance tonight, too. She wore a new blouse in a bright gold-and-teal print, and she had put on dangling earrings that looked like beaten brass shields. But she was still wearing her wedding ring. I wasn't sure what to think.

We walked home with Analemma afterward, and the road was so dark we had to light our way with a flashlight that Tony insisted we borrow. Every so often we heard the distant popping of fireworks. Some dogs couldn't stand them, but Analemma didn't even seem to notice. She pranced ahead of us happily, as if she were leading us home.

"That was a nice day, wasn't it?" Joan said contentedly as we walked.

"Yeah." I was a little surprised; I felt pretty good about it, too.

She linked her left arm through my right, drawing me closer. She smelled like woodsmoke; I probably smelled like it, too.

"Tomorrow morning Steph's coming to do some gardening, but I'm going to Berkeley to see a friend," Joan said. "I'll leave her check in the kitchen. Can you give it to her?"

"Sure." I felt a rush of excitement at the idea that I'd see Steph again—alone this time.

"We should have her over for lunch sometime. Ask her when she's available."

"Okay." I wondered whether she could detect the sudden racing of my pulse.

"You know you can ask me anything," she said quietly.

I tensed up and said, "I know."

"I understand you're not a little girl anymore, as much as I want to remember you as one."

I felt immediately self-conscious, and I didn't respond. I didn't have to, because fortunately at that moment my phone dinged. I pulled it out of my pocket to read the text. "It's from Tasha," I explained.

Tasha wrote: *Everybody says hi!!!!*

Attached to her message was a video, which was frozen because reception really was bad in the woods, but as we walked, it jerked into life. There was a group of people lit up by a bonfire, with a great swath of darkness behind them. Tasha must have shot it at a beach party. They all screamed in unison: "Hiiii, Ariaaaa!"

I recognized Haley and her sisters, and Tasha's little brother, and over on the right was a guy who looked vaguely familiar to me. Tasha's next text message cleared it up.

Look at Nathan!!

She sent a separate photo that was kind of grainy because of the low light, but it was unmistakable. There was Nathan, quirking an eyebrow at the camera, and I had to admit he did look cute. He had his arm around Haley, who had kind of a pained smile on her face.

I showed Joan the video of everyone saying hi to me, but I didn't show her the photo of Nathan and Haley.

Nathan was the first boy I kissed. I was fifteen. It happened the summer after freshman year, when I went to Martha's Vineyard for two weeks and stayed with Haley's family outside Edgartown. Tasha was at her family's cottage in Oak Bluffs, and we planned to meet up almost every day. Nathan's parents had rented the house next to Haley's, which shared the same private beach.

Haley, Tasha, and I had bought bikinis at the Chestnut Hill mall in preparation for the Vineyard. Mine was turquoise with white palm fronds printed all over. Tasha's was red-and-white striped, like a candy cane. Haley's was navy blue with white stars. I remember squeezing with them into a dressing room at Bloomingdale's, examining one another in the mirror and giggling. It felt like my whole body was exposed, breast and belly and thigh, but I also saw what I looked like, and I thought I looked good—finally. Haley and Tasha looked good, too, but I was the late bloomer in our trio, relieved to have caught up at last.

I remember Tasha asking, "You're sure I don't look too slutty?"

She was taller than Haley or me, and her long brown legs were already muscled like a marathoner's, since she did cross-country. Her breasts were bigger than ours, but her butt was almost flat—something Haley would later tease her about. That summer Tasha had her hair in long thin braids that she wore loose or wound up in a big twist at the nape of her neck. With her lush lips and high cheek-bones, I thought she looked like a model, not a slut.

"You look sexy," I assured her.

"You could never look slutty," Haley said. "But what about me?" She twirled in the dressing room, her blond hair flying out. She was petite and cute, with perky B cups and a round butt, and she bumped her hip against Tasha's and gazed up at her with a grin.

"You want to look slutty?" Tasha said, laughing.

"No," Haley said, pretending to be offended. "But what do you think?"

"You both look great," Tasha said, and she put her arms around us as we gazed at ourselves in the floor-length mirror.

Back then, none of us really understood what slutty meant, other than that it wasn't something we wanted to be called. We hadn't yet learned that the line between sexy and slutty was so thin it could move with a whisper.

I met Nathan one afternoon while Haley and I were walking from her house to where we planned to lay our towels out on the beach. He was part of a group of older teen boys playing volleyball nearby, and I eyed them through my sunglasses as I approached. They had the blond good looks of kids who went to boarding schools like Choate or Phillips and learned how to sail like a Kennedy during summers on the Cape. One boy in particular—he had sandy hair and a tight stomach and was wearing blue board shorts—seemed to notice me a couple of times. As we walked past, he actually turned his head to watch, and a volleyball came out of nowhere and smacked him in the shoulder.

I laughed. His teammates, who were ribbing him over not seeing the ball, noticed, and a few seconds later they pushed him out of the game toward me. He seemed slightly abashed, but not enough to resist their encouragement.

"Hey," he called. "You're distracting me so much I might as well say hello."

His smile was that perfect summer-boy grin—freckles, white teeth, blue eyes—slightly sheepish but mostly self-confident. He had a buoyant spirit I was drawn to right away. In those first couple of minutes while we introduced ourselves, I practically planned out the whole summer in my head. He'd buy me ice cream in the afternoons; we'd walk along the beach and he'd hold my hand. He'd kiss me at sunset as the water sighed onto the shore; I'd melt into him as he told me I was the most beautiful girl he'd ever known. By the end of the summer, he'd have fallen in love with me and would promise to visit in the fall. All this flashed through my mind even before I managed to say, "I'm Aria."

"Nathan. Have I seen you around here before?"

"I don't know," I said coyly. "Have you?"

His smile grew more flirtatious. "You gonna be around tonight?"

I wanted to say *Yes, absolutely*, but Haley and I had discussed how to act around boys and decided we shouldn't seem too eager. If you were too eager, they didn't want you. "Maybe," I said.

"Maybe, huh?" He leaned in a bit closer, and it seemed as if I could feel the warmth from his bare skin radiating at me. "We're having a bonfire tonight on the beach. After sunset. You should come."

My body buzzed with his nearness and the fact that *this was happening right now*. I was meeting a cute boy and he was interested in me and I was going to be kissed—I could feel it. "I'm here with my friends," I said a little breathlessly, and glanced at Haley. She was laying out her towel with her sunglasses on, and I wondered whether she was watching out of the corner of her eye.

"Bring them," Nathan said.

"Yo, Nate, game's not over yet!" one of his friends called.

He glanced over his shoulder and then back to me. "I gotta go. But come out tonight. We'll be right out here."

"Okay," I said, and then realized I'd agreed when I was trying to play it cool.

That night I wore a baby-blue sundress with spaghetti straps, and I probably should have worn a sweater because the wind off the Atlantic could get cold, but I wanted to look cute. I had washed my hair and let it dry naturally into waves, and then Haley sprayed some product in it to make it look "beachy." I put on makeup—eyeliner because it was dark, shiny lip gloss to make my mouth look kissable—and I thought the girl in the mirror looked great, if a little nervous. I had never kissed a boy before, and I was well aware of my lack of experience. I planned to change that.

I went to many more beach bonfires after that one, but because it was my first, it stands out in my memory like all first experiences. I still remember feeling like I didn't quite belong there with all those pretty, rich kids. I still remember feeling a little awkward when Nathan asked if I wanted to go for a walk down the beach, alone. I hoped that if he noticed the blush on my face he'd chalk it up to heat from the fire.

We stopped right before the beach curved around the bend, and Nathan took my hand as we looked out at the ocean. I gazed at the glinting black water and the spread of stars above, at the cloudy glow of the Milky Way and Cassiopeia like a W within it. I'd never felt this way before, as if every molecule in my body had turned into a vessel for anticipation. Nathan tugged me closer to him, and he said jokingly, "You sure you should be out here alone with me? You barely know me."

I looked up at him, his face a shadow in the starlight, and I said, "It's a little late for that, isn't it? Besides, maybe I'm the dangerous one." I felt like I was coming into some kind of power I hadn't known I had, but which arose as instinctually as holding my hands out to catch my balance.

"Dangerous how?" Nathan asked. "What are you going to do to me?"

After he said that, I had to initiate it. I reached up and put my hands on the back of his head to pull him down to me. I felt his surprise travel through him in a brief gasp, but he didn't resist, and then his lips were on mine and I thought: *This is it. I did it.*

For my first real kiss, I think I did a decent job. I tried to mirror his movements, my mouth pushing back against his. I was surprised by how focused I was on the technical details of the kiss. Were my lips too firm? Were my hands in the wrong places? I had expected something more—you know, fireworks—but when Nathan's tongue prodded my lips open, all I felt was a dim confusion at the bizarreness of having someone else's tongue in my mouth. A wet, slithering muscle I couldn't control, that tasted slightly sour. I realized he'd been secretly drinking beer. He pulled me closer, pressing our bodies together, and made a weird groaning noise in his throat that almost made me laugh. That was when I felt it between us, a hardness that hadn't been there before poking at my stomach, and I realized, *Oh my God, that's his penis.* My whole body flushed, half mortified, half pleased.

This was incontrovertible evidence that he liked me, and I think it was that knowledge that thrilled me, not Nathan himself. I didn't feel anything special when we kissed. I'd spent fewer than two hours with him, and I didn't know what kind of person he was. It didn't matter. I had planned to kiss a boy, and now I was.

I didn't resist when he urged me to sit down on the sand, and then to lie down, my dress becoming damp all along the back where the sand was wet. I didn't resist when he put his hands on my breasts; I didn't resist when he lay on top of me and rubbed his erection against my crotch. In a way I liked it, even though I had no feelings for him. I was both elated and distant, physically present but mentally detached.

I was relieved when he didn't try to take off my dress. I would have said no. I would have resisted then, but I was glad I didn't have to. After a while we got up, and I tried to brush the sand off my dress, and we went back to the bonfire. I remember Haley's and Tasha's glittering eyes smiling at me, and Haley whispering in my ear, "Your lip gloss is smudged."

During the rest of my two weeks on Martha's Vineyard, I saw Nathan several times. There were bonfires almost every night, and we'd sneak away to make out, moving gradually through the bases. Although I got used to the taste of his mouth, and I got used to the sensation of his erection pressing against me, I knew early on that I wasn't going to develop feelings for him. He was cute, but he didn't light a spark in me; there was only the satisfaction of knowing that I turned him on, and that wasn't enough.

Haley and Tasha seemed to be more into him than I was. They couldn't stop gushing about him—his abs and his hair and his smile—and sometimes I wondered if one of them actually liked him. But at the same time, they were so enthusiastic about me being with him. They went out of their way to make sure we had private time together, covering for me with Haley's parents when I got back late from a walk with Nathan. And they wanted endless details about the making out, which I did my best to provide.

I could tell that Nathan really did like me, and I was glad that

I was only on the Vineyard for a couple of weeks. If I was staying for the whole summer, like Haley and Tasha, I'd have to break up with him because I knew he wanted to do more than make out, and I didn't.

On the last night I was there, Nathan borrowed his parents' BMW to drive us to get ice cream in Edgartown. As we walked along the waterfront, looking out toward Chappaquiddick, he took my hand and said, "I want to keep in touch."

"Me too," I lied.

He had already friended me online, and my stomach sank at the idea of having to write back to him after I left. But I couldn't burst his bubble that night. I already felt guilty for letting him think I liked him. I didn't want to be a tease. So when he drove the car to an isolated parking area somewhere along the beach, I tried to act like I wanted him, too. I think I was too good at pretending, because he took my hand and put it in his pants and asked me to touch him, and I didn't know what to do except to do it. He reclined the driver's seat and I had to lean over toward him across the gear shift, which gave me a good view out his window at the ocean in the distance, all shifting shadows beneath the starry, blue-black sky. I tried to focus on that—the suggestion of white froth as the waves rolled onto the sand, the expanse of that moving darkness—until he made a strangled kind of sound and jerked in my hand.

Afterward he reached in the glove box for some tissues, which he gave to me so I could wipe my hand. I told him I should probably go back to Haley's house, and he seemed content to drive me back. I was relieved he didn't try to do anything more.

I didn't feel dirty, exactly, but I felt guilty, as if I had lied to him. He sent me messages for a couple of months after I left, but I responded very slowly, and then I stopped responding at all. I told Tasha and Haley that he had stopped messaging me. When they said

I seemed sad about it, I told them it was because I liked him, but he probably thought I was just a summer fling.

After the experience with Nathan, I decided not to date anyone at school. I didn't want my friends to get involved in any relationships I might have. I didn't want Tasha and Haley to ask me for details or to gush about any boy I might like. I didn't want to be the subject of gossip or rumors the way other girls were.

I broke my own rule too soon.

J oan was gone by the time I came downstairs on Friday morning. Analemma was sprawled on the rug in front of the cold wood-stove in the living room, and her tail thumped against the floor as I bent down to pet her. In the kitchen, Joan had left a check for Steph on the table, weighted down with the salt shaker.

I poured myself coffee, made toast, and took it all out to the deck, where I sat in the morning sunlight and gazed at the hills. It was going to be a hot day; I could feel the promise of it in the way the sun sank into my hair. In the distance, I heard the gate opening and closing. The metal latch dropping into place.

I couldn't see Steph from here, but there was something delicious about knowing that she was coming up the hill, and if I went around the house to look for her, I could see her. From my vantage point, it seemed as if I was alone, but I wasn't. Steph was close enough that if I called her name, she would probably hear me.

I sat on the deck for a while, listening. The gardening tools were kept in a shed just below the studio, and I heard the bolt on the shed door thrown open and then the low creak of the hinges. I heard the clanging of tools and the rumble of the wheelbarrow as it was pushed out into the yard. *Thump, thump, clang.* The door creaking again, closing. Footsteps and the wheelbarrow, trundling away.

Another few minutes passed, and then I went back into the

kitchen. Joan always had a pitcher of iced tea in the fridge, and there was a bowl of lemons on the counter. It was getting hot already, and Steph would probably be thirsty. I took out the lemon squeezer and some glasses and set them on the counter along with the iced tea, long spoons, and a tray of ice from the freezer. I didn't let myself think about what I was doing; I just did it.

Analemma ran ahead of me out the front door, and I followed more slowly with the two glasses of iced tea. The hill that the cottage was built into was terraced, and the brick path wound back and forth down the hill like a Z. I heard Steph greeting Ana before I saw her, and when I rounded the bend and Steph came into view, she looked exactly as I expected—baseball cap, shorts, sleeveless tee—but it still startled me: my imagination made real.

She looked up as she rubbed Analemma's back and smiled. "Hey."

"I thought you might want some iced tea," I said, and offered her a glass.

She was wearing work gloves, and she took one off to accept it. Our fingertips brushed together. "Thanks." She took a sip and then set the glass down on the stone bench nearby.

"Joan gave me this to give to you, too." I took the check out of my pocket and held it out to her.

"Great." She took it without touching me, and I was a little disappointed.

"She also asked me to invite you over for lunch sometime."

"That's nice of her," Steph said as she folded the check and put it in her pocket.

"She said any day would do, as long as it was after noon."

"I'll check my schedule at work and get back to her. Is she out? Her car's gone."

"Yeah, she went to Berkeley."

Steph went to sit on the bench, taking another drink of her iced tea, and gestured for me to join her. "Did you have a good time last Saturday?" she asked. Analemma nosed around the flower bed where she had been weeding.

I sat down beside her. "Yeah, I had a great time. Thanks for inviting me."

"Anytime." She glanced sideways at me, a mischievous expression on her face, and asked, "Did Mel try to make a move on you after we left?"

"That's private," I said with a hint of a grin.

"She did, didn't she?" Steph seemed to think this was hilarious. "I hope she didn't make you uncomfortable."

"Oh no. Mel is great."

"Good." She drank more of the iced tea; it was almost gone already. "You doing anything this weekend?"

"No. I'm helping Joan go through my grandpa's old papers, but that's more of an ongoing thing."

"She never says much about your grandpa. I only know he was a professor at Berkeley."

"Yeah, he taught astronomy. I'm sorting his research papers because she's using them in her art."

"Really? How?"

"I don't know. She won't tell me."

"What did he research?"

"Protostars. I can show you if you like." As soon as I said it, I wanted to take it back. Why would Steph want to see Grandpa's research notes?

But she said, "Sure, I'd love to see it. But I have to finish up here first."

"Oh, of course. Sorry. I'm distracting you."

"Happy to be distracted."

Did I imagine that look in her eyes? A hint of pleasure. I didn't imagine the buzz I felt in my body.

"But I do have to get back to work," she added, and then she set down the now-empty glass and pulled the work glove on again, returning to the flower bed she'd been weeding.

I wondered whether I should leave, but I didn't want to. Analemma had stretched out on the moss-covered brick path and was panting slightly in the growing heat.

"When did you start working for Joan?" I asked.

"About a year ago. She used to come to the Greenbrae Garden Center, where I work, and I'd help her there. Then she asked if I did gardening gigs outside my job."

"Were you here last summer?" My dad and I had visited last July, but Steph hadn't been around then.

"Yeah, I started in August."

She threw the weeds she had pulled into a yard-waste bag. A dark bloom of sweat dampened the back of Steph's shirt, and the short strands of hair along the nape of her neck were damp, too. I watched the way the muscles in her arms flexed as she worked, and then I realized I was staring and looked down guiltily. The glass in my hand was slick, and a droplet of condensation plummeted to the ground, leaving a splotch of water on the bricks.

"So—" she said.

"So—" I said.

She looked over her shoulder at me and grinned. "You go first."

"I was going to ask if you decided whether you're doing that concert in August with Roxy."

She straightened up to get the bag of fertilizer from the wheelbarrow. When she lifted it, I tried not to look at her. The way her koi tattoos moved.

"I haven't decided yet. If I get involved again, it could be—" She shook her head. "It's just a lot."

"What do you mean? Is there drama or something?"

"No. The band gets along fine. I'm just not sure if I have time to do the band and work, and I was thinking about finishing my music degree."

"You were getting a music degree?"

"An associate in fine arts at the community college. I have one semester to go, but I don't know when I can do it." She finished pouring out the fertilizer and returned the bag to the wheelbarrow.

"What's stopping you?"

She gave a short laugh. "Money. What else?"

"Aren't there scholarships?"

"Not for community college." She knelt down and began to spread the fertilizer around the plants. "At least not as far as I know. Anyway, I don't even know if it makes sense to finish the degree. I feel like life might be a better teacher."

"My mom has a music degree. She's an opera singer. She'd say it was worth it."

Steph looked up. "Your mom's an opera singer? Like professionally?"

"Yeah." Sometimes, when people found out about my mom's career, they thought I was making it up, but that didn't seem to be what Steph was implying. She seemed impressed, which made me uncomfortable.

"Where does she perform?" she asked.

"All over," I said vaguely. "She's in Europe this summer."

Steph sat back on her heels. "Touring?"

"No, she's at a festival. Sometimes she tours, but—I mean, the point is, she couldn't have done that without her degree. Maybe it's a good idea for you to finish yours."

Steph looked at me for a second and then returned to spreading the fertilizer around the plants. "Yeah, maybe. Or maybe it would be more useful if I get an accounting degree." She sounded a little bitter.

"I can't imagine you as an accountant."

"I can't either, but it might help with the rent."

I felt like I had screwed up our conversation somehow. "Well, you should do whatever makes sense for you," I said, trying to fix it. "Whether that means you finish your degree or get back together with the band. I just feel like if you have that talent, you should go for it. Otherwise you're suppressing who you really are, and that just seems wrong."

She smiled slightly, first down at the dirt, and then over her shoulder at me. "Thanks for the words of wisdom," she said.

I flushed. "Sorry. I mean, I didn't mean to be condescending."

"You weren't. I appreciate it. It's nice when someone believes in you."

I felt that warm flush spread down my neck as we looked at each other—as she looked at me. Her eyes bright, focused. Did I imagine the slight color on her cheeks, too?

"Enough about me," she said, turning back to the flower bed. "Tell me about you. You're going to college in the fall? What are you going to major in?"

"Yeah, probably either physics or planetary science."

"Really?" She sounded surprised.

"Why, you don't think girls can do science?" I teased her.

She laughed. "I never said that."

"It's just that people have assumptions, you know? Most boys take one look at me and think there's no way I could do math, even though I'm Asian. It's like their two stereotypes get crossed and they don't know how to deal with me."

"I'm not a boy," she said. She sounded amused.

After Steph finished the yard work, I put Analemma back in the house and helped her clean up. I hauled the yard-waste bag over to the trash area and carried the watering cans back to the shed, where Steph put away the wheelbarrow and tools.

"You still want to see my grandpa's notes?" I asked.

She took off the gloves and laid them on the shelf beside some empty pots. "Sure. I have a few minutes."

"I'm set up in Joan's old studio. Have you been in it?"

"No."

I led her up the back path toward the studio and opened the door. "She works in the house now, but she used to work in here."

Steph followed me into the studio, looking around. "Why'd she move into the house? This space is great."

"I don't know. It happened after Grandpa died."

By now I'd divided Grandpa's notes into three stacks on the worktable: unsorted, notes, and not-notes. Next to the not-notes stack was *Diving into the Wreck*, which I'd brought into the studio last time I was in here.

Steph pointed to the book. "Hey, Adrienne Rich. I love her stuff."

"I haven't read anything of hers except for this: I like it a lot."

"My favorite of hers is *The Dream of a Common Language*. Have you read it?"

"No, what's it about?"

"It's more poems." Steph gestured to *Diving into the Wreck*. "Like these, but gayer. She was a lesbian."

"Oh." I had assumed she was straight.

"I tried to write some songs inspired by her poems. One of them turned out okay. When I was with Madchen, we recorded it on our EP."

I could tell by the way she was downplaying the song that she was proud of it. "I'd love to hear it," I said. "Is it online?"

"No. We burned a bunch of CDs at Roxy's apartment and sold them after gigs. But tell me about your grandpa's work. This is it?"

I plucked the top folder off the notes stack and opened it to show Steph, who came over to stand next to me.

"He was researching protostars. They're stars in an early stage of formation," I explained. "Joan wanted me to separate out his research from his letters. I like seeing his handwriting."

"Do you understand all this?" Steph asked, gesturing at the math.

"Only sort of. I've taken calculus, so I can kind of see where it's going, but I haven't studied this. It's pretty advanced."

"Is that what you're most interested in? Protostars?"

"I'm actually more interested in planets than star formation. I'd love to study Earthlike planets."

"Like places we can travel to?"

"That's the first thing everyone thinks of," I said, smiling. "But we have to invent a way to travel a lot faster before we can do that."

"Warp speed?"

I figured she was joking, but I said seriously, "Maybe, but it's unlikely."

She leaned against the edge of the table and looked at me curiously. "Let's say we could go there—to these planets. Do you think there's life on them?"

"Absolutely! We've already found thousands of planets—and only from a really tiny part of the Milky Way. There are so many possibilities for life out there—and life out there might not be anything like what we know on Earth. There are a bunch of telescope missions in the pipeline at NASA that are going to make it practically guaranteed that we can find an Earthlike planet with life on it in our lifetime. I want to be part of that discovery." I stopped, realizing self-consciously that I sounded like a total nerd.

"You're really into this stuff," Steph said, smiling.

I shrugged. "Sorry not sorry?"

She laughed. "I bet you'd be interested in this movie we're watching this weekend. I can't remember the title but Lisa picked it out. It's a 1950s science-fiction movie. Lisa was almost a film major, so she likes to plan out little film festivals for us—I mean for me and Mel. We get together on Sunday nights and watch movies." Steph paused, then said, "You should come over. I bet I have an extra Madchen CD I could give you, and you could borrow my favorite Adrienne Rich."

It was a perfectly safe invitation—Lisa would be there, as well as Mel—but to me it felt, if not dangerous, then significant. "Are you sure? I don't want to crash your party."

"It's not a party; it's just a movie. It would be great to have you." She grinned. "And I know Mel would love to see you."

I was never going to say no, but I hesitated as if I had to think about it. If Steph were a boy, would my hesitation make her try harder? But she wasn't a boy, and she didn't look as if she doubted my decision. She simply looked at me, and I said, "Okay. Sure, I'd love to come."

"Cool. Give me your number and I'll text you my address." She pulled out her phone and handed it me to type in my number. "We usually start around seven and make pizza with Mel."

"Should I bring anything?"

"No, it's really low-key." She wrote a quick text message and a moment later I heard my own phone chime.

I pulled out my phone to read her message. It was just her address, no name. "Got it." When I looked up, she was looking at me with an odd expression on her face. "What?"

"You have a leaf in your hair."

"Where?" I ran my fingers through my hair, trying to dislodge it.

"Other side." Steph reached out with her left hand, her fingers sweeping through my hair behind my right ear, and even though she barely touched me, it felt as though she had stroked my skin from head to toe in one smooth motion. When she stepped back, she was holding a dry fragment of an oak leaf, and her face had a tentative expression on it, as if she wasn't sure if she should have done that. She carefully set the leaf on the worktable, and I wanted to pick it up and preserve it between the pages of a book, like evidence. Exhibit number one: The first time Steph touched me was because of this.

When I was a kid, my grandmother set up a makeshift studio for me in her backyard in Berkeley. She tacked up a piece of black roofing paper on the fence and gave me an enameled tray to use as a palette. She offered me brushes, but I liked to use my fingers. I remember the feel of smearing the bright paints across the rough surface of the paper. I never wanted to paint pictures of people or flowers or houses; I just loved sweeping different colors across the black background, as vivid and contrasting as possible.

Now I kept imagining the ocean in the Adrienne Rich poem. I was taken with the idea of trying to paint it.

Joan told me there were acrylic paints in the studio, left over from the last art class she had taught at the local community center. There was a roll of roofing paper, too, she said, stashed in the gardening shed. She still used it for classes because it was so cheap, and it held the paint well.

I went to the studio first, where I opened the cabinets to hunt for the paints. I found brushes and palette knives, trays with dried paint in the corners, jars of rubber cement and matte medium. I found a heavy, rectangular leather case with the word *Rolleiflex* stamped across the top, and realized this must be Joan's camera. At the very back of the cabinet was a jumble of plastic bottles and squeeze tubes filled with acrylic paint. I pulled them out and lined them up on the counter: ultramarine blue, raw umber, alizarin crimson, chrome yellow, titanium white, mars black. The bottles were covered in multicolored smudges and fingerprints.

I put away the stuff I didn't need, but kept out the camera to show Joan. Then I went to the shed, where I found the roll of tar paper wedged into a back corner. It was about three feet wide and seemed to weigh a million pounds. Once I maneuvered it outside, I found it was easier to roll it over the ground like a log than to carry it. I was rolling it into the studio when Joan called me from the deck.

I glanced over my shoulder and saw her waving the house cordless phone at me. "Your dad's on the phone!" she called.

I dusted off my hands—the paper still smelled a bit like asphalt—and went up the stairs to the deck. Joan handed me the phone and went back inside, while I sat down on the lounger. "Hi, Dad," I said.

He didn't have cell reception at the colony, so every Sunday he would go to the main lodge and call using their landline.

"Hi," he said. "How are things?"

"They're fine. How are you?"

"Same. I'm making progress. Are you still watching my dad's astronomy lectures?"

"Yeah. In the one I watched yesterday he was talking about analemmas—the path of the sun across the sky throughout the year. I forgot that's what Ana was named for."

"Oh, right. He would've loved Analemma. How is she?"

"She's good. Joan's neighbor Tony took her out for a hike with his dog this morning. Do you know Tony?"

"He's the one who did their built-ins, right?"

"Right." I wondered if Dad had any suspicions about Tony's feelings for Joan, but it seemed too weird to ask.

"I talked to your mother recently."

I tensed up. "You did?"

"She said she's coming to San Francisco to see you."

"She'll be on a layover to Hong Kong. She's not really coming to visit me."

He exhaled. "Give her a chance."

He was always asking me to give her a chance. I wondered how many chances he gave her before they divorced.

When I was about twelve, I found a folder of newspaper clippings about my mom in the bookcase in my dad's office. In one article, she was on the front page of the *Boston Globe*'s arts section in an off-the-shoulder black dress, her shiny black hair hanging down in a long straight sheet. Her lips were dark red, her eyes dramatically lined, and the headline read "Alexis Tang Gives 'Carmen' an Asian Twist." She had played Carmen when I was seven years old. I hadn't been allowed to see her performance, but I remembered it had been a big deal.

Inset in the article was a smaller photo from the production itself, with my mother in costume onstage. She wore a red bustier and a ruffled red skirt, and she held up the hem with one hand while she sang, bare legs on display.

I stared at those two photos for a long time: In the larger one she was all elegance; in the second she was all sex appeal. It was disconcerting to see her in the bustier, her cleavage and skin exposed, but she was arresting in both images. I wondered if I could ever look like her. My hair wasn't as black as hers, and it wasn't as straight. My features were softer, as if someone had taken a photo of her face and blurred the lines.

I read the article several times. She told the *Boston Globe* it was long past time for color-blind casting in operas; there was nothing stopping her from playing Carmen if she could sing in French as well as any other soprano. "Why should being Chinese exclude me from taking this role?" she said to the *Globe* reporter. "The language of music, like the language of love, is universal."

The day I found that article I had been angry at my mom for something she'd said to me over the phone. Dad asked me, after the call, to give her a chance to explain, but I was too mad to listen. When I read the *Globe* interview, though, I was so proud of her it hurt.

I put the article back into the folder, and I put the folder, with its worn edges, back where I'd found it. I never asked my dad why he was keeping press clippings about my mom, but it made me suspect that he still loved her.

Over the phone Dad asked, "Are you there?"

"Yes."

"Are you still angry about the summer?" He sounded resigned.

I realized that I wasn't anymore. "No, I'm over it," I said. Maybe that video from Tasha had cemented it. It hadn't made me wish I was on the Vineyard at all. And tonight I was going over to Steph's apartment, and the thought of it made my heart race.

"I'm glad. Your grandmother told me you've been making some new friends in the area?"

"Yeah."

"Want to tell me about them?"

"One of them does yard work for Joan—you met her, actually. The others are her friends."

"They're older?"

"Maybe by a couple years," I hedged.

"These are girls, right?" Dad asked, sounding suspicious.

"Yeah, Dad. They're girls."

"Okay. Sorry," he said sheepishly.

"Don't worry about it." I wasn't about to tell him they were lesbians.

"I'd better get going. I'm in a good spot in the book. I think I'm on track now."

"Okay. Good luck."

"I'll talk to you next week. I love you, Ari."

"Love you too, Dad."

Later that afternoon, I brought the Rolleiflex into the house. Joan was in the living room reading a book when she saw it. "Where'd you find that?" she asked.

"It was in the studio. Is this your old camera?" I sat down beside her on the couch and handed it to her.

"Yes. I'd forgotten where it was. It's been so long since I've used it."

She unsnapped the cover to reveal a black box with silver knobs and levers, and two lenses stacked on top of each other. It wasn't that large and fit comfortably in two hands, but its weight and square corners made me think of those giant old cameras where photographers would cover themselves with a cloth to look through the hood.

"How does it work?" I asked.

She removed the lens covers and pushed up the top of the box, then pressed something that caused a circular glass piece to pop out. "You look down through the top of it," she said, showing me. "This is the viewfinder. Hold it in your lap and look through it. You can focus it with this knob here."

I bent over the top of the camera and realized the glass piece was a magnifier. As I turned the focusing knob, I saw the blurry shapes of the living room come into focus the same way Mars or Venus would sharpen when I'd focus on them through a telescope. A refracting telescope would invert the image, and similarly, the Rolleiflex flipped it horizontally. The woodstove was on the other side of the living room when I looked at it through the viewfinder.

"Does it still take pictures?" I asked.

"It might need some cleaning, but probably. I don't have any film, though."

The camera—with its knobs and levers, its focusing hood and twin lenses—felt like a time machine. I carefully placed it on the coffee table. "Can I ask you something?"

"Of course."

"Why'd you stop using the studio outside?"

She looked surprised by the question. "I didn't mean to. After your grandpa died, I missed him so much. For a long time, I couldn't work. And then when I wanted to work again, the studio felt so far from him. I used to go out there to be alone. He never came out there. He wanted to give me my space." She had a distant expression on her face. "I started using your grandpa's office because I was going through his files, and it just stuck. I like being in his space. I like being able to see what he saw when he worked there. It gives me a different perspective." She looked at me and said, "I'm glad you're using the studio now."

"Don't you want to ask me what I'm doing out there?"

A smile. "Would you like to tell me?"

I thought I did, but as soon as she asked, I felt a kind of defensive constricting inside me. "Actually, I don't know if I do."

Joan nodded. "It's good to keep it to yourself until it's ready. Give it time to incubate on its own, without other people's opinions."

"When will I know if it's ready?"

"You'll learn. Sometimes I've said things too soon, and it's been ruined. I could always tell Russ, though. His knowing never ruins anything. He never judges. He just listens."

I didn't know whether Joan's use of the present tense meant anything. Sometimes it seemed as if Grandpa were right there beside her, just out of sight. I glanced over at the stairs that led to Grandpa's office. I almost expected to see him standing there.

Steph and Lisa lived in a two-story apartment building that looked like a 1950s-era motel. It was on a block lined with older cars and bungalows in San Rafael. I parked next to a manicured hedge in front of the building, checked my phone again for the apartment number, and gave myself one last glance in the rearview mirror. I'd pulled my hair back in a ponytail and put on a smear of neutral lip gloss, aiming for casual, and now I worried my lips were too shiny. I grabbed a tissue from my purse and rubbed some of the gloss off, which only made my lips seem pinker and more swollen. I looked like the girl in the pictures Jacob had taken.

I crumpled up the tissue and got out of the car.

Steph and Lisa's apartment was on the ground floor in the corner, where the building bent like an L around a courtyard with a dry fountain. The windows were covered with half-closed blinds, and through them I could see the flickering of a TV. I pressed the buzzer and didn't wait long before the door was opened.

"Hey," Lisa said. She was holding a PBR in one hand. "You found us."

The door opened into the living room, where an overlarge blue-and-white sectional, across from the TV, took up the majority of the space. A couple of movie posters were tacked up on the wall over the sofa: *The Wild One*, with Marlon Brando on a motorcycle, and *Mädchen in Uniform*, with two women looking pensively past each other. A breakfast bar separated the living room from the kitchen, where I saw Steph and Mel bending over something on the counter. They looked up as I came in and waved at me, but didn't leave the kitchen. Their hands were white with flour.

"Aria!" Mel called. "How've you been?"

"Good. How about you?"

"Even better now that you're here," Mel said.

"You want something to drink?" Lisa asked.

"Sure." I followed her toward the kitchen. It was U-shaped, with the breakfast bar on one arm, the sink and refrigerator across from it, and the stove and a narrow dishwasher crammed into the short side. Lisa edged into the small space and opened the fridge.

"Diet Coke or beer?" Lisa asked.

"Diet Coke, thanks."

Lisa held a can out to me and then went around to lean against the front of the breakfast bar. I joined her, sliding onto one of the two stools.

"Did you get pepperoni?" Mel was saying. "We were out of it last time."

"Yeah," Steph said. "I'll get it." She went to the fridge while Mel began to stretch the dough on the floured counter.

"Can I do anything to help?" I asked.

"No, we got it," Steph said. "Mel and I have been making pizza since when? High school?"

"Since we used Boboli crusts," Mel said.

"So glad we evolved," Steph said.

"We? You mean *me*?" Mel looked at me. "I make the dough now."

"I can't cook," Lisa said. "I let them take care of it."

"You make a mean Kraft macaroni and cheese," Steph said.

Lisa smiled at Steph. "That's right, baby."

She was pretty with that smile, but even as I thought that, I felt a prickling of jealousy. I opened the Diet Coke and realized she hadn't given me a glass or any ice, and then I realized I'd sound like a princess if I asked for some. I drank it straight from the can, the bubbles fizzing so sharply on my tongue that I could taste the chemicals.

The movie we watched was called *It Came from Outer Space*. It was about an amateur astronomer who spots a meteor striking the desert near a small Arizona town.

"This is a rare cinematic masterpiece," Lisa said dryly. "It's different from most 1950s sci-fi movies. They were almost all about people freaking out over nuclear war or Communists secretly invading America. You know, *Invasion of the Body Snatchers* stuff. This one is about aliens who don't actually want to harm us. They crash-land here on accident and need to repair their ship before they go home."

"Like E.T.," Mel said.

"Sort of," Lisa said. "There's also some mind control and kidnapping."

The film began with the astronomer—a white guy in a tweed suit whose name I immediately forgot—driving out to the desert, searching for the crashed meteor. His fiancée, Ellen, who was impeccably dressed 1950s-style, went with him in his convertible.

"Steph said you want to be an astronomer?" Lisa said to me.

The astronomer on-screen was clambering over the lip of the meteor crater. "Yeah," I answered. "But if I were him, I would not go climbing into that hole alone."

Despite the movie's extremely tenuous connection to actual science, I was enjoying it. Lisa said parts of it had been filmed in the Mojave Desert, and the alien-like Joshua trees and craggy rocks, shot in black-and-white, had an otherworldly quality. In one scene a telephone repairman climbed to the top of a telephone pole and listened to the strange alien sounds coming through the wires, which made me think of that Jodie Foster movie *Contact*. When the aliens finally showed up, they were magnificently bizarre creatures with tentacle-like limbs and one giant, bulbous eye—and they left trails of glitter instead of footprints.

"It's a gay allegory," Mel said suddenly. "The aliens are drag queens."

Lisa laughed. "Just you wait."

Toward the end of the film, the astronomer followed the glitter trail through Ellen's apartment (she had been kidnapped by the aliens) to a closed door. He flung it open to reveal an empty closet.

"Look!" Mel cried, pointing at the hangers. "She's out of the closet!"

"You think Ellen being kidnapped by aliens means she's queer?" Lisa said. "That's a messed-up interpretation."

Mel shrugged. "I just call it like I see it."

Steph caught my eye and grinned.

After the movie, Lisa went out to the courtyard to smoke. I tried to help Mel and Steph put the dirty dishes into the dishwasher, but the kitchen was so small we kept bumping into one another. I ended up back on the stool outside the kitchen, where I couldn't help but notice how run-down the apartment was. The beige linoleum, printed with fading tan flowers, was peeling up along the edges. The white stove had electric burners, the black coils embedded in stained metal bowls. The fluorescent-light panel overhead was smudged with black spots where the corpses of dead insects had left indelible stains.

Steph opened the fridge and took out more beers, handing one to Mel and offering me another Diet Coke, which I refused. I asked for some water instead.

"I'm going out front for a minute," Mel said. "You wanna come?"
Steph shook her head. "I'm good."

Mel glanced at me, but I also shook my head. "I didn't know you smoked," I said.

"Not cigarettes," Mel said with a grin.

"Oh," I said, feeling stupid.

But then Steph said, "You wanted to borrow that book, right?"

"Yeah," I said gratefully, and as Mel went outside, I followed Steph to the back of the apartment, past the bathroom and into her and Lisa's bedroom.

There was a single queen-sized bed, unmade, with pale blue sheets rumpled up in the center. A nightstand stood on one side, and wedged between the bed and the window on the other side was a narrow desk. Beneath the window was a bookcase crammed full of CDs, books, and stacks of papers that I realized were musical scores. Two guitars were in the corner. I recognized the acoustic guitar in its case from the open mic, and there was a shiny white electric guitar on a stand. On the dresser I saw a framed photo of Steph with her arms around Lisa's waist, her head resting on Lisa's shoulder. Steph was smiling only slightly, but Lisa looked radiant—as if this was the one place she had always wanted to be.

Steph was sitting on the edge of her bed, pulling out a thin blue paperback from the bookcase. I went to join her, and the mattress sank softly as I sat beside her. I made sure to leave several inches between us.

She gave me the book and said, "This is the one I was telling you about."

The spine was cracked, and the book opened on its own to a series of poems titled only with roman numerals. I flipped back a page and read the title: "Twenty-One Love Poems."

"I think the CDs are in here," Steph said, opening the closet. It was jammed with clothes—hers and Lisa's—and shoes piled on the floor. She reached up to the shelf above the clothes and pulled down a cardboard box. Inside it was a mess of spiral notebooks, yellow bubble envelopes, Sharpies, and tape. She opened one of the envelopes and said, "I forgot about these." She handed me a postcard-sized flyer for Madchen, and I realized the name must be related to that movie poster on Steph's living room wall. The postcard featured a photo of the band taken on a beach. Steph was on the left, dressed all in black, with her hair gelled into a fauxhawk. Roxy stood next to her in a hot pink tank top, ruffled black miniskirt, and those steel-toed boots. On either side of them I recognized the other band members, Talia and Jasmine.

"Here it is," Steph said, pulling a CD out of another padded envelope. "I still have a few."

The CD cover used the same photo, with MADCHEN printed across the center. "Can I borrow this?" I asked.

"You can have it. I'm not selling them anymore."

"Thanks." I stacked the CD on top of the book, and when Steph didn't ask for the postcard back, I tucked it inside.

As Steph returned the cardboard box to the shelf, she said, "I hope you had a good time tonight? Hope the movie wasn't too weird."

"It was weird, but I liked it. It was unexpectedly philosophical."

"What do you mean?"

"Remember the beginning? It starts with that voice-over where they're like, *Welcome to this town in Arizona, where everybody is so sure of the future.*" I pitched my voice lower.

"*Future voice,*" she intoned, turning back to me with a smile.

"Exactly. But then the future turns out to be not so certain. They thought they knew what would happen, but nobody knew anything."

"That's why I don't plan ahead. If you plan too much, you'll just disappoint yourself."

"But you have to make some plans. Otherwise how can you work toward your goals?"

She laughed slightly. "I bet you have your whole life planned out."

"Not my whole life. But definitely the next few years."

"You didn't know where you'd be this summer."

"True," I admitted.

"Disappointed?"

I was still holding the Adrienne Rich book and the CD, and I pressed the hard corner of the plastic case against my fingertip, reminding myself that this was real. I was in Steph's bedroom, and she was looking at me with a curious light in her eyes, a smile on the edge of her mouth, not quite there, but maybe I could tease it out.

"I'm not disappointed," I said softly. "Not anymore."

There was the smile.

listened to the Madchen CD on the way home in Joan's car. Two of
the four songs were fast and angry, a third was more mid-tempo,
and the fourth was contemplative and a little sad. It was called
"Twenty-One," which made me think this was the song inspired by
the Adrienne Rich poems.

The music was very different from Steph's open-mic performance,
but of course it would be different. At the open mic she'd only had an
acoustic guitar. Madchen reminded me of Metric, but less polished.

I thought I heard Steph singing harmony behind Roxy, and then
on "Twenty-One," Steph sang the chorus alone.

You drove me to another place
To sleep in your arms
You said you waited for me
You said you chose me

There was something plaintive about it, as if Steph resented the
person who had chosen her. Was it Lisa? Did it mean something about
their relationship? I could spin a whole story out of those few lines.

The next morning, I listened to the CD again as I drove to Corte
Madera. I wanted to buy some bigger brushes for painting, and Joan

told me about an art supply store on Sir Francis Drake. I played "Twenty-One" on repeat until I had the lyrics practically memorized. *You said you chose me*, Steph sang over and over.

After I bought the paintbrushes, I stopped at the Starbucks next door for an iced chai. It was late morning by then, and when I got back to the car, the interior had heated up. I turned on the engine and the AC, and Steph's voice came out of the speakers. I had parked facing Sir Francis Drake, and across the street I saw a sign for the Greenbrae Garden Center. It took a second, and then I remembered that was the place where Steph worked.

I could go over and say hello.

Immediately I felt my heartbeat quicken, as if I were preparing to commit some kind of crime.

What would I say?

She might not even be there.

I backed the car out of the parking spot and drove to the shopping center exit, where I turned left to head back to Woodacre. I approached the garden center on the right. It was a one-story building with a big fenced-in area in the back. Through the fence I saw rows of plants, bags of soil, stacks of pots, and then I passed it and couldn't see it anymore.

I could go back.

Sir Francis Drake was a busy four-lane divided road with shopping centers on either side, but there were also single-family homes and apartment buildings behind fences and hedges. A middle-aged man was pushing an old mower across a tiny lawn in front of a white bungalow. Trash barrels were lined up on a side street, where a yellow VW Bug pulled up to the intersection. I glimpsed the driver's hands on the steering wheel. Four construction workers were sitting on a low concrete wall outside an apartment building, eating their lunches, their orange hard hats lined up beside them. None of these people knew what I was thinking as I drove past, and I felt sharply disconnected from them—from everything—as if I were in a parallel universe that mirrored this one but could not influence it.

According to the many-worlds theory of quantum mechanics, there is an infinite number of universes. They exist independently but in parallel to our own, so each of us may have an infinite number of replicas living in other universes. When I first learned this, I wondered if each version of myself lived exactly the same life, or if sometimes different versions made different decisions. And if one made a different decision, wouldn't that set off a chain reaction of different decisions? Wouldn't those different decisions transform us into different people? Or were we still the same person at heart?

"Twenty-One" started to play again.

At the next stoplight I made a U-turn.

Greenbrae Garden Center had a big parking lot that was about half full. I pulled into a space, switched off the engine, and sat there in silence, looking in the rearview mirror at the store's entrance. People were coming and going, pushing carts full of flowers and tools.

It would probably be weird for me to show up at her work. I could back the car out and leave without anyone knowing. I didn't want to seem desperate.

I checked my hair in the rearview mirror. I didn't have any lip gloss with me, so I licked my lips.

I got out of the car and realized I was wearing my cutoffs again. I rolled up the bottoms, cuffing them high on my thighs. Looking at my dim reflection in the car window, I adjusted my tank top, and then I headed into the store.

I immediately saw the flaw in my unplanned visit: The place was huge. I passed spinning racks of seed packs, aisles of rakes and spades and ceramic pots, a carousel of gardening hats. The employees wore brown aprons with *Greenbrae Garden Center* printed on the front, but I didn't see Steph anywhere.

I walked through the store to the vast backyard. Beneath the angular plastic greenhouse roofs were rows of flowers and plants that I didn't know, and even more pots spread out on a long, low platform. They were glazed in violet or Mexican blue or goldenrod, the colors bright as jewels.

An employee who was pricing the pots asked me, "Can I help you find anything?"

"No thanks, I'm just looking," I said automatically, and then wondered if I should have asked for Steph. What if I couldn't find her? What if she wasn't working at all?

But I wanted this to be accidental. Getting someone else involved made it feel planned, and I didn't have a plan.

I kept searching. At the back of the yard, the plastic roof ended, leaving the open area baking under the bright sun. Here there were pallets of soil and fertilizer and rocks, but still no sign of Steph.

It was too hot out here, so I headed back to the covered area. Down the aisle to my right a middle-aged blond woman was pointing at something on the ground, and as I approached, I realized she was gesturing to a person who was nearly hidden behind a cart full of plants. When the person stood up, it was Steph.

Once I saw her it felt inevitable, even though a second before it had seemed impossible. She didn't notice me until the woman left with another plant in her basket. Steph was clearly expecting another shopper with another request, and the moment she recognized me, her entire expression changed, polite blankness swept away by surprise.

"Aria? What are you doing here?"

I gave her a tentative smile. "I was across the street, and then I remembered you work here. Hi."

"Hi." She smiled back. She began to move small pots of white and purple flowers from the cart in the aisle to the platform beside her. I walked down the aisle and looked at the plants; I was pretty sure I'd seen them in Joan's yard.

"What are these?" I asked.

"Impatiens."

"Impatience?"

"No." She pulled a stake out of one of the pots and handed it to me. *Impatiens.*

"Oh. I don't know much about plants." I gave the stake back to her, and her fingers brushed mine as she took it.

"That's what I'm here for." She glanced up at me as she worked, and there was something knowing in her expression as she said, "So, are you here to broaden your knowledge of plants?"

There was a teasing tone in her voice. I knew she was giving me an opening to flirt with her, and I felt a thrill go through me.

I knew how this worked with boys. There was a kind of offering I could make, an invitation for them to look at me. I'd smile at them for longer than was strictly necessary, sit a little closer than I needed to, accidentally-on-purpose brush against them. I wasn't entirely sure how to do that with Steph, who wasn't a boy, and always at the back of my mind lurked the knowledge that Lisa existed, but when I looked at Steph and she looked at me, something happened to push all reason aside. As if my body had already made a decision without any input from my brain.

I sat on the edge of the wooden platform next to the rows of impatiens, stretching my legs across the aisle. I saw her gaze drop, sliding over my limbs. My shorts were almost too short to sit in, but I didn't unroll them. I crossed my ankles, my fingers curling over the rough edge of the platform, and said, "I listened to the Madchen CD. My favorite is 'Twenty-One.' You sing the chorus on that, don't you?"

A tinge of pink rose in Steph's cheeks, but it was so faint I might have imagined it. "Thanks," she said. "Yeah. It's the song I told you about."

"I thought so."

"Did you read the poems, too?"

"Not yet, but I'm going to read them. Thanks for letting me borrow the book."

"Anytime."

We were looking at each other again, and her hand came so close to my thigh as she placed the potted impatiens on the platform, the tiny pink blooms limp and defenseless. Maybe she would brush her hand accidentally against my skin. The thought of it made a thrill go through me, as if she already had touched me, and I remember thinking that we were looking at each other for far too long—this was getting obvious—and then Steph seemed to shake her head slightly and broke the gaze. She shifted, straightening up to push the cart a little farther down the aisle, because the platform near me was full now, and she had to stock the next section.

I was a little disappointed. She wasn't looking at me anymore. I started to wonder if I'd gotten this all wrong, but she said nothing and I said nothing. I heard the sound of carts rolling and the hollow thunk of someone placing a terra-cotta pot on the ground, and a woman asking loudly, "Where are your gardening gloves?"

And then Steph said, "I have my lunch break in half an hour. If you want to hang out here for a while, we could get something to eat."

She met my eyes again, directly, and just like that my disappointment vanished.

"Okay." I stood up, brushing the dirt off the back of my shorts, and when I turned around to walk away, I knew she was watching.

Steph suggested we go to the In-N-Out by the freeway. She led me to a blue Toyota truck that looked like it was from the 1980s, parked in the employee lot beyond the pallets of rocks. On the doors I saw the faded outlines of letters that had been peeled off; they spelled NICHOLS LANDSCAPING.

Steph got in and reached across the cab to push up the passenger side lock. I climbed in, and the hot vinyl seat burned against my thighs. "Ow," I said, and scooted to the edge.

"Here, you can sit on this," Steph said. She pulled out a spare Greenbrae Garden Center apron from behind her seat.

"Thanks," I said, and tucked it beneath my legs.

She started the engine, and I looked for the button to roll down the window, only to realize the truck was old enough to have a hand crank. I turned it, squeaking, to let in the still, hot air.

"The sign that used to be on the car door—Nichols Landscaping," I said. "Does your family have a landscaping business? Is that how you got into . . ." I gestured at the garden center as she drove us out of the employee parking lot.

"Sort of. This was my dad's truck. He had a landscaping business, but he died when I was twelve."

"I'm so sorry," I said quickly.

She shook her head. "You didn't know. My aunt Christy tried to keep the business running for a while but it didn't work out. She gave me the truck when I turned sixteen. It was already old then, but it still runs." She rapped her knuckles on the tan plastic dashboard. "Hopefully for a while longer, anyway." She turned left onto Sir Francis Drake and nodded toward the shopping center. "So were you really across the street before you came in?"

She sounded as if she thought I was lying—that I'd made that up as an excuse to see her. And she'd asked me to lunch anyway. "Yes, I was really across the street," I said, pretending to sound indignant.

"I went to buy some brushes at the art supply store." I now remembered my iced chai, probably totally melted in Joan's car.

"For your grandma?"

"No, for me."

"I didn't know you painted."

"I don't. Not like Joan anyway. I painted with her when I was a kid, but I haven't really painted anything in a long time."

"What made you want to paint now?"

I didn't know how to explain it to myself, much less to Steph. It was more like an instinct than any conscious desire. "I guess . . . why not try something new?" I was looking at her and she glanced sideways at me for a second, and when our eyes met, I wondered if what I'd said sounded suggestive.

She smiled slightly. "Why not?" she echoed.

"What makes you want to write a song?" I asked.

She turned onto a side road so we could go under the highway overpass. In-N-Out was on the other side, just outside a shopping center that contained a Trader Joe's. Dad and I had gone to it before.

"It depends," she answered. "For the song I sang at the open mic, I was going for a different sound—acoustic, Americana-type stuff." She glanced at me as she said, "I wanted to try something new."

"Did you write all the Madchen songs?"

"No. Roxy wrote a couple and I wrote a couple. But the whole band worked on the music together." She turned into the In-N-Out drive-through lane. There were four cars ahead of us. "I thought we'd get it to go to save time," she said. "There's a nice place to park down the road where you can see the bay. I go there for lunch sometimes."

"Sounds good."

We were quiet for a while as the line inched forward. A young couple came out of the restaurant with a tray of food and sat down at one of the tables near the drive-through. The girl was blond with glossy pink lips, wearing short jean shorts and a pink tank top. I could see the blue straps of her bra. The guy, dressed in a 49ers jersey and baggy shorts, quickly stuffed a bunch of fries in his mouth.

Steph saw me watching them and said, "So, do you have a boyfriend? You never told me." She added with a smile, "Or a girlfriend?"

The second part of her question made my whole body go hot. "Not right now," I answered, trying to sound nonchalant.

Out of the corner of my eye I saw the girl at the table unwrapping her burger, lifting it to her pink lips. I looked down and noticed that the twin cup holder wasn't built into the dashboard; it had been velcroed beneath the ancient tape deck. Steph shifted in her seat, and I wondered if she was going to ask me something more. I wanted her to, but I was also afraid she would.

But then she said, "I think I'm going to do the concert."

I looked at her in surprise. "You are?"

She was gazing at the Prius in front of us, one hand resting on the steering wheel, the other on the gear shift. She pulled us ahead. "Yeah. It's just one day, and Roxy and I wanted to do it last year, but we didn't get in. I didn't realize she tried again."

"Are you excited?"

She made a face that was sort of a grimace. "I don't know. I mean, I want to do it. I like playing with the band. But if I do it, will I want to do it again? I've done a couple open mics and they're just not the same. I don't think I like performing solo."

"I know you said there were reasons you couldn't be in the band, but it seems like if you like it that much, and the band wants you back . . ."

I saw her grip on the steering wheel tense, and then she deliberately let it go. "It's not that simple. I have to think about whether it's good for me and Lisa."

"Shouldn't she want you to do what makes you happy?"

Steph's jaw clenched.

"I'm sorry," I said. "I shouldn't be butting in."

"She gets jealous," Steph said unexpectedly.

"Of the band? Or Roxy?"

Steph pulled the truck forward to the menu, and through the speaker a slightly scratchy voice said, "Welcome to In-N-Out. Can I take your order?"

We both asked for the same thing: cheeseburgers animal style, with fries and Diet Cokes. I pulled my wallet from my purse and extracted a twenty-dollar bill, holding it out to her. After a second of hesitation, she took my money. I was faintly disappointed.

"I'll get change," she said, and pulled the truck forward again. We weren't quite at the pickup window yet. "I understand why she's jealous," she continued. "It's a little weird to be in a band—and it's not like Madchen was well-known. We were barely anything, but people come to shows and look at you, and they have ideas about you, and they want things from you. It probably sucks to see that and be on the outside."

I thought about my mother and that *Boston Globe* article my dad had kept. I had been too young to witness the way he reacted when he saw her onstage, but he never struck me as the jealous type. Had he felt like he was on the outside? I wondered if that was part of why they'd divorced.

Steph looked at me. "I didn't mean to unload that on you."

"No, I get it. I can see how it would be hard to deal with."

Finally, we were at the pickup window, and Steph passed me the food to hold while she paid. The smell of french fries made my stomach growl. Then she handed me fifteen dollars in change and drove out of the drive-through lane.

"It's just down here a little ways," Steph said as she turned onto the street. We passed the road that led back under the overpass; we passed the entrance to a trailer park; and then suddenly on the left, water appeared, dotted with small grassy islands.

"What is this place?" I asked. "I've never been here."

"I don't know. I think it's some kind of marshland. It connects to the bay. You can't see it from here but over to the left is the ferry terminal at Larkspur."

The 101 freeway was directly to our right, but it was elevated above the road, so as long as we weren't looking at it, we could be on a remote stretch of the coast. Steph pulled into a little parking area facing the water and turned off the engine. The low roar of the freeway sounded almost like the ocean.

I handed over her lunch and opened my own, and for a while we were busy with the food. The burgers and fries came in paper trays, into which I squeezed my packets of ketchup. I had a sudden memory of dipping fries into a paper ketchup cup, sitting at a hard red-and-white plastic booth inside In-N-Out. Dad had been the one who taught me to order my burger animal style, and now as I picked mine up, I remembered the taste just before I bit in: the tangy pickles mixed with minced grilled onions, the toasted bun, the slice of tomato that always wanted to slide out and escape. This was the second burger I'd eaten with Steph this summer.

"I always forget how good this is," I said between bites. "I wish there was an In-N-Out where I live."

"There is, for this summer." She took a sip of her drink.

"I guess we'll have to come back." I said *we* without thinking, and I saw her eyes brighten when she heard it. I felt a warmth in me that had nothing to do with the summer heat.

It was a surprisingly intimate experience to be sitting beside her, the ancient vinyl seats creaking whenever we moved. We didn't say much because we were eating, and I was excruciatingly aware of the movements of my mouth. The crispy-soft texture of the meat as

I bit into it, the creamy-vinegary taste of the sauce, the saliva in my mouth, the flavor on my lips. I saw her right hand reaching for her drink, lifting it from the cup holder, her fingers shiny with french fry oil. I didn't intend to finish my fries but of course I did, and afterward I licked the salt from my fingers.

We stuffed the cheeseburger wrappers into the paper sacks, crumpling up the trays and fitting them inside, too. "Here, I'll take it," Steph said, gesturing to the trash can at the edge of the tiny parking lot.

I handed my bag to her, and she opened the door and walked over to the trash. Beyond her the water tossed off light like diamonds. She came back to the truck and got in, and we sat there in silence. It felt like a good silence. I could say something, but I didn't have to. She leaned her head against the headrest. Her eyelashes were dark and thick.

After a while she turned to look at me and said, "I have to get back to work."

"I know."

She smiled that tiny smile again and reached forward to turn the key in the ignition. Her right hand seemed to move toward me—I could see it coming to rest on my knee, her fingers sliding over the soft skin of my inner thigh—but her hand only came to rest on the gear shift between us.

All the way back I could feel her phantom hand on my leg, even though she had never touched me.

On Tuesday I wanted to drive back to the garden center, to linger in the flower aisles until I saw Steph. I imagined her pulling her brown apron off, folding it, catching my eye as if she expected to see me there. We would get into her truck and she would drive us somewhere—it didn't really matter where—but I imagined redwoods rolling past the windows, which meant we were heading west past Woodacre and toward Point Reyes. I would look over at her and we'd be laughing, the windows open and wind whipping my hair back as if we were in a movie, and she would reach out and put her right hand on my thigh.

I wanted to text her, but every message I started turned into a fantasy.

The flowers you planted are dying, you need to save them. She'd show up and we'd go to the shed, and instead of taking down the spade or the watering can she'd run her fingers through my hair to extract another errant leaf, and then her hand would cup my face. I could feel her palm on my cheek.

Do you want to go out for another burger I'm so hungry. We'd go to the Fairfax Grille again, just the two of us, and after we ate our dripping Marin burgers we'd go out to her truck, and she'd lean across the gear shift and her lips would taste like salt.

Once I hovered my finger over the send button for a good long minute, wondering what she would do if she got a message from me that said *I have to see you, please come over.*

I deleted the message. I didn't even leave Joan's house for fear that I'd be compelled to case out Steph's neighborhood on the off chance she wasn't working and might be sitting outside, waiting for me.

I was possessed by thoughts of her that made me want to do stupid, embarrassing things. I wasn't myself.

took the paintbrushes I'd bought into the studio, but now that I had them, I didn't know what to do. They stayed in their plastic wrappers on the counter next to the paints. I turned the camping chair away from the TV in the corner and toward the view out the windows. I sat down in the chair and opened up *The Dream of a Common Language*.

On the title page was an inscription: *To Steph—Don't give up on your dreams*. I couldn't read the signature, but it looked like a *J* followed by a squiggle.

I reached for my phone and texted her: *Who gave you the book of Rich poems? Just curious.*

As soon as I sent it—part of me pleased that I'd come up with a legitimate reason to text her—I felt stupid and wished I hadn't.

She didn't respond immediately. I opened the book again and began to read. "Twenty-One Love Poems" weren't twenty-one separate poems, but a connected narrative, a story about two women who meet in New York City and fall in love. Their relationship seemed to end ambiguously; I wasn't entirely sure what happened. One poem was unnumbered and titled "The Floating Poem," and this was the only one that fit my idea of what a love poem was supposed to be: centered on physical desire. I ran the words around in my mouth as if I were tasting something new. They were lush and round, like berries. If I were to paint them, they would be ripe orange and pomegranate red.

My phone dinged, making my heart race.

Steph wrote: *Ms. Silva, my high school English teacher. She gave it to me when I graduated.*

I stared at her message for some time before I responded. *I'm reading the 21 love poems. Is your song inspired by number 15? The lyrics sound like some of those lines.*

Several minutes passed before she replied: *Not exactly, but sort of. It's hard to explain by text. I get off work in an hour. Want to meet up?*

A burst of excitement went through me. I forced myself to wait for a minute. While I was counting off seconds, I remembered Joan had gone out for the afternoon, taking her car, and I had promised to walk Analemma. A flash of disappointment was followed by a sudden new idea.

Do you want to come here? Joan's out and I told her I'd take Analemma on a hike. You could come with us.

I waited, barely breathing, for what felt like the longest thirty seconds of my life. Her response was brief: *OK.*

By the time Steph arrived, I'd put on sneakers and changed my clothes twice. When Analemma started barking, I grabbed her leash and my sunglasses, and we went out to meet Steph.

She was coming up the path and bent down to pet Analemma, who bounded up to her. "You look ready to go," she said, and Analemma barked. Steph laughed. "Wow, all right," she said, and then she looked up at me from beneath the brim of her baseball cap, smiling. "Hi."

"Hi," I replied. Analemma dashed down to the bottom of the path to wait by the closed gate, her tail whipping back and forth excitedly.

"After you," Steph said, and she stepped aside so that I could brush past her and put Analemma on her leash.

A SCATTER OF LIGHT

"I thought we'd take the short loop up to the fire road," I said. "It's just a couple of miles. Have you ever hiked up there?"

"No. Sounds good to me."

As we walked, Analemma ranged ahead on the leash, sniffing at plants and patches of the ground. Not far from Joan's house, I turned onto a single-lane road. We passed the gates to other houses built up into the hillside, but except for us the road was deserted.

"Can I ask you that question again?" I said. We weren't looking at each other as we walked, and maybe that made it easier to talk.

"About the song?"

"Yeah. I wondered if it was inspired by a specific poem."

"Not just one poem, more like the whole group of them. I wrote it last year when I was about to turn twenty-one, so that's why it's called 'Twenty-One.' And I guess I was thinking a lot about relationships, and how much work they are, and 'Twenty-One Love Poems' is about how Adrienne Rich's relationship with another woman is a lot of work. You have to choose to be in the relationship, because the rest of the world doesn't make it easy."

"Do you believe that?"

"The world is definitely not set up for queer relationships."

"True, but I mean do you believe that relationships are a lot of work? I always thought that if you're in a relationship with someone, it should work on its own. You shouldn't have to force it."

"I don't think forcing anything is a good idea, but yeah, you have to work at it."

I wanted to ask if her relationship with Lisa was a lot of work, but instead I said, "Some things can't be forced, anyway. Like chemistry. You either have it with someone or you don't."

"You think so?"

We arrived at the trailhead, and Analemma led the way through the metal gate onto the trail.

148

"Of course, don't you?" I said. "Isn't it obvious when you're attracted to someone?" I looked at her through my sunglasses, which made it feel safer to ask this question, but she only smiled slightly and didn't meet my eyes.

"Sometimes it's obvious, yeah," she said.

I felt like I was too close to saying something I shouldn't. Analemma was sniffing at the little yellow flowers growing along the side of the path, and I used it as an excuse to bend down and look at them.

"Joan told me these are named something kind of funny," I said. "I can't remember."

"Monkey flowers. They grow all over around here." Steph bent down and plucked one of the blossoms; it was about the size of the tip of her thumb. "Supposedly they're called monkey flowers because they look like monkey faces, but I don't see it." She offered me the little bloom. "Do you see it?"

I carefully took the flower from her fingertips. I studied the interior of the bloom, the butter-yellow petals soft and pliant, the tiny white-tipped stigma at its deep gold core.

"I don't see it either," I said. When I looked up, she was looking at me, and even though I was shielded by my sunglasses I felt a flush come over my face.

Analemma tugged on the leash, and I let her pull me onward. When Steph wasn't looking, I slipped the flower into my pocket. It was only a little yellow monkey flower, but I felt as if she had given me something much more significant.

The trail wound up through groves of trees—Douglas fir, Steph said, like the kind you buy at Christmas, and California bay laurel—and then through grasslands that smelled like hay. Some of the trail was quite steep and rocky, and although Analemma had no trouble, Steph and I had to pay attention. As we climbed, it felt as if time had stopped and we were in a little bubble of forest and hillside.

"Can I ask you something else?" I said. "You don't have to answer if you don't want."

"Sure," she said from behind me.

"When . . . when did you know you're . . . queer?" The word *queer* sounded strange to me, like a slur, but Steph had used it so I thought I should, too.

"I'm not sure if there was a light bulb moment," she said. "In retrospect, it should've been obvious. I used to have these really intense friendships with girls. I'd save up all my money to buy them stuffed animals and unicorn stickers in elementary school."

"Unicorn stickers?" I said, laughing.

"Hey, they loved them. I was really popular."

"So you've always known?"

"No, I mean . . . I knew I didn't like boys the way the other girls did. But I didn't know it was possible to like girls. This is kind of embarrassing, but I don't think I really knew until *The L Word*."

"Really? When was that?"

"I was thirteen. It came out the year after my dad died. I used to go online in the middle of the night and torrent the show."

"I've never seen it. It's not on anymore, is it?"

"No, it ended a few years ago. It wasn't that great—some of it was offensive—but it . . ." She laughed. "It explained a lot."

The trail emerged onto the fire road, which ran along the ridge, and we stopped to catch our breath. There were a couple of huge coast live oak trees up here, with twisting branches and spiny-edged leaves that rattled like tambourines in the wind. It was a clear day, and the view was spectacular—360 degrees of golden-brown hills dotted with dark green trees and brush, the blue sky above, and the shine of water to the southwest. Joan had told me it was Kent Lake, and I pointed it out to Steph.

"You can see how dry everything is," she said. "The only time it would be green is right after the rainy season, and we've been in a drought for years."

"I didn't know that."

"Yeah. It's global warming. Sorry to be a downer."

"No, I get it. Would you ever leave California? Isn't it supposed to fall into the ocean?"

Steph shook her head. "This is my home. If it falls into the ocean, I'll probably fall with it."

Analemma tugged on the leash, and we continued on, heading for the other fire road that would circle back down to Joan's house. After a while I said, "I don't think I've seen any TV with queer people in them. There's Ellen, but that's just her. I don't think it counts."

"Not even *Glee*?"

"I've never been into that."

"*Grey's Anatomy*?"

"Not really my thing either."

"What is your thing?"

"*The Walking Dead*? *Alien*? I guess I like monsters."

"Horror is very queer."

"Is it?"

"Hello, vampires."

"Oh! I remember now I used to watch *Buffy* reruns when I was a kid. I was probably too young for it. Willow was queer, wasn't she?"

"Definitely. I used to torrent those, too. I'm surprised my parents never caught me and figured out I was queer."

"They don't know?"

"No, they know. I mean I used to watch so much gay TV on the desktop computer in the den in the middle of the night, but they never noticed. I did wipe the history, but still."

A mountain biker came toward us, his tires kicking up dust, and I pulled Analemma to the side while he passed.

"When did you come out to your parents?" I asked.

"It was kind of an accident. When I was fifteen I started dating this girl at school, and my mom saw us kissing outside the 7-Eleven. She didn't take it well."

"I'm sorry." But all I could think about was Steph kissing a nameless girl outside a convenience store. A Slurpee staining her lips red.

"It was a long time ago."

I wondered who the girl had been and what had happened to her. "Is your mom okay with it now?"

"Not really."

I hadn't expected that answer. "Are you okay with that?"

Steph shrugged. "My stepdad is religious and a straight-up asshole, so as long as she's married to him I don't think she can change her mind. They kicked me out when I was seventeen."

"That's awful," I said inadequately.

"I wanted to leave anyway."

She acted as if it hadn't been a big deal, but it must have been huge. I couldn't even imagine my parents doing that to me, and the vast difference between my childhood and what Steph had dealt with seemed to yawn between us. I felt as if I owed her some kind of revelation of my own at the very least, but she didn't ask me any questions.

Analemma was sniffing around a bush where tiny white flowers were in bloom, and Steph said, "That's toyon. The flowers will turn into red berries in the fall, like holly berries."

I went along with the change of subject. "What's that one?" I asked, pointing at another bush nearby with red limbs and flat oval leaves.

"Manzanita," she said.

We continued along the ridge while she named the other plants she knew: yerba santa, buckbrush, sagebrush. When we came to the fire road that descended down into Woodacre, I turned onto it. Analemma caught sight of a lizard on a rock and sprinted, snapping the leash out of my hand. "Analemma!" I shouted, running after her. She disappeared down the road and into a grove of trees, finally stopping at a fallen log in the shade, her tongue lolling out while she panted. I picked up the leash from where it trailed onto the ground, about to scold her, but she gave me her big brown eyes and sloppy grin and I couldn't be mad.

The trees around us had reddish bark that was peeling away in long, paperlike strips from a green trunk beneath. I heard Steph crunching down the trail and then into the grove behind us. I turned to her and asked, "What are these trees called? They're so weird looking."

"Madrones. It's like you can see inside them, right?" She went over to one of the trees and rubbed her fingers against the green interior.

And then I knew what I wanted to tell her, and before I could lose my nerve I said, "I don't think I'm straight."

I have a crush on you, I thought, as if I were a twelve-year-old, and I blushed even though I didn't say the words out loud.

Steph turned away from the tree and toward me. She gave me a sympathetic look, and I felt that flutter in my belly that I was beginning to recognize as belonging to her: that warm purr, that fizzing lift.

"How long have you known?" she asked.

"I don't know," I said. *Since I met you.*

She nodded gravely, as if that were normal.

I don't remember what we talked about after that. My head was full of what I'd said to her and what it meant for me. I wondered if I should download some episodes of *The L Word* just to make sure, or maybe I could find those Willow episodes of *Buffy* and compare myself with her.

And then there was Analemma to manage; we encountered another dog on the road as we returned to civilization, and Analemma didn't like a lot of other dogs. By the time we got back to the house and I checked my phone, we'd been gone for over an hour. Joan's car still wasn't back.

I thought about inviting Steph inside, but she said she should go home; she was meeting Lisa for dinner, and it was already after five. So I let Analemma in through the gate and then walked Steph to her truck.

"Are you working tomorrow?" I asked.

She nodded. "Every day this week."

"When do you come back to do the yard?"

"Not till next Friday. I'm here every other week. We should do that lunch, though. How about next Wednesday? I have the day off."

"I'm sure that'll be fine." I was a little disappointed, though; next Wednesday was a whole week away.

"You should come to movie night on Sunday again."

A surge of excitement. "Are you sure?"

"Yeah, of course. And keep in touch if you want to talk or anything."

She came toward me with her arms open to hug me goodbye, and I knew it was a completely normal thing to do, but it was also the first time we hugged. Did she realize that? Her arms went around me, and she smelled slightly metallic, like sweat. I felt her hands on my back through my T-shirt, her palms and fingers splayed out across my spine. I felt the press of her breasts and hip bones against me, her warm body, and I had to fight the urge to pull her closer.

Then she stepped back and opened the door of her truck, and I waved goodbye as if I didn't want to climb in right after her. I forced myself to go back through the gate and not stand there watching her drive off, but I listened until the sound of the engine faded into nothing. As I walked slowly up the path to the front door, I slipped my hand into my pocket for the keys and felt something soft inside. It was the yellow monkey flower, only slightly squashed from its journey.

7:43 PM

Steph: *Checking in. You ok? That was a big thing you did*

7:44 PM

Me: *I'm ok. Thanks for asking!*

7:52 PM

Steph: *Of course. Been there*

F riday morning, I cut off a big piece of roofing paper and tacked it to the bare wall inside the studio. It was uneven, not quite a rectangle, and as I stood there looking at it, the blackness seemed to become a doorway to somewhere else. I saw a diver descending into the deep, and I wondered what she hoped to find.

My phone dinged from the counter, making me jump.

But it was a message from Haley. I hadn't heard from her in so long I almost didn't believe it was really her. She'd sent a mirror selfie as if it were proof of life. She wore a black strapless minidress with a satin corset-like top, and she was in her parents' house on Martha's Vineyard. She wrote: *Do you like this dress on me? I can't decide if it's too goth.*

Another photo followed; this one showed her from the back. She had pinned her blond hair up, which revealed a string of star tattoos on her left shoulder blade that she'd gotten right before we graduated. They seemed to burst out of the dress in a mini-fireworks display, shading from dark red to gold to yellow.

Almost automatically, I responded: *What's it for?*

She texted back instantly: *NYC. I'm going for the weekend, planning to check out my new neighborhood by NYU!!*

I wrote back: *Looks good on you. Not too goth but definitely edgy.*

Thanks!! she wrote, and that was all.

I put the phone down, feeling irritated, and returned to the black paper. But now I couldn't concentrate. Haley and I hadn't been in touch since graduation. Was everything back to normal now? I didn't know if I wanted that.

My phone dinged again, and I flinched. I stared at the black paper for a minute longer, before my curiosity over what Haley was sending now drove me to pick it up. But this time it was Steph.

In n out?

When we were sitting in her truck looking out at the water, eating our burgers, I told her about Haley and Tasha, which somehow led me to show her the video from the Fourth of July. And then I told her how I was supposed to be spending the summer on Martha's Vineyard, but I had been uninvited because of the Tumblr photos. She didn't look shocked and she didn't interrupt, and I realized I hadn't told anyone about this before. I had been embarrassed and angry, but now the embarrassment had faded and my anger had dissipated. The photos were probably still on Tumblr since you could never entirely delete something from the internet, but with every passing day they got buried under more posts. It wasn't a funny story—not yet, and maybe it never would be—but it didn't hurt anymore.

When I finished, Steph said, "Now I understand why you seemed so down when you first got here."

"I did?"

"Yeah. I'm sorry that happened to you."

She reached over and put her hand on my knee. She squeezed it very lightly, as if to comfort me, and then she moved it away and picked up her Diet Coke. It happened so fast I almost thought I'd imagined it, but I felt her fingerprints on me, as if they'd been tattooed on my skin.

Steph texted me a photo of the poster for the Golden Gate Queer Music Festival. A bunch of bands were listed in the lineup, and right there second from the bottom was Madchen. She wrote: *8/3 in SF. You coming?*

I replied: *Wouldn't miss it.*

I started to cover the roofing paper with blue acrylic paint. It had a rough surface, and the paint clumped on it, but I liked the effect. It was too blue, so I mixed in red to make purple, and then black at the bottom. I took a photo of it and sent it to Steph, writing, *I don't know what I'm doing.*

She wrote back: *I like it.*

On Sunday night, I went to Steph and Lisa's apartment for movie night. I brought a pint of salted caramel ice cream from the Scoop in Fairfax, and Mel said it was her favorite flavor. Steph sat on the opposite end of the sofa from me, with Lisa snuggled against her. She didn't mention that we'd met up a few times that week already, so I didn't bring it up either. I told myself it didn't mean anything; there simply wasn't an opportunity or a reason to mention it. But it felt like a secret, and I liked having a secret with Steph.

Lisa had chosen the 1956 *Invasion of the Body Snatchers* to watch. In the movie, humans were replaced by aliens who took on their exact physical appearance, hatching out of gooey pods that reminded me of the eggs in *Alien.* The aliens in *Invasion* looked just like their human counterparts, but were devoid of emotion.

"They're zombies," Steph said.

"No, they're Communists," Lisa said. "They represent the fear

that Communists could be anywhere—they could be your neighbor!"
She made a face and pretended to be freaked out.

"People are still scared of Communists," Mel said. "It's capitalist
propaganda. We should all be communists—hello, national health
care."

"But Communism in the fifties wasn't good," I said. They all
looked at me, startled, and I said, "China—Communist China—that
was bad." I didn't know much about Communist China, but I knew
that my mom had left it for a reason.

"That's not what I'm saying," Mel said.

"Well, what are you saying?" I asked.

"Capitalism institutionalizes inequality," Mel said. "We need na-
tionalized health care, better labor practices—fuck, the restaurant
industry is insane."

"Yeah, I agree with you," I said, "but that's not what this movie's
about. They're afraid of the Soviet Union and the People's Republic
of China."

"You think their fears were justified?" Mel asked, surprised.

"Hang on," Lisa said, pausing the movie. "It's more complicated than what either of you are saying. They're not afraid of
the Soviet Union and China—or maybe they are, but that's not
what the fear of Communism in this film is about. It was the Cold
War, right? Anticommunism was also about expanding American
democracy." She put finger quotes around *democracy*. "In other
words, American imperial power. And if the Commies are bad,
then we're good."

"Well, that's a lie," Mel said.

"It *is* propaganda, in a way," Lisa said. "But Aria has a point, too.
People in China and the Soviet Union totally suffered under their
Communist governments, but we didn't really know what was going

on. It's not like the internet existed back then. So we could make up shit about them—the idea that they're all faceless masses obeying their leaders, like these emotionless pod people." She gestured to the movie, where a crowd of pod people were chasing the lead characters down a road.

"So, it's bad propaganda," Steph said.

"It's uninformed propaganda," I said.

"Or maybe it's art," Lisa said, and started the movie again.

Afterward, as I was getting ready to leave, I asked Lisa, "How did you know all that stuff about Communism?"

"I took a film class about classic science-fiction movies and the Red Scare," she said.

"Oh yeah, Steph said you were almost a film major. How come you decided not to be?"

"I didn't really decide not to be," Lisa said, sounding disgruntled. "I just didn't finish college. Not worth the money."

In mid-July, I got my housing assignment from MIT. In a little over a month I'd be leaving, and Steph would stay here. Maybe we'd keep in touch after I left, and she'd come visit me. I imagined us in Cambridge in the winter, walking down Mass Ave together in the snow, our breath blooming cloudlike from our mouths. She'd be cold because she was from California; I'd lend her a scarf and gloves. When we came inside, I'd brush the snow from her shoulders.

Maybe she'd break up with Lisa. If I came to California at the holidays with my dad, maybe we'd meet up at In-N-Out again, drive to that stretch of marshland together, and in the quiet of the truck cab she'd tell me she wanted to be with me. Long distance. I imagined phone calls then: me lying on my dorm-room bed, hearing her voice in my ear late at night. She'd send me new tracks that she recorded with Madchen. Maybe she'd write a song about me.

I felt as if we were cocooned in *maybe*. Maybe when we talked about Adrienne Rich's *Twenty-One Love Poems*, we were talking about something else. Maybe when I climbed into the cab of her truck, I wanted to do more than talk. Maybe when she lingered at Joan's on Friday mornings, she wanted something more, too.

The day that Steph came over for lunch, I put on the summer dress I'd brought with me, but I was worried it made me look like I was trying too hard. I cycled through jeans and shorts and my limited collection of tops, discarding the ones that Steph had already seen, which was most of them. I knew I was obsessing too much over this, but it was hard to stop. The lunch felt official in some way, as if Steph and I were coming out as a couple, even though I knew that was a fantasy. The longer I changed my outfits, the longer the fantasy lasted.

And then Analemma started barking, and she was here.

Steph had brought a loaf of crusty bread. She handed it to me like an offering when she came through the door, then bent down to greet Analemma. When she straightened up we shared an awkward hug, hampered by the bread in my hands.

"You look nice," she said.

I had put the summer dress back on moments before she arrived. "Thanks," I said. I was happy she noticed, but a little embarrassed to be so much more dressed up than her. She was in jeans and a Greenbrae Garden Center T-shirt. "Are you working later?"

"Yeah, I picked up a closing shift."

We were looking at each other, and I felt as if she had something on her mind she wanted to say, but then the moment passed and nothing was said. Maybe she was nervous about the lunch, too.

We went upstairs. I took the bread into the kitchen to slice while Steph went to greet Joan on the deck, where she was grilling salmon. They came back inside together, and Joan started issuing instructions on how to finish putting together the salad. The tension I'd felt about what might or might not happen began to dissipate in the wake of carrot peeling, avocado scooping, and table setting.

As I sliced lemons on a cutting board by the sink, Joan came over to rinse off the tongs. "You look lovely," she said. "I haven't seen that dress before."

"It's the only dress I brought here," I said, and then wondered why I'd admitted that. I glanced swiftly at Steph, but she didn't seem to have heard. Joan merely nodded.

When the food was ready, we ate it on the deck under the umbrella. Steph was different with Joan around. More earnest, respectful. They talked about the drought and its impact on wildfires in the state. They talked about the Fourth of July, which gave me the chance to show the photo of the papier-mâché unicorn to Steph, her head bending over my hand. They talked about baseball and whether the Giants could ever repeat their World Series sweep from last year.

I started clearing the plates in the middle of their baseball conversation, and decided to bring out dessert. Joan had stocked up on the Scoop's Fourth of July flavor—vanilla swirled with blueberries and raspberries—which they made only once a year. Dad always made sure to get it if we were here in July, and as I peeled back the lid on the pint I remembered the last summer we'd had with Grandpa. Standing with him on the sidewalk outside the Scoop one summer night as we waited in line, little kids clutching their dripping cones nearby. Christmas lights had been strung from the trees and they seemed to wink like fireflies.

I heard Joan saying my name out on the deck, and I blinked back to now. I stacked up bowls and spoons and the ice cream and went outside.

"Why didn't you tell me?" Joan was asking Steph.

"Tell you what?" I asked, setting the bowls on the table.

"That she was a musician," Joan said. "I was just telling Steph that I didn't know until you told me."

Steph looked a little embarrassed. "I guess it just never came up. And it's not like it's my job—I just do it on the side."

"That's where it starts," Joan said.

"She has a CD," I said as I scooped out ice cream.

"It's just four songs with my old band," Steph said.

"That shows commitment, though," Joan said. She accepted the bowl of ice cream I offered her. "Thank you." She picked up her spoon and asked Steph, "What happened to your band?"

"Nothing. They still exist, but I'm not in it anymore."

"But she's going back for one show," I said.

"One show only," Steph said.

I wondered whether Lisa had put her foot down. I handed Steph a bowl of ice cream. "Fourth of July flavor."

"Thanks," she said.

"Why only one?" Joan asked.

Steph looked uncomfortable. "I have to pay the rent."

"Ah," Joan said. "I understand. I was very lucky that Russ's pay-check enabled me to keep making art."

I took a bite of my ice cream. Grandpa said Fourth of July was his favorite flavor, partly because you could only get it once a year. *The rest of the year you think about it longingly,* he told me.

"Would you have stopped if—if your husband hadn't supported you?" Steph asked.

"I can't imagine he wouldn't have supported me," Joan said.

"There were some years when I wasn't making any art, but that was because my children were very young and I needed to be their mother."

"I thought that's when you started photography," I said.

"Yes, but not right away. When your father and Aunt Tammy were very little, I was focused on them. There wasn't time for much else."

"Were you upset about having to give up art?" Steph asked.

Joan smiled. "No. I wouldn't trade that time for a permanent exhibit at MoMA. But I'm from a different generation than you two. I grew up believing I'd become a wife and mother, and even though I went to art school, I thought I'd stop all that once I had children."

"What made you start again?" Steph asked.

"My children," Joan said. "I began taking pictures of them because they were so expressive. I wanted to capture some of that. Russ was the one who encouraged me to show those early pictures to a photographer friend of mine, and he gave me some really good feedback. I realized I wanted to do more. So, I got a better camera and taught myself how to use it, and I set up a darkroom and learned how to make prints. It went on from there."

"Her photos are amazing," I said to Steph. "Have you seen them?"

"Only the ones in the house," Steph said.

"Do you still have that catalog?" I asked Joan.

Joan nodded. "It's in the bookcase in the living room."

I went to find it and brought it outside. It was from a retrospective show of Joan's work at a San Francisco gallery in 2005. I turned it toward Steph and opened it to the first image. It was a black-and-white self-portrait of my grandmother outside a ranch-style home in Boulder, Colorado, and behind her in the living room window was the blurry face of a child that I knew to be my dad. Joan was wearing a 1970s-era shirtdress with muted diagonal stripes that seemed to radiate out from the horizontal lines of the house. She looked faintly impatient. Below the photo the caption read: SELF-PORTRAIT, BOULDER, 1973.

"You look so young in this one," I said.

"I *was* young," Joan said. "In that picture I'll be thirty-two forever."

Steph was paging through the catalog, looking at pictures of my dad as a kid running through the sprinklers, Grandpa setting up a telescope in the backyard or flipping a steak on the grill, Aunt Tammy with a scowl on her face at the swimming pool.

"These are great," Steph said. "They're definitely expressive. But the pictures are about more than capturing that, aren't they?"

"Yes," Joan said. "What do you think they're about? I'm curious."

"They're about . . . family," Steph said. "Whatever that means."

"In a particular context," Joan said.

"Middle-class, white picket fences," Steph said.

Joan was nodding.

"It's very subtle," Steph said. "The ways you're pushing back against that."

I was sitting across from her as she turned the pages of the catalog, so I saw the images go by upside down. The double exposure of Dad and Aunt Tammy that was also framed in the guest room. A self-portrait of Joan on a foggy beach. Aunt Tammy high on a swing set, her skirt like a kite. Steph flipped past an Asian woman in something like a spotlight, her eyes looking straight at the camera, and just as she turned the page, I recognized my mother.

Had I forgotten that picture existed? I almost reached out to make Steph go back, but she had already moved forward to photos of people I didn't know. Another Asian woman, this one with teased hair in an eighties power suit on a street littered with firecrackers; an old white man who seemed to be floating above a box; and then the paintings. The early ones, from the 1960s, were entirely abstract, but they began to transform in the nineties into the semi-figurative landscapes she made in the early 2000s.

"Why did you switch from photos to painting landscapes?" Steph asked. "They're so different."

"I see them as a very natural progression, actually," Joan said.

"What do you mean?" Steph asked.

Joan considered for a minute. "You have to remember that the photos aren't necessarily about the people in them—just like you said. They expressed things I wanted to say. When I made those pictures I think I wanted to stop time. The kids were growing up so fast, and in a photograph, they stay that age forever. But then they grew up, and . . ." She waved her hands and frowned. "I'm not explaining this right. I've realized—over time—that all my work is about time. When I started—you remember, Aria, I told you I did that performance art. That was about ephemerality, how quickly time passes. The pictures were a way of stopping time. Instances. I liked making them, but then I started to want to express the slower passage of time. Deep time, like through geological processes. Painting landscapes enabled me to do that because—well, the landscapes, the shape of rocks, the way water cuts through the land—all of that is deep time. But also, the act of painting allows me to show time passing in physical ways. The paint itself, brushstrokes, impasto—it shows motion, gestures. You can make light and shadow appear to move across the canvas with techniques of illusion. And it's physical—a photograph of a painting doesn't do it justice, but if you're standing there in front of the painting in real life, you see the work of the hand on the canvas in the brushstrokes, the way the paint is applied. It's very obvious that it was physically constructed by a person. The artist. I think I'm increasingly interested in showing the physical marks of the artist. Handwriting, fingerprints. I suppose it's also a way to freeze time, but in a way that's more obvious to the viewer." She laughed. "And of course, that counteracts the slow passage of time that I said I was interested in, so you might think I'm contradicting myself, but it's all one thing." She made a circular gesture with her hands. "All of it is linked together in ways that I can't really describe."

I felt as if I were on the verge of understanding what she meant. It reminded me of Grandpa, who told me we could travel back in time by looking at the stars. It took millennia for the light of some stars to reach us, so when we saw them from our vantage point here on Earth, we were actually seeing the past.

"No, thank you for all that," Steph was saying. "I really appreciate hearing about it."

Joan took a sip of iced tea and said, "I've gone on for too long. Tell me about your music. Have you always written songs?"

Steph nodded. "Yes, but when I was little, it was just music. We had an old guitar at home, and our neighbor gave me lessons for a couple years. I started writing songs with lyrics when I was twelve."

"What were the songs about?" I asked.

Steph laughed self-consciously. "Uh, well, the first one was about this girl I had a crush on, but I didn't know it was a crush back then. And then I sang it to her—"

"Oh my God," I said.

"Courageous!" Joan said.

Steph grinned. "It was a mistake. That's when I learned that people don't like it when you write songs about them. Like, they might say they'd like it, but if the song doesn't show them exactly the way they want to be shown, they can't handle it." She grew serious. "And then, even if the song isn't about them, people see themselves in it when they shouldn't. I don't know what to do about that. Like with your portraits—didn't people ever get mad if they didn't look the way they wanted?"

Joan smiled as if she'd heard this question before. "It depended on who was being photographed and whether they understood what I was going for. I think sometimes it was my fault. I needed to be clearer with them about what I was trying to do. But you can't always explain yourself clearly, and sometimes people don't understand because they're clinging to an idea of themselves, and any disturbance to that idea is devastating."

"What if it's not even about the person who gets upset about it?" Steph asked. "Like, sometimes I've written songs that start from personal inspiration, but it changes in the process. And ultimately, it's not about that personal experience at all, but the people who see themselves in it—they still think it's about them."

"You can't worry about other people's feelings about what you're creating," Joan said. "That will suffocate you. You have to do what your heart desires."

Joan and Steph were so focused on their conversation, it was as if I wasn't even there.

"What if what your heart desires hurts someone else?" Steph asked.

"Sometimes you can't avoid that," Joan said, "because people have feelings, and other people's feelings aren't always congruent with ours. But here's the important thing when it comes to art. This is what I've learned: The art is greater than you and your feelings. You have to serve it. It is not you. Some people will never understand that, but you need to surround yourself with people who do understand it. And *you* need to understand it yourself. Whatever you're creating may come from within you and your life, but then—almost like a child, it comes out of your body and it grows up and walks away. It walks away and affects other people you don't know and have never met. That's the beauty of it, and the reason I keep trying new things. You never know who it will affect."

Steph had to go to work. The ice cream bowls were scraped clean, and Joan stacked the three of them together, the spoons ringing against the porcelain like bells.

"Steph," I said, "will you take a picture of me and Joan?" I held my phone out to her.

"Sure," she said.

I leaned in, and Joan put her arm around me, and we smiled.

"I took a bunch," Steph said, handing the phone back.

"Thanks."

"Here, give it to me," Joan said. "Let me take a picture of you two."

She told us to stand together by the railing so that we weren't backlit.

"Aria, turn toward her just a little," Joan said. "Yes, just like that."

I felt like I must look totally awkward, my elbows at all the wrong angles, but when I saw the pictures, I was surprised. Joan had taken a few in a row, like Steph, but she had guided us into a story. First, we were stiff, the empty space between us somehow highlighted. Then, I was turned toward Steph while we both smiled self-consciously at the camera. Finally, Joan had caught Steph gazing downward, looking almost shy, while I looked at the camera with a question in my eyes. That one was my favorite.

O n Friday when Steph came over to do the yard work, she told me that Roxy was having a house party the following Friday night. "Do you want to come?" she asked as she put away the gardening tools.

I was standing outside the shed, leaning against the edge of the door frame. "Who's going to be there? I probably won't know anybody."

"Don't you go to parties to meet people? Everybody you met at the Dyke March will be there, plus more people you don't know. Roxy knows everyone."

My phone chimed and I pulled it out of my pocket. Tasha was due back from France today and I was wondering if she would text me, but it wasn't Tasha. It was an email from my mom with the details about her trip to San Francisco.

"Bad news?" Steph asked.

"No, just my mom."

"From the look on your face it doesn't seem good."

"She's visiting San Francisco next week. I'm going to meet her at her hotel." I scrolled through the email. "The Fairmont."

"Fancy."

"That's my mom."

"She's not coming up here?"

"No." I put the phone in my back pocket and moved out of the way as Steph closed up the shed.

"I get the impression your relationship with your mom isn't all that great," Steph said.

"We're not that close. She's not around much." Steph and I walked around the house and started down the path to the street.

"Do you think she'd be okay with you coming out to her?" Steph asked.

"I hadn't thought about it."

"I'm not saying you have to, I was just wondering how you think she'd react."

"I don't think my mom is conservative. She'd probably be okay with it, but I can't imagine telling her. Like, what do you do, just say it?"

Steph stopped at the front gate. "It depends on the situation but yeah, basically. Have you thought about telling your grandma?"

The idea alarmed me in a way I hadn't expected. "No."

"Maybe you should start with her, not your mom," Steph suggested. "Joan has always been fine with me."

I must have looked dubious because Steph said, "You don't have to say anything to anyone till you're ready." Then she added, "So, you're coming to Roxy's party?"

I liked the way she was looking at me, with that smile in her eyes. "You want me to come?" I asked.

The corner of her mouth curved up. "Yes."

A warm curl in my belly. "Okay, I'll come."

She stepped toward me to hug me goodbye. "I'll see you on Sunday for movie night."

"See you Sunday," I said.

I wondered if I would ever get used to hugging her. It never felt casual.

Lisa was noticeably grouchy on Sunday night. When I arrived, Steph and Mel were making pizza as usual, but Lisa was out in the courtyard, smoking. "We're watching *Forbidden Planet*," she told me as I approached.

I wasn't sure whether I should go into the apartment without her or whether she expected me to keep her company. "What's it about?" I asked.

"Dudes go to an alien planet, discover one hot lady who swims naked and a machine that produces monsters from the subconscious. Sorry, spoiler alert."

"Sounds . . . unique."

"It's inspired by Shakespeare's *The Tempest*."

"Oh." I knew nothing about *The Tempest*.

Lisa inhaled on her cigarette but didn't invite me to sit down with her. I went inside, where Mel and Steph were silently putting the pizza into the oven.

"Hey," Mel said, sounding relieved at my arrival.

"Hi." I went over to the breakfast bar and leaned over it, asking softly, "Is Lisa okay?"

"She's had a rough day," Steph said shortly, but didn't meet my eyes.

When Steph was turned away, Mel mouthed at me, *They had a fight*. I nodded and went to put the ice cream I'd brought—cardamom—in the freezer. When Lisa returned from the courtyard, we all tried to pretend as if everything was normal.

The movie could have been viewed as a campy comedy, with its 1950s-era robot named Robby, who was kind of a cross between a butler and an iPhone, but none of us laughed. The sole woman in the movie, Altaira, was the daughter of the scientist who had been stranded on the forbidden planet. She grew up with only her father for company, and when a starship full of young spacemen landed, she was immediately smitten by the handsome commander. Altaira was so innocent she didn't know that skinny-dipping and wearing very short dresses was apparently inappropriate. The men couldn't resist her allure, which was obviously her fault.

"How things have changed," I said after the commander told her to dress more conservatively.

"Yeah, this is bullshit," Mel agreed.

But the movie wasn't only about slut-shaming. It turned out that the aliens who had once populated the planet had built a machine that could make the subconscious real. When the scientist interfaced with the machine, the monsters in his imagination stepped into the real world—and terrorized it.

Lisa watched the whole movie with her lips drawn into a flat line, saying nothing. I wondered if she had chosen it in advance or if it was a spur-of-the-moment choice.

After we cleaned up our plates and glasses, Mel said she was heading home early. I decided to go, too, since it didn't seem like a great time to linger in Lisa and Steph's apartment.

As Mel and I walked down the street to our cars, I asked, "Do you know what's up with them?"

"Not really."

"Is it about the concert? I was wondering if Lisa doesn't want Steph to do it."

"I don't know."

"I keep wondering why they're still together if Lisa doesn't support Steph's music."

Mel didn't respond right away, and in that silence, I wondered if I had made a mistake. I was about to walk it back when Mel said, "Steph and Lisa have history together."

"But you shouldn't just stay with someone because you have history together."

"I've known Steph since the sixth grade. When her parents found out she's queer, they didn't accept her the way mine accepted me. Steph ended up getting kicked out of her house, and Lisa took her in. Lisa is basically the reason Steph had the chance to do music in the first place."

I was chagrined. "Oh."

"I think it's hard to understand any relationship from the outside."

We arrived at the Honda and stopped. Mel put her hands in her pockets and rocked back on her heels.

"Sometimes I don't understand it either," she said.

"Really?"

"Yeah, but it's none of my business. If Steph wants to be with Lisa, that's her choice."

"Yeah, of course," I said, although Mel's conclusion was unsatisfying to me.

"I better go," Mel said, and hugged me goodbye.

I realized that Steph hadn't hugged me tonight. She had barely looked at me. I thought about that as I got into the car, wondering if there was any significance to it. I was about to put the key in the ignition when my phone rang, and I pulled it out of my purse. It was Tasha.

I answered because it was after midnight on the East Coast, and she never called this late. "Tasha?" I said.

"I can't do this anymore," she said. Her voice was thick, as if she had been crying.

"What's wrong?"

"Haley and I had a fight."

"What happened?" For a moment she didn't say anything, and I heard her breath hitching. "Are you okay?"

"I don't know." She sounded miserable. "I don't know what to do."

"About what?"

She took a deep breath. "Haley and I have been fighting all summer."

"You have?" I wasn't sure if I was surprised. The Fourth of July video and the weird, disconnected texting had felt a little off.

"Yeah." She paused. "I don't think I can talk about this over the phone."

"Okay. Do you want to FaceTime or something?"

"I need a break from Haley. Can I come visit you?"

"In California?"

"Yeah. You're not doing anything, right? I found a cheap ticket and it leaves on July thirty-first. I'd only be there Wednesday through Sunday."

That was the weekend of the Queer Music Festival. I gazed out the windshield at the quiet street outside Steph and Lisa's building. I couldn't see the apartment from here, but I imagined that I could feel Steph's presence nearby. If Tasha came to visit, would I have to introduce her to Steph and Lisa and Mel? What would I tell her? The idea was unsettling.

"Don't sound so excited," Tasha said as I continued to be silent.

"Sorry, I have to ask Joan," I said quickly. "But it's probably fine." I did want to see Tasha. Didn't I? "I'll ask her first thing tomorrow."

"Thanks," she said, sounding relieved.

After I ended the call, I drove past Steph and Lisa's building on the way out of the neighborhood. I glanced into the building's court-yard, but it was deserted. They were probably inside. I wondered if they were arguing or if they were making up, and what making up looked like.

The Fairmont Hotel was a giant white palace on Nob Hill bristling with international flags, and as I pulled the Honda Civic beneath the front awning, I felt as if I should have searched for the service entrance somewhere out back. But the valet took my key and handed over a ticket with a smile, so I forced myself to pretend that I belonged and entered the hotel.

I was early for lunch with my mom. I thought about calling her to say I was downstairs, but then I saw a sign for the ladies' room across the lobby. I could check my appearance first. I headed across the marble floor and pushed open the heavy wooden door. Inside, it smelled like flowers.

I studied myself critically in the gold-framed mirror over the sinks. I was wearing the one dress I'd brought to California—a black-and-white floral print with spaghetti straps—which now reminded me of that lunch with Steph and Joan. I'd pulled my hair back in a ponytail and put in small silver hoop earrings. I smoothed back some flyaway strands of my hair and retouched my lip gloss. I told myself I looked fine.

The last time I saw my mom was in April, when she came to Boston before heading to Vienna. I had met her at the Fairmont Copley Plaza, where she'd taken me to dinner in the hotel's plush restaurant. I remembered sitting in a leather armchair so deep it felt like it was swallowing me. After our food came, she told me she'd been offered the opportunity to perform at the Munich Opera Festival in some kind of groundbreaking role in July. I wasn't paying close attention until she said, "I won't be able to come to your graduation because we'll be in rehearsals. Is that all right with you?"

I hadn't known until that instant that I had long imagined her at graduation standing beside my dad. She would be beautiful, impressive. Without her there—

When I didn't respond, she said, "If it means a lot to you, I can change my schedule for you. People tell me American high school graduation is a big deal, but you've never given me the impression that you care that much about it. College graduation, yes, but high school . . . Do you want me to come?"

This wasn't the first time she had missed something important to me because of her career. The disappointment was familiar. "No, it's fine," I said, trying to ignore the sinking feeling that pulled at me. "It's just high school."

She attempted to hide her relief, but I hadn't missed it.

Now my mouth was suddenly so dry I turned on the cold water and cupped my hand beneath it to drink. Water dribbled down my chin and splattered onto my dress as I straightened up. I grabbed a thick paper towel to soak up the liquid. As I pressed it against my chest, I became aware of the racing of my heart. I flattened my hand there. I thought I could feel it thudding against my palm, ready to run.

I didn't call her. I found a seat in the lobby facing the elevators and pretended to look at my phone while I waited.

I saw my mother before she saw me. She had an unmistakable stride that I recognized through the group of tourists in front of the concierge desk; she walked as if she were onstage. She was wearing a sleeveless black sheath dress, so simple it must have cost a fortune, and heels. She might have flown in late last night from New York, but that would never have stopped her from looking her best.

When she spotted me in the lobby, she waved. I got up to meet her, and we hugged stiffly.

"Hi, Mom."

She smelled of a light floral perfume, more sharp than sweet. I was instantly back in her New York apartment at a cocktail party where I didn't know anyone, but everyone there knew I was her daughter.

She held me at arm's length to examine me, her smile turning pensive. "You look tan," she observed. "Are you wearing sunscreen when you go outside? You have to be careful to watch your complexion."

I stepped out of her grasp. "Thanks for your concern."

I expected her to give me her disappointed look, but instead she said, "We're so close to Chinatown I thought we'd go have dim sum. I haven't had good Chinese food in months!"

I was surprised. "Okay."

She smiled and reached out to tuck a strand of my hair behind my ear. "I've already called an Uber."

The Town Car smelled overpoweringly of pine air freshener. Mom unrolled the window as we descended a steep hill toward the bay. The driver turned right onto a street with worn-looking three-story buildings.

"My cousin Eddie and his family used to live around here," Mom said. "He told me it was very close to the Fairmont. I invited him to join us, but he's out of town."

"How come you've never told me about him before?" I asked.

"I'm sure I have. You must not remember."

Mom rarely talked about her family, and I'd only met her parents once, when they came to New York on vacation. I was thirteen and couldn't speak Chinese, and they didn't speak English. Mom had quickly tired of translating, so I mostly remembered not understanding what they were saying.

"How exactly are you related?" I asked.

"He's a distant cousin. Eddie and his family live out by Livermore. They don't come into the city much these days. Oh, I almost forgot—he sent me something to give to you." She opened her purse, but soon frowned. "I must have left it in the hotel room. You'll have to come back with me after lunch. Remember I told you one of your Chinese cousins was an engineer? He sent some photos of her."

We crossed some cable car tracks and continued downhill toward the Transamerica building and into Chinatown. It was strange to imagine anyone from the Chinese half of my family living here. I wondered what it would have been like to grow up in Chinatown.

The driver turned left onto a block lined with streetlamps shaped like miniature pagodas. It was crowded with cars and pedestrians, and strings of red lanterns hung overhead. We passed shops selling souvenirs and cheap T-shirts, handbags by the dozen, and jewelry stores displaying gold on red velvet cushions. Finally, the car turned right and pulled over, double-parking outside the Great Eastern Restaurant.

"Here we are," Mom said. "Eddie recommended this place."

I climbed out, and the smell of Chinatown was so familiar: fried noodles, roast duck, and the hint of bitter herbs. All Chinatowns seemed to smell the same, whether I was in Boston or New York or here.

Mom finished paying for the Uber on her phone and headed for the restaurant. I followed her in.

We were seated at a round table for eight, but because the

restaurant was only half full, we had the table to ourselves. Mom ordered chrysanthemum tea, and it appeared within seconds, along with thick vinyl menus and a long dim sum card and pencil. She reached out to pour the tea with her left hand, holding it with a kind of showy grace, and I couldn't help but notice the giant diamond on her ring finger.

She saw my surprise, and she said, "Andrew proposed." An uncharacteristic flash of nervousness crossed her face. "That's part of the reason I wanted to see you in person, so that I could tell you."

I didn't know what to say. She'd had a string of boyfriends since she and my dad divorced, but she had never remarried. I thought she'd never marry again, but now that seemed like a childish fantasy based on romantic notions about my parents' relationship. Andrew Leung was her most recent boyfriend; they'd been together for a little more than a year. He was a Hong Kong Chinese banker who divided his time between New York, Hong Kong, and Geneva, and I'd only met him once—last New Year's Eve in New York. He was, as far as I knew, the first Chinese man my mother had been in a relationship with.

"I hope you can be happy for us," she said. Her normally smooth forehead was creased by a few worry lines.

"Congratulations," I said, but I couldn't make it sound genuine. I barely knew him. Most of my mother's previous boyfriends had tried to ingratiate themselves with me, but Andrew hadn't. I considered that a mark in his favor.

She twisted the diamond ring back and forth, making it glint in the light. "He's a good man," she said a bit defensively. "I haven't been with a man who understands me so well since I was married to your father. I never thought I'd find that again. I want you to know that."

A hot lump lodged in my throat. I had never heard her speak of my dad like that.

At that moment the waiter appeared, and my mother began to speak to him in Chinese. I heard her mention some of the dim sum items I liked, but I didn't understand the rest. Then she looked at me and asked in English, "Do you want anything to drink? Water?"

"Diet Coke?" I said, and the waiter nodded curtly before taking the menu and dim sum card away.

Mom took a sip of her tea and said, "Now, where were we?"

"Your engagement," I said. The word sounded foreign to me.

She unfolded her napkin and spread it on her lap. "Yes. I think we're going to have a winter wedding. We stayed in such a wonderful hotel in the Swiss Alps last January that we're thinking of going back. Wouldn't that be lovely?"

"That sounds nice," I said, but my stomach twisted.

"We're just going to have a small wedding. Close friends and family. Neither of us is young anymore." My mother laughed as if she were making a joke. "Andrew and I would love for you to be in the wedding. Will you?"

The worry in her eyes couldn't be acting, could it? Even if it was, how could I say no?

"Sure," I said, and her eyes actually gleamed as if tears had risen in them. I looked down quickly and unfolded my napkin across my lap. I felt as if I were betraying my father.

"Thank you. It means a lot to me—and to Andrew. I want you to get to know him. He's a good man and he's very successful, and that gives me some freedom now to only take on the roles that I want."

I'd heard my mother talk about this before. Sometimes she had to take roles she wasn't entirely in love with because she needed the income. She was certainly a success—no one in the opera world would deny that—but opera wasn't Broadway or Hollywood, and my mother had a lifestyle she wanted to maintain.

"That also means you won't have to worry about MIT at all," she continued. "I know you've committed to taking on some loans, but I can take care of that now."

"You don't have to do that," I said quickly. "Have you talked to Dad about it?"

"Not yet. I wanted to talk to you first, because it's your life, not your father's."

My Diet Coke arrived, and I unwrapped the straw and slid it into the drink.

"I don't want you to graduate with so much debt," Mom said.

"I'll think about it." But at that moment I was sure I'd say no. I didn't want to owe her anything.

She sighed. "I know I haven't always been there for you."

There was something in her tone that made me wary of what she might say next.

"I know I haven't always been a good mother," she continued.

I went rigid in my seat.

"I want things to change between us," she said. "I want you to understand that the money would be a gift. Now that I have Andrew, I can give you more support. Before, I had to make sure I could pay all my bills, but now I can make sure you have the best life possible."

The shine of tears in her eyes, the self-conscious pink in her cheeks—it was too much. I couldn't look at her. I felt spotlighted by my mom's attention in a way that embarrassed me.

The waiter suddenly appeared with a tray full of dishes, and my mother sat back, blinking rapidly and touching the corners of her eyes with her fingertips. There was a bamboo steamer of fluffy white barbecue pork buns that I knew she'd ordered for me, because she never ate them. Deep-fried rice dumplings filled with savory pork. Pan-fried turnip cakes drizzled with oyster sauce. A plate of stir-fried water spinach. A large platter of yellow noodles with steaming seafood on top.

"So much food!" she said with a shaky laugh. "You'll take some back to your grandmother." She reached for the serving spoon and began to cut into the noodles, placing a portion on my plate along with shrimp and squid.

"Thanks," I said automatically. The noodles were crispy on the outside but soft and chewy on the inside, and they were difficult for me to manage with the chopsticks.

"Do you need a fork?" she asked.

"I'm okay," I said, but my mom signaled to the waiter to ask for a fork anyway. When he laid it beside my plate, I ignored it.

I hoped my mother wouldn't return to what she'd been talking about earlier. I was afraid I would burst into tears. I concentrated on chewing each bite thoroughly so I wouldn't choke.

Mom placed more shrimp on my plate, then added water spinach, telling me I needed to eat some vegetables. Another steamer basket was delivered, this one filled with shrimp-and-chive dumplings, the green flecks visible through the translucent wrapper. Mom dipped the dumplings in chili oil and ate them delicately.

I remembered going to dim sum with her in New York. I remembered huge, loud restaurants packed with Chinese diners, and the carts pushed between tables by old Chinese women, steam rising when they opened the lids on their stacks of bamboo baskets. Mom always ordered shrimp dumplings for her and pork buns for me.

Her ring sparkled as she lifted her teacup and took another sip. As she put it down, she said, without looking at me, "I should have been there for you when you had that situation with your boyfriend."

I was disoriented by the change of subject. And then I realized she meant Jacob. "He wasn't my boyfriend," I said.

She looked at me sharply. "He wasn't?"

I shouldn't have said that. "It doesn't matter. It's fine."

She laid her chopsticks across the rim of her plate. "Who was he?" she demanded.

This tone I understood. We were back on familiar ground. "It doesn't matter," I repeated crisply. I gave up on my chopsticks and picked up the fork.

She shook her head. "I should have taught you better. I've been too busy with my own life. Were you trying to get my attention? You can't do that with strange boys—"

"I didn't do it to get your attention! And he wasn't a stranger. I didn't think he would do what he did."

"That's your biggest mistake—you didn't think! You need to think before you act."

"It's not my fault," I snapped.

I had said the same thing to her over the phone on the morning of graduation. She'd called while Dad and I were driving to the high school, and just when I thought she was going to express regret over missing my graduation, she said, "You need to be on your best behavior today. Don't give them anything else to talk about."

After I told her it wasn't my fault, I hung up on her. She hadn't called back.

"You *chose* to be with that boy," she said now. "What made you trust him? You need to learn some judgment. You should be with someone who appreciates you for your mind, not your body."

I stabbed one of the shrimp dumplings with my fork, but I couldn't bring myself to take a bite. "You don't understand," I muttered.

"I don't?" My mother leaned closer to me and said in a low voice, "It's been very hard for me to find love because I lost my roots. I wanted to have company when I was in Vienna or London or New York. I made some bad decisions, too. I tried to keep them away from you, but I know I didn't do the best job. But I was lonely. I want you to learn from me—from my mistakes."

I let the fork clatter onto my plate. I grabbed my Diet Coke and almost dropped the slippery glass. My fingers were trembling.

To my shock, my mother reached out and took my hand in hers. "Look at me," she said. Her face was flushed, her eyes focused fiercely on me. "This is important," she insisted, squeezing my hand tightly.

I felt like I couldn't breathe. I wished I could end this conversation as easily as I could end a phone call.

"You need to find someone who loves you for who you are," she said. "You're a beautiful girl. Many men will want to be with you. But most of them will be wrong. You need to wait for the right one. Andrew is the first Chinese man I've ever been in a relationship with. I don't know why I've waited so long. He speaks my language. I want you to find someone who speaks your language."

My mom's hotel room had a stunning view north toward Coit Tower and the bay. I stood at the window, gazing down at the city in miniature, while Mom searched through her bag for the photos she wanted to give me.

"Here they are," she said triumphantly, pulling out a white envelope. She sat down on the padded bench at the foot of the bed, and I took a seat beside her while she opened the envelope.

There were two photos: one in black-and-white, the other in color. She handed me the color photo first, which showed a group of people gathered around a white cake on which *Happy 60th Birthday Lily!* had been written in red frosting. Mom was on the edge of the group, and she looked both younger and a little softer.

"This was in 1997," she said, "when I went to Los Angeles to audition for the LA Opera."

In 1997, I'd been two years old, and my parents had still been married, living in an apartment in Cambridge while Dad finished his PhD. She must have left me with him to fly across the country for the audition.

"Lily is Eddie's older sister," Mom continued. "She had her sixtieth birthday party when I was in town, and they invited me along." She pointed at the woman standing in the center, wearing a light blue shirtdress with a white belt. She had shoulder-length black hair and her arm was around an older woman who looked a lot like her, but had white hair.

"Who's that? Her mother?"

"No, I think that's . . ." Mom turned the photo over and I saw there were names written on the back. "That's Judy Fong, Eddie and Lily's aunt. That's right, Judy also worked at that lab."

"Really? She's so old."

"She was retired by 1997, but yes, I think they both worked there since the 1950s."

I took the photo and studied it more closely. I realized Lily was the only person looking at the camera; everyone else was looking at one another as if they were still figuring out where to stand. "Who are the other people?" I asked.

Mom pointed to the thin, white-haired man beside Judy. "That's her husband, Francis, and next to him is their son and daughter-in-law, and that little girl is Judy and Francis's granddaughter."

"Is that Eddie?" I asked, pointing at the man on the other side of Lily.

"Yes. And that's his wife. Their children were grown by then, so they weren't in LA. Eddie came down for Lily's birthday."

Mom passed me the second photo. "This is Lily and Judy at work in the 1960s."

The black-and-white photo showed a younger Lily and Judy standing in front of a bank of ancient computers, the kind I'd seen in documentaries and movies about the Apollo program.

"Is Lily still working at JPL?" I asked.

"I think she must be retired by now. Eddie's seventy-five, and she's older than him. She can't be working anymore."

"I wonder if Aunt Tammy knew them."

"You'll have to ask her." Mom handed me the envelope that the photos had come in. "These are for you. If you ever want to get in touch, Eddie left his email address in there, too. He knows everyone in the family. I'm sure he'd love to hear from you."

Inside the envelope was a small piece of folded paper. I pulled it out and found a brief note.

Dear Aria, I hope you enjoy these photos of your ancestors. Please write to me anytime. Your first cousin twice (!) removed, Eddie Hu.

He had written an AOL email address beneath his name.

"What does 'twice removed' mean?" I asked.

"I don't really know. My grandfather was Eddie's uncle, so his father was . . . my great-uncle."

"When did they come to America? They must have come before you."

"Yes, I think Eddie's father came before World War II. So, that branch was here long before me."

"They were here in the 1950s?" I thought about the movies I'd been watching at Steph and Lisa's.

"Yes, in San Francisco."

I studied the group photo again, looking at Lily and Judy. I realized Lily was on her own; she didn't have a husband beside her. I wondered if it had been too difficult for her to work at JPL and have a family. I wanted to ask my mom if that career pressure was why her relationships had been so short-lived—until now. But that wasn't the sort of question I could ask her. Instead, I said, "How did you know Andrew was the right one?"

Her face softened into a smile. "Everything made sense. It was easy, no obstacles." She added, "That's how you'll know, too."

B ack in Woodacre, I took Joan's catalog off the shelf again and flipped through to the photo of my mom.

Now I remembered it. She was doubled, and the places where her two bodies overlapped were transparent, as if she were part ghost. One Alexis was looking slightly to the left, and the other Alexis was gazing straight at the camera. She wasn't wearing any makeup. I wasn't used to the bareness of her lips, the soft shadows beneath her eyes. It felt so intimate to see her like that.

Beneath the picture, the caption read: ALEXIS TANG, 1997. It was the same year she'd gone to Los Angeles and met our engineer cousin. I got the photos Mom had given to me out of my purse. I took out the group shot and compared the way she looked in the small color photo with the black-and-white portrait that Joan had taken. They showed the same person, but it was remarkable how different she looked in each one. The color photo showed her the way she appeared on the outside, but the portrait seemed to show the way she looked on the inside.

I heard Analemma's claws clicking down the stairs from the third floor, and a moment later Joan's footsteps followed.

"You're back," she said as she came into the living room. "How was your mother?"

I hadn't decided if I would tell her, but then the words just came out. "She's engaged. To this guy in Hong Kong."

Silence. Joan came around the couch and sat down beside me. "How do you feel about that?"

I gazed down at the two pictures of my mother. "She says she's happy, so I guess I'm happy for her."

"It's all right to have mixed feelings."

"I don't know what my feelings are."

"That's all right, too." Joan reached for the catalog and slid it toward herself. "I forgot about this picture."

"She gave me this other photo today." I showed her the snapshot. "Same year, same person, but she looks so different."

"They were different days, different cameras, different photographers. Different purposes."

"What was your purpose?"

"Oh, I think . . . I just wanted to capture your mother. I wasn't doing as much photography by then. But she was so vibrant—is so vibrant. Has so much personality. She was very open to what I wanted to do."

"Did she like it?" I asked.

"Your mother is an artist," Joan said. "She understood it."

5:13 PM

Steph: *You're still coming to Roxy's party tomorrow night right?*
I'm driving down with Lisa but you can grab a ride with Mel

5:14 PM

Me: *I'll be there! Can't wait*
Steph: *Me too xx*

went to the mall to hunt for something new to wear to the party. I flipped through tops at Madewell and Free People and finally at Nordstrom with increasing frustration, because everything seemed too straight somehow. I ended up buying a loose gray tank top with a sheer back, and at home I tried it on with jeans and a pair of black leather ankle boots I bought on sale. My black bra showed through the back of the shirt, and I thought about Steph seeing me, and I suddenly felt like I'd made the wrong choice. The shirt was too obvious. I took it off, and then I stood there in my bra and jeans and had no idea what to do.

In the mirror over the dresser I looked like I was about to cry. I pressed my fingertips beneath my eyes. I told myself I was being ridiculous. It was a shirt.

I put it back on. I turned back to the mirror. My hair was loose and wavy. I was wearing my silver hoop earrings. I'd put on heavy eyeliner and mascara, and a new dark red MAC lipstick. Tasha and Haley would be surprised by my new look, but when I looked at myself, I saw who I wanted to be.

Mel blasted classic Missy Elliott in the Jeep on the drive down to the city. She was hyped up, bopping her head in time to the beat. "If I stay over tonight," she said over the music, "you can get a ride back with Steph and Lisa."

"So, you and Roxy . . ."

She shot me a grin. "It's gonna be a good night. I can feel it."

The bass reverberated through the Jeep's speakers and into my body. The vibration like a hand on my back urging me to make a move.

Roxy lived in the Mission south of 24th Street. When Mel pushed open the front door, Daft Punk spilled outside from big speakers in the living room. People were already filling the space with Solo cups in hand. Mel knew a lot of them; she said hello as we walked through, and because I was with her, they said hi to me too even though they had no idea who I was. Lots of tattoos, bright pink or blue hair cut short or shaved on the sides. Short-sleeve button-downs printed with little birds, ripped jeans, battered sneakers or Docs. They were mostly women, but I also saw a few people who were more androgynous. No Steph.

Roxy was in the kitchen wearing a black vinyl miniskirt and a black-and-red silk corset, along with her boots. She was pouring a giant bottle of rum into a punch bowl, but put it down when she saw Mel and opened her arms. Mel had been holding two six-packs of Sierra Nevada, but she handed them to me so she could step into Roxy's hello kiss.

Behind Roxy, I recognized Jasmine from the band, standing at a laptop plugged into the sound system. She caught my eye and grinned while Mel and Roxy's kiss went on.

"Where do these go?" I asked Jasmine, holding up the beer.

She pointed toward the back door. "Out on the deck. You'll find it."

The deck had been hung with white Christmas lights, and a metal bucket the size of a small bathtub was filled with ice and beer and bottled water. I added the beers Mel had brought, then found a bottle opener nearby and opened one. A speaker was perched on a stool, and Pharrell was singing about getting lucky. Down in the yard, lawn chairs were set up in clusters. People I didn't know were talking and drinking, but toward the side of the yard I saw Lisa smoking, and then I saw Steph.

It was dark already, so I couldn't see her clearly, but I felt as if she saw me. I felt as if she watched as I came down the stairs from the deck and crossed the yard. I hadn't seen her in three days. I tried to play it cool.

"Hey," I said.

We hugged. Her body was warm against me, her hands sliding from the back of my bare shoulder down my spine. She was wearing some kind of cologne, spice and citrus.

"You look amazing," she said in my ear.

Her breath made a shiver go through me. I was sure she felt it.

Steph introduced me to the people she and Lisa had been talking to. She introduced to me to more of their friends who drifted into the yard for a cigarette or a beer, but their names were swallowed by the noise of music and increasingly loud conversations. They probably all thought I was queer, and when I realized this I felt a thrill, as if a mask I'd put on had suddenly become my real face.

After a while Steph noticed that I was peeling the label off my beer instead of drinking it, and when I admitted I didn't really like it, she took it away and reappeared a few minutes later with a cup of punch and Mel and Roxy in tow. The yard was growing more crowded now, and people were shouting over the music, and I realized Steph was drinking my beer.

Talia came out and joined us, and Mel asked her about her work. Talia was a student at the Art Institute, and she lived in the flat upstairs. "I'm painting everyone I know," she yelled at Mel. "You should sit for me!"

I was aware at all times that I was only a few feet away from Steph. I saw her hand on my beer, her mouth at the bottle's small curved lip. The punch was so strong, but it went down like candy. I finished my first cup.

Lisa was tugging at Steph's hand, pulling her toward the steps to go back inside. She turned back toward us and I could read her lips in the Christmas lights hanging above: *Let's dance.* Janelle Monae was on, and we all followed Lisa back into the house and crowded into the living room, where the lights had been turned down low and the furniture was pushed against the walls. The music was so loud it muffled all my thoughts. Rihanna, Nicki Minaj, their voices demanding. Mel pulled me into the middle of the floor, and we were dancing together. Roxy joined us, laughing at the cheesy moves Mel was making. Roxy's hair smelled like apples, and as we danced together, I felt like she'd tell me what I should do if I asked, but I couldn't put my question into words.

M.I.A.'s "Bad Girls" came on; the bass thumped. Lisa was shimmying up against Steph and I turned away so I didn't have to see it. I bumped into a woman with short bleached-blond hair and backed away, mouthing, *Sorry.* She was wearing a black muscle tee that exposed tattoos of vines crawling up her biceps. She looked at me, really looked, and when she put one hand on my waist to pull me closer, I let her. Her other hand followed, and soon she was angling her hips so that I had to move with her. I was intensely aware anyone could see us—including Steph—and my heart thudded with the beat. The back of her shirt was damp with sweat; I felt her thigh pressed against mine. She bent her face close to me, and I knew what she was about to do, but at the last moment her mouth slipped to my ear and she asked, "Do you want to get some air?"

"Yes," I shouted back, and she took my hand and I let her lead me out of the living room.

Her name was Casey. She said she was friends with Roxy from SF State, and I told her I knew Steph. We grabbed bottles of water from the ice bath and went down to the yard looking for a quieter corner. We ended up in the back next to a shed painted with a mural that I couldn't make out in the dim light. My ears were ringing from the music. When I leaned against the wall of the shed, Casey leaned in.

The last person I'd kissed was Jacob. I'd never kissed a woman before, but here was a woman who clearly wanted to kiss me. She was softer than Jacob—her lips, her tongue, the touch of her hands on my waist, pulling me into her. I could recognize that she knew how to kiss me with her whole body, not just her mouth, but I felt like I was splitting inside. Half of me was kissing her back and the other half was shrinking away.

I didn't know Casey. I wasn't even attracted to her. She was an experiment for me.

I felt like a monster.

I pulled away, dragging her hands off me. "I'm sorry," I said. "I'm really sorry." I fled before she could do anything, practically running back toward the house.

I saw Steph and Lisa in the yard, Lisa gesticulating with her cigarette. I thought I saw Steph's gaze flicker toward me, but I didn't go to them. I went upstairs and back inside. There were people everywhere, and they all seemed to be getting in my way on purpose. I pushed my way through the kitchen and into the living room. The floor seemed to heave as everyone in the room danced to Kelly Clarkson's "Stronger." They were all singing the chorus in unison.

I had to get out of here. I edged around the room, trying to avoid people's drinks as they raised them in the air. I kept feeling Casey's hands on me. Why had I let her? I felt sick about it, as if I'd cheated on someone. On Steph.

Behind me there was motion, as if someone were coming after me, and I was afraid it was Casey. I pushed through the crowd faster, and finally I reached the front door. I burst out onto the front stoop. The door to the second-floor flat was propped open with a shoe, and I glimpsed Christmas lights wrapped around a banister leading upstairs.

I went inside, climbing up to a dimly lit living room. The music was muffled up here, although the bass still reverberated through the floor. A few people were lounging on a wide L-shaped sofa, talking quietly. They glanced at me as I appeared at the top of the stairs, and then went back to their conversation.

Tealight candles had been placed along the floor, lighting the way down a hall past another kitchen to more rooms. I followed them, expecting to find a bathroom to hide in, but the door I opened led into what seemed to be a storage room.

I went in and pushed the door almost shut so I could still peer out through the crack. No one had followed me. I took a deep breath to calm the pounding of my heart, and I smelled paint. I turned around. In the dim light through the single window, the room gradually took shape. Large paintings were hanging on the walls: portraits of big, shadowed faces. An unfinished canvas was attached to an easel by the window, and when I went to get a better look, I thought I recognized Roxy. This must be Talia's work. But she hadn't painted these portraits in naturalistic colors. Roxy's eyes were gold, her hair purple. Another painting showed a woman with spiky orange hair and blue skin.

The door opened, and I whirled around.

Steph stood in the doorway. "Are you okay?" she asked.

Now I was sure that she'd seen me with Casey. "I'm fine," I said, feeling guilty.

Steph came into the room and shut the door behind her with a click. "I saw you with . . . Did she do something?"

My stomach dropped. "No. Everything's fine."

"Did you want to hook up with her?"

Her tone was sharp. I realized, suddenly, that she was jealous. Her face was barely lit in the shadowed room, but I didn't need to see every detail to recognize what she was feeling. It seemed palpable in the air between us. Inevitable.

"No," I said. "I only want you."

I felt as if I'd lit myself on fire.

Steph said nothing, and her silence made me bold. I took three steps across the floor of the small room, and I was standing right in front of her. I smelled the spice-and-citrus scent on her skin, now cut with cigarette smoke.

She could have stopped me, but she didn't.

I put my arms around her neck as if we were slow dancing in a high school gym. I felt the swaying of her body into mine as if we were moving to music. In my new boots we were the same height. It was as though gravity were conspiring with us because I didn't feel like I was standing on firm ground until her mouth met mine.

have replayed this moment in my memory over and over. It has, over time, been honed down to a few bright fragments.

The cold, bright taste of her. Ice and lime.

The fine soft hairs on the back of her neck, my fingertips raising them from her skin in an electric charge.

Her hands sliding around my back to press me into her, and she feels so good I forget everything else. There is only her.

er phone rang. It was loud and insistent, and at first, we ignored it. Her hands were slipping beneath my shirt, raising goose bumps on my skin, and then suddenly she backed off and I was standing in the middle of the tiny room, blinking, while she stared down at her phone.

"Shit," she said. "Fuck."

I was dazed. "What's wrong?"

"Lisa left."

"What?"

Steph's phone shed a ghostly light over her face. Behind her, the painted pink eyes of the blue-skinned woman seemed to glare at me. I moved toward Steph and reached for the phone, but she pulled it away before I could see the message.

"What happened?" I asked.

"If she took the car, I—I don't know."

She was at the door before I understood what she was doing, and now the door was open and she was leaving.

"I'm sorry," she called back to me. "I have to go find her."

She was gone.

I was stunned. I could still feel her mouth on me. I ran out into the candlelit hallway and into the quiet living room. Everything looked the same as before. I didn't see Steph, but one of the people on the sofa noticed me and pointed at the stairway, and I realized it was Talia. She looked knowing, and I went downstairs before she could say anything.

Steph was out on the sidewalk, gazing down the street. She began to run, and I went after her. She stopped at the end of the block, where she stared at an empty parking space on the street.

"She took the car," Steph said flatly. "Fuck."

Mel gave Steph the keys to her Jeep. "I'm staying," she said. "You can borrow it. I hope Lisa's okay."

I said goodbye to Mel because there was no way for me to get back to San Rafael and my car if I didn't leave with Steph. I thought being alone with her on the drive would lead to something more—at least an acknowledgment of what had happened between us—but she was grim as we headed out of the city. She told me she and Lisa had fought, and Lisa had gone home angry, and then she didn't say anything else.

I couldn't make sense of it. She had kissed me, but now she wouldn't even look me in the eye. I felt like she had punched me in the stomach, and an ache began to build there, a combination of frustrated desire and bewilderment. The longer we were silent, the harder it was to break it, and I ended up saying nothing the whole way to Mel's house.

She pulled up behind the Honda and left the engine running. "I'm sorry," she said. "I shouldn't have—"

"Don't say it," I muttered. I got out and slammed the door shut before she could respond. My eyes burned as I walked to the car. As soon as I was in, Steph drove off. I sat there alone in the dark, tears spilling out of my eyes.

When I got back to Woodacre, the house was dark, but the motion-sensor outdoor lights snapped on as I opened the gate. The ferns on the side of the path were washed in whiteness, all their color leached away.

I opened the front door, and Analemma came down the stairs to nose at me. I petted her half-heartedly and went upstairs. She followed as I went to my room and dropped my purse on the dresser and took off my boots. The world seemed to wobble, and I realized I was hungry.

Analemma followed me into the kitchen. I opened the fridge and saw the brown paper bag from lunch with my mother. There were still a couple of steamed buns left. Moving automatically, I took one out and wrapped it in a damp paper towel to microwave it. When it was ready, I sat down at the kitchen table and pulled apart the steaming white bun, revealing the glistening red barbecued pork inside. Analemma put her head on my thigh hopefully. There was something about the mournful look in her golden-brown eyes that startled a laugh out of me.

"You are shameless," I whispered, and pulled out a piece of pork and fed it to her.

She continued to drool onto my thigh while I took my first bite.

Sometimes a memory will overtake you so unexpectedly it's as if you've been instantly transported back in time. I was eight years old and Tasha was at our apartment in Wellesley after school, and we'd just eaten some pork buns. My dad had brought them back from Chinatown in Boston and reheated them for us.

Afterward, when my dad shut himself into his office to write, we went into my bedroom to play house. Tasha wanted to be the mommy, and even though I didn't want to be the daddy, I told her I would because Tasha only ever wanted to be the mommy.

Tasha said, "You have to come home from work, and I'll bring you a drink," and I knew this was because after school we sometimes watched a TV show in which the dad came home from work, calling, "Honey, I'm home!" The mom always appeared in an apron and greeted him at the door with a kiss and a cocktail. I couldn't get enough of watching the dad settle his kids' inconsequential arguments while the mom served up a casserole dinner. The show had been mesmerizing to me because it felt like the opposite of my parents. They were always rushing here and there, packing suitcases, bringing home takeout, and closing doors behind which they had tense-sounding conversations. And now they were divorced. The parents on the TV show were exotic in comparison, and always, in every episode, they kissed each other hello.

Maybe that's why I suggested to Tasha, "You have to kiss me when I come home."

In my memory, I came through the door of my bedroom and called out, "Honey, I'm home!"

Tasha, waiting inside my room, came to greet me holding a plastic tumbler full of water. She beamed as she said, "Welcome home, dear." She had tied one of my sweatshirts around her waist with the sleeves, like an apron, and I had to put down the empty leather briefcase we'd borrowed from my dad's closet before I took the tumbler from her. Then I approached Tasha for the kiss, and right before I leaned in I knew I shouldn't kiss her like this, and I put my hand over her mouth to create a barrier, my palm against her lips, and I kissed the back of my hand.

I had forgotten about our game until that night in Joan's kitchen, with Analemma still drooling on my leg, and the pork bun steaming on the napkin in front of me. I couldn't eat any more. I fed the rest to Analemma and went to bed, still hungry.

The ringing sounded like an alarm and I jolted awake, scrabbling for my phone, which for some reason was in my bed under the covers. When I finally found it, the screen said DAD. I meant to silence the call, but I accidentally hit the wrong button. I heard his tinny voice through the speaker: "Aria? Are you there? Can you hear me?"

I sighed and lifted the phone to my ear. "Hi. Yes I can hear you."

"Sounds like you're half asleep." He laughed. "It's almost noon."

"Really?" I blinked and looked toward the window. The blue curtain was outlined by bright sunlight that made me squint.

"Up late?" he said, sounding amused.

The party. Steph. *Shit.*

"Aria?"

"Sorry, yeah, I'm here." I sat up, rubbing my face.

"I'd offer to talk later but I only have the landline for a brief time."

"Okay."

"How was lunch with your mom?"

I groaned involuntarily. "Do we have to talk about that?"

"She called me afterward."

The blankets were hot and scratchy, and I shoved them away. "What did she say?"

"She told me she's engaged. And she told me about her offer to help pay for MIT."

His tone was too even. "How do you feel about it?" I asked carefully.

"I'm happy for her," he said, but he still sounded so neutral that I wondered if he was lying.

"Really?"

"Of course. I'm glad she met someone she wants to marry. But how are you feeling about it?"

I wished desperately that we weren't having this conversation. "I don't know. I haven't been thinking about it."

"She's very glad you've agreed to be in their wedding."

"What was I supposed to say?"

"You could've said no."

"No I couldn't."

He exhaled. "It *is* your choice. If you need me to tell her that, I will."

I felt tears well up in my eyes. "Dad, can we please talk about this later?"

"It's not a good idea to avoid it."

"I'm not avoiding anything, I'm just—I just woke up. That's all."

"She's really trying now," he said, ignoring me. "Her offer to help with MIT is very generous. I would think about accepting it."

"I don't want to be beholden to her."

"It's her money to give. She gave you as much as she could in the past, and she's still trying to."

"Why are you always defending her?" I snapped. "She left you, didn't she?" I flinched as I heard my own words, but I couldn't stop.

"How can you expect me to forgive her for what she did to you, and to me?"

"That's not fair—"

"You've never even gone on a date with anyone since you guys got divorced. Aren't you still in love with her? Isn't that why you can't finish your novel?"

There was total silence over the phone. In rapidly dawning horror, I realized what I had just said. "Dad, I'm sorry—"

"Aria, your mom and I split up twelve—no, thirteen years ago," he said. He sounded tired. "I'm not in love with her anymore. And she's not the reason I've been having trouble with my book. But it's almost done now."

I couldn't tell if I was relieved or disappointed. "Really?"

"Yes, really." He exhaled. "I'm sorry if I've given you the impression that I still wanted to be with your mom. I really don't."

I was uncomfortable. "We don't have to talk about this."

"No, we do. If this is what's holding you back from working things out with her, we do. Listen. Your mom and I have both moved on, and I *have* gone on dates since we divorced. I don't tell you everything, Ari. Nothing serious developed because—well, I've been busy." He gave a short, rueful laugh. "I had five years of writer's block, and tenure to go after. And I had you to take care of. I didn't have the time or the inclination, and probably I would have made some bad decisions if I let myself get involved with anyone seriously. It's been my choice. It's not your mom's fault."

"But you had those newspaper clippings and—"

"I had what?" He sounded confused.

"I—I just thought you still loved her." It hurt so much to say those words.

"I do love her," he said firmly. "I'll always love her. She gave you to me."

My eyes grew hot. "Dad, I want you to be happy."

"Oh, sweetie, I am happy. I'm so happy to talk to you about this. I'm sorry we haven't talked about it before. I had no idea you— Maybe I should have had an idea. Maybe I've been clueless about everything. Your mom would certainly have said so." He took a quick breath. "Look, it's going to be fine. Your mom and I agreed a long time ago that we're not meant to be together. It was a hard decision—I admit that. Maybe I let it show too much when you were younger. But I'm past it now, I really am. I'm happy that your mom has found someone. I hope you'll be happy for her, too."

I leaned against the wall and stared at the sunlight glowing through the curtains. "Okay," I said finally. "I'll try."

In the living room, Joan was sitting on the couch with a bunch of photo albums spread out on the coffee table. Analemma, who was lying on the rug, raised her head when I came in, and Joan twisted around as if surprised to see me.

"Hi," I said. "You're not working this morning?"

She blinked, and then the surprised expression on her face cleared. "My goodness, for a moment there I thought you were Alexis."

I sat down on the couch beside her. "Are you okay?"

"I'm not feeling well," she admitted. "I thought I was fine when I woke up, but my head started hurting." She picked up a mug of herbal tea that was on the coffee table, and it shook slightly as she sipped from it.

"Did you take some ibuprofen or Tylenol? Can I get you any?"

"No, I took some."

"Maybe you should lie down."

She seemed to consider that. "Do you know what I was doing with these photos last night?" she asked.

I glanced down at the albums. They looked like the ones we'd found in the basement. "No, I wasn't here last night, remember?"

Joan's forehead wrinkled as if she were puzzled. "You weren't." It wasn't quite a question, but it worried me.

"Did you take them out for your work?" I pulled the closest album over to me and opened it. I recognized the snapshots from Hawaii. There was the photo of Grandpa and his colleagues on top of the mountain.

Joan said, "Russ says they're building an infrared telescope there."

I glanced up at the present tense. "Are you sure you're okay? This photo was taken a long time ago."

Joan looked briefly confused, and then she shook her head. "What am I thinking? I probably should go lie down."

She stood up and I put a hand on her elbow as she wobbled. "Do you want me to call a doctor?"

"No, no, I just need to rest a bit." She headed for the stairs.

"Let me help you." I got up to follow her, and Analemma followed me.

"I'm fine," Joan snapped.

I halted in surprise. Analemma went over to her and nudged her left hand. She looked down at Analemma and her expression cleared, then she looked at me.

"I'll be fine," she said more gently. "I'm going to go rest. I didn't sleep well last night, that's all."

I watched her slowly climbing up the stairs, Analemma following just behind as if she could catch her if she fell. I wondered if I should insist on helping. When she shut the bedroom door, I turned back to the coffee table. The photo album was still open, the picture of

Grandpa on the mountain waiting like a portal to the past. I decided that if Joan didn't feel better after her nap, I'd insist on calling the doctor.

I made myself a lunch of scrambled eggs, heavily buttered toast, and very strong coffee. I ate it out on the deck under the umbrella, wearing my sunglasses. I felt like I had an emotional hangover.

But all was quiet here, normal. On this deck looking out at the brown-and-green hills, there was no trace of what had happened last night. Maybe it didn't happen at all. Maybe I was living my life in multiple universes, and I was the only one who could move between them. In the universe that contained this house, I was Joan's granddaughter, and I was going to check on her in a few hours to make sure she was okay. Last night had taken place in another universe—one where I was not myself. That universe contained Steph-and-me, if that was a thing. All our lunches at In-N-Out were in that universe. The quiet inside her truck cab was in that universe.

I remembered kissing her. I tried not to, but I couldn't stop. I didn't know it was possible to want to be in a place that ached like a bruise.

I was restless. Kelly Clarkson's "Stronger" was stuck in my head on a loop. I changed into hiking clothes and left Joan a note saying I was going up to the fire road. I wondered if I should take Analemma, but there was no sound from Joan's room and I didn't want to disturb her if she was sleeping. I grabbed my earphones and a bottle of water and headed out.

I put on Lana Del Rey because she seemed like the opposite of Kelly Clarkson. The fire road was busy with Sunday mountain bikers, and I kept to the side as I walked. It was warm, and when I stopped to take a drink of water, I felt sweat trickling down my back beneath my tank top. I had forgotten to put on sunscreen, and the possibility that I'd burn seemed fitting. I turned off the unshaded fire road as soon as I could, taking a small unmarked trail downhill. I wasn't sure where it would end up, but I figured it didn't matter. I had my phone.

And then it rang. I pulled it out of my back pocket, and I was both surprised and unsurprised to see Steph's name on the screen. For a moment I thought about not taking her call, but before it was too late, I swiped to answer.

"Hello?" I said.

"Hey. It's Steph."

"Yeah."

"I'm sorry about what happened."

I didn't say anything.

"I didn't mean— I don't want you to think I don't—" She sighed. "We're still friends, right?"

A hiker was coming up the path toward me, so I stepped off the trail. I was surrounded by those trees with the peeling bark. I couldn't remember their name.

"Aria?"

"What do you want me to say?"

"I feel like I hurt your feelings. I didn't mean to do that. I want you to—I want to be friends."

"That's all. Friends." The word sounded so strange to me now, the *s* on the end like an insinuation.

"You know we can't be more than that." She actually sounded apologetic.

"Because of Lisa."

"Yeah."

"What happened when you got home?" Pushing on the bruise.

"That's between me and Lisa."

"You're still together."

"Yes."

"But you want to be my friend."

"Yes. What happened between us—" She made a frustrated sound. "Look, I was there. I know what happened. I can't deny I wanted it, but I'm not—I'm with Lisa. You and I can't be more than friends."

My heart began to race. *I can't deny I wanted it.*

When I said nothing, she continued: "I would feel so bad if you took this the wrong way. I know you're just coming out, and it's got to be a confusing time for you. I didn't mean to fuck it up even more. I really want you in my life. Let me make it up to you."

Beneath the curling red bark, the trees' green interiors looked like skin, soft and supple.

I asked, "What do you mean?"

"Tomorrow . . . let's talk in person."

"Where?"

"Do you want to meet for dinner in Fairfax? How about at the Thai restaurant?"

I felt all the blood in my body pulsing in response to her voice. I put my hand on the nearest tree's green skin. It was cool and smooth. *Madrone*, I remembered. These were madrone trees.

"What do you say?" she asked. "Tomorrow night?"

I had hesitated to respond, but there was never any chance I'd say no. "Okay."

"Great. How about seven? And there's no movie tonight. Sorry about that. We just need some time."

I wasn't surprised. "Okay."

"But I'll see you tomorrow."

"Tomorrow," I repeated.

The call ended, and Lana Del Rey was singing "Gods & Monsters."

That ache: If I could bottle it, it would make you drunk.

angkok Thai was only a couple of buildings down from Bolinas Café, where Steph had performed during that open mic. I got there way too early and sat restlessly in Joan's car in the parking lot until the appointed time. I had been reluctant to tell Joan I was meeting Steph for dinner; it felt like she'd be able to tell it wasn't a casual thing, and if she was still feeling bad, I wasn't even sure if I should go. But I hadn't had to tell her anything. That morning Joan said she felt fine, and she made plans to go to Spirit Rock that night with Tony. He picked her up at a quarter to six to take her to the community vegetarian dinner before meditation.

At seven o'clock, I went into the restaurant and got a table for two. I tried to read the menu, but my thoughts kept cycling back to Steph. Tasha would call me obsessed. She was arriving on Wednesday, and I hadn't decided yet whether I would tell her about Steph. The question was paralyzing.

Steph texted to say she was stuck in traffic. I went back to thinking about what I should say to her. I'd imagined a dozen different ways to spin what had happened: *It was a mistake; I didn't mean it; I'm sorry; I regret it.* But none of them were true, because I didn't think it was a mistake and I didn't regret it. Steph had been the first new person I met here, and then we'd run into each other again at Safeway as if it were fated. That's what I wanted our relationship to be: fated.

I'd been seated at the table for more than ten minutes—painfully aware that I was alone because the waitress kept stopping by to refill my water glass—when Steph came through the front door. She saw me right away, which wasn't particularly extraordinary since the restaurant was small and mostly empty, but it still gave me a thrill to meet her gaze across the room. She looked nervous, too.

"Sorry I'm late," she said, sitting down across from me.

"It's okay." I wondered what she had told Lisa about her plans tonight.

When the waitress came over, Steph ordered pad Thai with shrimp. I ordered the next item on the menu, pad see ew with beef. We made small talk while we waited for the food. Paintings of Buddhas and lotuses hung on the walls, and a group of elderly Fairfax hippies was seated nearby. The restaurant was so brightly lit that it felt wrong to talk about what had happened between us in Talia's dark room.

When the food came, we ended up splitting our dishes. Steph fumbled with her chopsticks. "Sorry, I'm a chopstick amateur," she said.

"Stick with me long enough and you'll learn," I joked, and then my face burned. I was such a fraud. Not only an Asian fraud, but a lesbian fraud, too. I had no idea what I was doing. I felt as if my whole body had just turned into a swarm of bees, and I had to concentrate on taking one bite after another so I could hold myself together.

Beef. Rice noodles. Carrots. Tasteless.

Slowly, I came back to myself. I drank some ice water. My chair was slightly unstable beneath my body; one of the legs was shorter than the others. Steph was eating with her eyes lowered to her plate, avoiding my gaze.

By the end of the meal, we still hadn't brought up the elephant in the room, so after the waitress took away our plates, I said, "I know we have to talk—"

"I've been thinking—" Steph said at the same time.

We both stopped. I said, "Go ahead."

Steph grimaced. "Okay." But she didn't speak for several moments. I heard someone across the small restaurant break into laughter, and the clink of a fork against a plate. Steph dropped her gaze to the clump of noodles she'd dropped on the table. "I made a mess," she said.

"They'll clean it up."

"I'm not sure I was talking about the food."

The waitress brought the check on a small plastic tray. I pulled my wallet out of my purse as Steph took her money out, too. "Split it?" I asked.

"Sure," Steph said.

We each laid down cash; neither of us needed change. We had both come prepared, as if we'd mutually agreed to make this part, at least, easy. The waitress appeared moments later to pick up the money. She had been watching us all night with a curiosity that seemed to go beyond making sure our orders were correct, and I hadn't figured out if it was because I was Asian and there weren't many other Asian people here, or if it was because she couldn't decide if Steph was a boy or a girl. I'd noticed that Steph got confused looks sometimes, and it struck me that if I were her girlfriend, I would be part of that confusion. The two of us together could be perceived as either a stereotype or a mistake.

"Do you need change?" the waitress asked.

"No thanks," I said.

"You want to go?" Steph asked after the waitress left. "We can talk in my truck."

"Okay."

It was almost dark outside, and Steph pointed toward the parking lot across the street. "I'm over there at the end." She led me to the far side of the lot, where her truck was parked facing a big bush that blocked the lot from the street on the other side. She climbed in first and then reached over to unlock the passenger side door.

When I got in, the cab smelled faintly of french fries. The bush in front of the truck gave us a sense of privacy, and after a few moments the dome light clicked off, leaving us in the dark cab. There was no more putting this off.

"I know you're with Lisa," I said.

"I don't want to mess things up," she said at the same time.

"I don't want to mess things up either," I said. "For you or for us. I mean, I'm leaving on August twenty-first. I won't even be here. I wasn't trying to start anything, I really wasn't."

Fraud.

"I wasn't either," she said.

"It just happened."

Did it?

"Yeah."

"I'm sorry if I've made trouble for you and Lisa," I said. "I really am." The voice inside me was quiet. Was that the truth?

"I know," she said. She was a silhouette outlined by the distant streetlights, and I wished I could see the expression on her face.

"I meant it when I said I'm not trying to mess that up for you," I said. "I know you love her, and you have a life here, and I'm leaving in less than a month, and all I want is—I don't want to lose you. I—I like you." I felt possessed by a sudden, clear-minded sincerity. A fierce urge to reveal myself. "You made me realize something I never knew. I'm so grateful for that."

She didn't speak for a long moment. Instantly I was mortified. I had told her I *liked* her, as if I were thirteen.

And then she said, "I like you, too." There was a smile in her voice.

I whispered, "Really?"

"Yes," Steph said, but this time she didn't sound happy. She let out a breath. "The thing is, Lisa and I—we've had our issues. I love her, but . . ."

She didn't finish her sentence, and I could barely breathe. I wanted to touch her so badly.

"I didn't plan any of this," I said. My desire was overwhelming.

"Me either."

I let myself reach for her. Her right hand was clenched on her thigh. I loosened her fingers, lacing them with mine. There was a moment where she resisted, and I wondered if this would be the end of it—and then she lifted her free hand and tucked my hair behind my ear. Her touch sent tingles over my scalp. In the quiet of the truck cab, I thought I could hear the racing of my own pulse. The rustle of fabric as she shifted in her seat, leaning toward me. The hitch in her breath, so close I could feel it on my face.

And then we were kissing.

It was different this time. After that first taste, there had been time to develop an appetite. Now I was starved for her. We were separated from each other by the shape of the truck's bucket seats and the gear shift, jutting up unwelcome between us. It was uncomfortable and made for awkward maneuvering, but it seemed a tiny price to pay for this time alone in the dark with her.

woke up with the memory of Steph imprinted on my body in the way I ached for her. Every single nerve buzzed with new awareness.

I met her on Tuesday after work. I climbed into her truck and she drove us across Sir Francis Drake to Starbucks, where we got iced coffees. Then we drove around to the back of the shopping center and parked by the loading docks.

Our drinks sweated in the cup holder while we kissed. She smelled metallic; her skin was salty.

"What are you doing tomorrow?" she asked after a while.

"Tasha's coming," I said. The thought of not seeing Steph, of not touching her, seemed intolerable.

She ran her hand over my thigh. "I'm still coming over to do yard work on Friday," she said. "Will Tasha be there?"

"Come early. Maybe she'll be asleep."

"Are you going to tell her?"

"I don't know."

I pulled her face to mine. We didn't have enough time.

met Tasha at the Marin Airporter stop in San Rafael on Wednesday morning. It had been less than twenty-four hours since I'd seen Steph, but my body felt like it was in withdrawal. I was jittery, but the shuttle was pulling into the parking lot and I had to get out of the car.

I spotted Tasha in big sunglasses and a Spelman hoodie, pulling her carry-on behind her. She'd colored her dark hair red at the tips since the last time I'd seen her.

"Tasha!" I called, waving.

When she saw me, she headed in my direction. I met her halfway, and when we hugged I smelled her coconut lotion. It brought me back to graduation day. I remembered staring at the shiny acetate of the gown over my knees and the freshly cut grass at my feet, uncomfortably relieved that my mom wasn't there to see the way everyone was avoiding me.

Tasha said, "It's so good to see you." When we parted, she had a strange expression on her face—mingled excitement and anxiety. "How are you?"

I remembered Steph asking me the same question yesterday, a smile in her eyes. I had answered her with a kiss.

"I'm good," I said, and in that moment the words felt true.

In the car, I asked Tasha to tell me about France. We were almost to the freeway on-ramp when she pointed out the window and asked, "Is that an In-N-Out?"

I saw the red-and-yellow sign in the distance. "Yeah."

"I've never eaten there. Isn't it supposed to be a thing?"

"Yeah, it's good."

"Can we go?"

"Right now?" The idea of going there without Steph startled me.

"Sure, why not? I had a weird breakfast on the plane but it's past two on the East Coast. I need lunch!"

"Okay," I said, and headed for In-N-Out.

In the restaurant, we slid into a hard plastic booth while we waited for our orders to be called. Steph and I had never eaten inside. Tasha said she wanted to go to the beach while she was here. I kept glancing at the doors as if Steph might walk in at any moment.

"And San Francisco," Tasha was saying. "Can we go there?"

"Sure," I said, and I remembered the Queer Music Festival. "Actually, there's this music festival I want to go to on Saturday in Golden Gate Park. I know one of the bands that's playing. The guitarist is Joan's gardener."

Speaking about Steph, even without using her name, made my pulse race. I waited for Tasha to ask me about Joan's gardener, but our order number was called and we had to go get our food. Then Tasha insisted on taking selfies with our burgers and posting them on Instagram to mark the occasion. I wanted to text my photo to Steph, but then I'd have to explain to Tasha who she was, so I didn't.

I'd ordered my burger animal style as usual, but it didn't taste as good as it normally did. I felt Steph's absence beside me almost physically, as if the lack of her had become a charged current thrumming against my skin.

Later, when Tasha went to the bathroom, I sent my photo to Steph and wrote, *Wish you were here.* She replied immediately: *Me too. X*

When we approached the garden center, I was tempted to stop in, pretend I needed to buy some plants for Joan. Steph would be in the flower section, or maybe restocking pots. I imagined the surprise on her face as she saw me, the way she'd hug me a little too long.

"The light's green," Tasha said.

"Oh, sorry." I accelerated too fast through the intersection and Tasha jerked forward against her seat belt. "Sorry!" I said.

"Are you okay?" she asked. "You were totally out of it back there."

"I'm fine." I looked in the rearview mirror. I couldn't see the garden center anymore.

Tasha and I had slept over at each other's houses countless times before. It shouldn't have felt weird for us to sleep in the same bed, but that night when she climbed in next to me, I noticed the sway of her breasts beneath her tank top. I looked away quickly, suddenly aware of the way the mattress sank in the middle. If I wasn't careful I could roll into her.

"Is something bothering you?" she asked.

"No, why?"

"You've been a little . . . I don't know. Off."

"I think I'm just tired," I said.

She shifted onto her back. "I'm not sleepy," she announced. "I think all the travel has screwed up my sleep. My body can't figure out what time zone I'm in. Hey, remember when we were in middle school and we'd stay up all night watching bad cable TV?"

"Don't forget the cheese puffs."

"Yeah. Haley would never eat them." She sounded a little sad.

I rolled onto my side, away from Tasha, and turned off the lamp. I imagined Steph in bed behind me, her mouth on my neck. Steph wore a sports bra, as far as I could tell. I'd never really touched her breasts.

"We're going to the beach tomorrow?" Tasha said.

"Yeah," I said.

"Hope it'll be warm enough. I want to swim."

"Tasha, I'm sleepy. Sorry, can we talk tomorrow?"

She sighed. "Yeah, yeah. I'm gonna read on my phone. Good night, dork."

I smiled. "Good night."

But now I couldn't fall asleep. I was remembering Steph's hand cupping my breast through my T-shirt in the darkness of the truck cab. The memory of it alone made a charge go through my body.

Joan suggested we go to Bolinas Beach, although she warned us it wouldn't be that warm. "I doubt you'll want to swim," she said. She showed me the route on Google Maps. "Drive carefully. The road is pretty winding."

Tasha was a little subdued, and I wasn't sure if it was due to jet lag or something else. She put on her swimsuit under shorts and a T-shirt even though it was still only in the mid-sixties and cloudy.

We stopped at Lagunitas Grocery & Deli to buy lunch, and while Tasha was ordering her sandwich, I checked my phone to make sure I hadn't missed any texts from Steph. Nothing. I fought the urge to text her anyway.

In the car, Tasha played DJ, skipping from "Call Me Maybe" to "We Are Young" and "Come and Get It." The pop songs felt fake to me, as if we were pretending to be happier than we were. When Rihanna came on, I asked Tasha to forward to the next track, and she didn't ask why.

Bolinas was a small, hippie beach town that I'd visited before with Dad, but I barely remembered it beyond a vague memory of surfers in wetsuits outside a café. The access to the beach was down a residential street lined with cedar-shingled houses. I parked a couple of blocks from the water, and when we got out, we could see it as a shivering gray light at the end of the street.

The beach was mostly empty, although one family was making a day of it with a bunch of beach chairs and a big red cooler. Tasha and I walked about five minutes down the sand and spread out our blanket. I began to open the lunch bags. "We should take a picture and send it to Haley," I suggested.

"Maybe," Tasha said.

"But we always do that." I sat down cross-legged and unwrapped my ham-and-cheese sandwich.

Tasha sat down beside me and dragged a towel out of the bag to cover her bare legs. I had worn jeans and a sweatshirt, and I could tell she was cold. "I should've listened to your grandma," she muttered. "This is not summer weather."

Out over the ocean I saw the last traces of the marine layer hovering in a faint haze. "Not like it is in New England," I agreed.

She took out her sandwich, folding back the paper deliberately as if she were practicing origami. "There's something I have to tell you."

The tone of her voice was so serious that I became worried. "What's wrong?" I asked.

She spoke quietly, her eyes downcast. "We were together. Haley and me. But we broke up."

I wasn't sure if I'd heard her correctly. "What?"

She took a bite of her sandwich, chewed methodically, and swallowed. She still wasn't looking at me. "We were dating. Well, not dating. We were kind of secretly hooking up because Haley wasn't really okay with it, and I kept hoping that she'd come around—that maybe this summer once we left high school she'd realize it was fine." Tasha took another bite of her sandwich, but midway through chewing it she grabbed a napkin and spit it out. "I'm sorry," she said, her voice catching. "It's fine, but I can't eat right now."

This was why Tasha had flown all the way out here. For the first time in a long time, I stopped thinking about Steph. I saw the slightly darker freckles on the brown skin of Tasha's cheeks, and the redness at the rims of her eyes. All the little things I'd seen but not understood about her and Haley: the way they'd sit leaning against each other, their constant texting, and then the way they suddenly avoided each other. It was a revelation.

I set down my sandwich and scooted over to put my arm around her shoulders, pulling her close to me. "Tash, I'm so sorry," I said.

I felt her trembling against me.

"After graduation Haley told me it 'wasn't her.' " Tasha made air quotes as she spoke, and she blinked fiercely. "She said she couldn't be with me anymore, and she'd only been doing it because she was my friend and she loved me 'as a friend' "—the air quotes again—"but that's all. She said she was just confused the whole time."

Tasha reached for a bottle of water, and I let her go. She took a couple of sips and seemed to sag toward the ground.

"By the time I got back from France she was dating a guy she met this summer," she continued. "She brought him with her to Mad Martha's. It was supposed to be just the two of us—we were supposed to talk about it. But she brought him without telling me he was coming, and I—I *hate* him."

Tasha had always been the nice one among the three of us, the one who wouldn't say a mean thing about anyone, but now she spit out the words with a vehemence that shocked me.

She seemed to suddenly realize she was talking to me, and she looked at me in a panic. "Are you freaked out?"

"No, absolutely not," I said quickly. "I'm sorry. I feel like I should have known. You two were so close back in the spring. Why didn't you tell me?"

"I wanted to but Haley didn't, and I kept hoping she'd come around and we could tell you together."

I remembered now that neither of them had had prom dates. They'd told me they were going stag because of the Jacob situation and wanted to support me. I asked, "Did you two go to prom together?"

Tasha winced. "Well, not exactly. We went to prom alone, together."

"I can't believe I never got it," I said. "You must have thought I was so stupid."

"No, I didn't," Tasha insisted. "I mean, it's not like you'd think it was an option, right?"

The question almost made me laugh. "No, I guess not."

"Are you sure you're okay with this?" Tasha asked tentatively. "You're not—you don't think it's weird?"

"It's not weird," I said. I put my arm around her again, and she dropped her head onto my shoulder. I knew this was a chance for me to tell her about Steph, to make her feel less alone, but the words stuck in my throat. I told myself I didn't want to trample on her news, that I was being unselfish by letting her have this space.

woke up just after sunrise on Friday morning. Tasha had stayed up late reading again, and I left her fast asleep in bed. Outside, the trees seemed to float in the misty dawn light as I walked from the house to the studio.

Inside, my unfinished painting was still tacked to the wall, a panel of dark, smudged purples and blues on black, like a well of bruises. I thought about the Bernice Bing painting with the figure floating in the upper left, and wanted to add something similar. I rummaged through the acrylic paints in the cabinets and pulled out yellow and orange and red. I loaded up one of the smaller brushes and painted a circle in the upper left in yellow, as if it were a sun. It was too bright, so I darkened it with some orange. That looked like an egg yolk, which I didn't like, so I took the red and trailed some lines from it, which made it look like a bleeding egg yolk.

It was all wrong. It looked like a kid's painting.

I put my fingertip on the orange paint, which was still wet, and smeared it vigorously. I liked the way the yellow and orange partially mixed, so I smeared it some more. I ran my fingers over the red, too, weaving orange trails into it like wavering sunbeams.

I stepped back. It still looked like a kid's painting, and not even a good one. *I'm so stupid,* I thought, *to believe I can do this.*

My phone dinged. I went to the sink and scrubbed my hands, and as I watched the colors swirl down the drain, I thought about the painting of the blue-skinned woman watching us as we kissed for the first time.

I dried my hands on a paper towel and finally let myself pick up my phone from the worktable. The text was from Steph. It was just after seven.

Be there soon.

Earlier, I had taken my clothes into the bathroom to avoid waking Tasha while I got dressed. Now I went into the house to brush my teeth and change out of my paint-spattered T-shirt. I put on a lacy pink bra, and the thought that Steph might see it made my skin tingle.

I knew what Steph and I were doing was wrong. Everyone would say so. Lisa would definitely say so, but she seemed irrelevant to the way I felt. I didn't want to hurt her, but I had convinced myself she'd never know. Our universes would not cross. Today was August 2, and I was leaving in nineteen days. We had less than three weeks left together.

When I heard the creak of the gate, all my senses went on alert. I forced myself to wait for three full breaths. Then I went out to the shed, where I knew she'd go first, and when she rounded the corner of the house, I was waiting.

"Good morning," she said. She was dressed for yard work, but I thought she'd taken extra care with her hair.

"Hey," I said. "Do you want to come see the painting?"

She smiled. "Sure."

She followed me back to the studio, and once she was inside, I closed the door. "I screwed it up," I told her, gesturing to the bleeding egg of the sun.

She walked over to it and squinted at the paint. "What are you aiming for?"

"I have no idea."

She turned back to me, but she didn't make a move. Her smile had vanished, and she put her hands in the pockets of her cargo shorts as if to stop herself from touching me. So I went over to her and lightly rested my hands on her waist. I leaned in to her space. She smelled like citrus shampoo.

"I have to work," she said softly.

"Five minutes," I suggested.

She exhaled, and her hands came out of her pockets and went around my back. When we kissed, her mouth was minty.

Five minutes turned into ten, our bodies pressed together, her hand sliding up to cup my breast through my shirt. I covered her hand with mine and squeezed, and her breath caught in a low gasp. I liked that sound. I wanted to hear it again, and I wanted her to touch my skin, so I started to pull off my shirt, but she stopped me.

"Five minutes," she whispered, and moved her mouth to the hollow between my neck and collarbone.

Her tongue was warm and startling, and I held her head there, pulling her as close to me as I could. I shivered as her teeth scraped against my skin. She lifted her head and kissed me again, and now her hand was under my shirt and pushing aside the lace cup of my bra. Her palm was warm on my breast, her thumb rubbing my nipple until all I could feel was the stroke of her finger.

There was no way to fake this. I was 100 percent present in my body, every millimeter of my skin alive, a liquid ache between my legs. It made everything that had happened before this moment seem like a mirage. This—Steph's hands on me and her kiss and her body beneath my fingers—this was the realest thing I'd ever felt.

On Saturday, Tasha and I arranged to meet Mel in Golden Gate Park at a fountain near the band shell. When we arrived, Lisa was leaning on the edge of the fountain beside Mel, smoking a cigarette. It disappointed me to see her. I realized I'd been hoping she and Steph were still fighting, and that she might not show up.

I introduced Tasha to Mel and Lisa, and then asked, "Where's Steph?"

"She's backstage with the band," Lisa said. "They're second in the lineup." She seemed a little tense.

"Let's go find a spot," Mel said, and Lisa stubbed out her cigarette.

Tasha and I followed them down the plaza toward the concrete band shell at the far end. A crowd was already forming. A big banner that read SAN FRANCISCO QUEER MUSIC FEST 2013 hung over the stage, and when she saw it, Tasha took my arm and dragged me to a halt.

"Queer music fest?" she whispered. "You didn't tell me."

"Is it okay? The band that Steph's in is—they're all queer."

Tasha narrowed her eyes. "Yeah, it's fine." She glanced at Mel and Lisa, who had gone ahead without us toward the front of the crowd. "They're queer, too?"

"Yeah." I hesitated. "Lisa is Steph's girlfriend. Steph is Joan's gardener."

Tasha gave me a sharp look. "Somehow you've been spending your summer with all these lesbians and you didn't mention it to me?"

I tried to shrug it off. "It didn't seem relevant. It's not like I knew about you and Haley."

Tasha relented. "True. Okay, let's go to a queer music festival."

Roxy and Steph were magnetic onstage. Roxy was wearing a white ribbed tank top and a stretchy black miniskirt over hot-pink fishnets and her boots, and as she sang she kept sliding her eyes toward Steph, who was circling her like a tiger. There was an unmistakable connection between them, and the way Roxy looked at Steph, that hungry glint in her eyes, would make anyone think they were together—or were about to be. Steph was in jeans and scuffed boots and a black muscle shirt, the white electric guitar glossy in her hands as she played toward the sway of Roxy's hips. Every so often Steph would step up to her own mic to sing backup, but when they got to "Twenty-One," I realized it was a duet. By the end of the song, Roxy and Steph were singing into the same microphone, their faces so close together they'd barely have to move to be kissing.

At the beginning of Madchen's set, we were on the side of the crowd, but soon we were all surging into the pit in front of the stage to yell and dance to the music. I was mesmerized by the chemistry between Steph and Roxy. It felt like a luxury to be able to look at Steph in public, because everyone else was looking, too. Once, I glanced at Lisa and saw her watching Steph and Roxy's performance with an increasingly frosty expression, and even though I had no right to feel sorry for her, I did. I could understand why Lisa would be jealous of Roxy, but to me jealousy seemed pointless here. Roxy and Steph were putting on a show, and it was a good one. I remembered the picture of my mother dressed up as Carmen, the look in her eye like the one in Roxy's. It was more than permission to watch, it was an invitation.

After they finished their set, Madchen came out to sell merchandise at the tables set up near the food trucks. Tasha said she wasn't hungry, so I went over to buy some tacos and a water for myself. When I returned, Tasha and Mel were seated on a bench under a tree.

"Where's Lisa?" I asked.

"Bathroom," Mel said.

I unwrapped my taco, and Mel and Tasha went back to talking about the show. I had wondered if Mel would be jealous like Lisa, but she didn't seem to be. I ate my taco—al pastor, with hot salsa—and watched the crowd milling in front of the merch table as my tongue burned. I caught glimpses of Roxy, Jasmine, Talia, and Steph signing CDs.

"I'm not exactly straight," Tasha was saying.

Startled, I tuned back in to her conversation with Mel.

"Really?" Mel exclaimed. "Dude, I didn't know."

"Why would you? It's kinda new to me, too."

"New, huh? Should I ask for the story?"

"I had a thing with one of my friends. That's all. She says she's not gay." Tasha's nonchalance was hard-edged.

"What 'thing'?" Mel asked. "I need more details before I can accurately assess this. Was it just you, was it mutual, what?"

"Oh, it was mutual," Tasha said. "I mean, we hooked up."

MALINDA LO

"By 'hooked up,' do you mean you made out with her? Or did you have sex? Sometimes girls hook up with other girls, you know, and it's not like they're queer."

I was taken aback by the directness of Mel's questions, but Tasha didn't seem to mind. Maybe it was easier for her to talk about these things with a near-stranger.

"We had sex," Tasha said. "And she was definitely a willing participant."

"Hey, TMI," I said. "Don't forget I'm here."

Tasha glanced at me. "Sorry! I know this is probably weird for you, but she asked."

Mel chuckled. "So what happened then?"

"She freaked out and said she's not gay."

"That sucks."

"Yep."

Mel reached over and patted Tasha's knee. "I'm sorry."

Tasha gave a short laugh. "Me too."

"She still loves you," I said.

"As a friend," Tasha noted bitterly.

"I know you didn't ask for this, but let me give you a piece of advice," Mel said. "Don't get involved with your friends."

"Too late for me," Tasha said.

"For the future," Mel said. "Because there will be a future, and when you start to fall for Aria, just say no."

"Don't worry, I'm not in any danger of falling for Aria." Tasha looked at me and grinned. "No offense."

"Hey, what's wrong with me?" I joked.

"You're like my sister," she said, making a grossed-out face.

There was something about the way she said it—ribbing me as if we were in middle school—that made a wave of relief wash over

235

me. Things between us were going to be okay. It must have showed on my face, because Tasha suddenly looked serious and put her arm around me and said, "I mean it, Ari. You know I do."

It felt like we had to wait forever for the crowd to clear away from the merch table. Lisa returned with tacos and a Mexican soda. On the band shell stage, another band was performing—a skinny man and a short woman who sounded like a Tegan and Sara knockoff. Tasha and Mel hit it off after Tasha's confession, and I half-heartedly participated in their conversation about Mel's first girlfriend (her name was Lucia), while I was increasingly distracted by Steph behind the merch table. I saw her smiling at a girl who wanted a CD signed; I saw her glancing at Lisa, and then quickly at me. I would've missed it if I hadn't been watching.

When the moment finally came, it was anticlimactic. Steph had to greet Lisa first, with a kiss, and they stood together for a while before she came over to hug me delicately, keeping her distance. "Thanks for coming," she said. I wanted to pull her closer but I knew I couldn't. I could never do that in public, and despite a flash of despair, I also felt a thrill about the secret between us.

"This is Tasha," I said.

"You guys were great," Tasha said.

"Thanks," Steph said.

Roxy was kissing Mel, and Talia yelled at them to get a room. Roxy flipped her off. Lisa appeared at Steph's side and snaked her arm around Steph's waist.

"Let's go watch the other bands," Lisa said. She looked tired, as if she hadn't slept much the night before, but now that Steph was with her she seemed to relax.

I forced myself to turn away from them, and I caught Tasha

eyeing me. "Are you sure you don't want to get a taco or something?" I asked.

"Maybe a soda," Tasha said.

"Let's go," I said. I didn't want to be there anymore.

There was an after-party at a club in the Haight after the festival ended, but Tasha and I couldn't go because we weren't twenty-one. Instead we went to dinner at Burma Superstar, a restaurant Tasha picked after reading about it on some foodie blog.

The parking was atrocious, and I had to channel my inner Masshole to wedge the car into a spot on a street five blocks away.

"We should've called an Uber," Tasha said.

"I don't have that," I said.

"I do."

"Well, next time you can call us a car."

Finding parking had taken a while, and by the time we got to the restaurant, there was an hour-plus wait. We signed up on the clipboard and went back out to Clement Street to wait along with everyone else. The fog was rolling in, and I realized that when people said "rolling in," they really meant it, the mist unspooling from the western end of the street as if it were on wheels.

"So," Tasha said, "do you have a thing for Roxy?"

I was surprised. "Roxy? No. I mean, she's hot—everybody thinks she's hot."

Tasha looked at me and nodded. "Yeah. So not her. Steph, then?"

I was taken aback. "What?"

Tasha's eyebrows lifted and she nodded slightly. "Yep. Okay, Steph. Your grandma's gardener."

I stared at her, my chest tightening.

"It's okay," Tasha said. "It's me, remember? I've known you since we were kids. I could tell by the way you looked at them onstage. It was one or the other."

I exhaled. "Shit. You could tell?"

Tasha seemed puzzled by that. "Yeah. It's fine. Did I not just come out to you?" She shook her head. "Everything makes a lot more sense now. I couldn't understand why you wanted to go to some indie music festival. And she's cute. I mean, she's got the look if you like that kinda thing."

"What kind of look?"

She shrugged. "You know. Boyish, guys' clothes. What do they call it on Tumblr? Genderqueer? I don't know the right words. It works for Steph."

"You think so?" I said, a little too eagerly.

Tasha rolled her eyes at me. "Girl, you have it bad. Yes, aesthetically speaking, she works the look. Do you want to do a mash note about her now?"

I laughed involuntarily. "Tash, I didn't mean to keep it a secret, I just . . ."

She waved it off. "I get it. You have a crush. It's a little weird at first."

"Yeah, it's . . . it's a little more than a crush."

"What do you mean?"

I hesitated. "She—we've been hooking up."

"Shit. Aria!" Tasha's eyes were so wide. "She's with Lisa, right?"

"Yeah. I know, it's not good."

Tasha gave me a knowing look. "But?"

I winced. The fog was creeping closer to us, and a gust of damp wind ruffled my hair. "I really like her," I said.

"I can tell."

"How am I supposed to change the way I feel?"

"You're asking me?" Tasha sighed. "I don't know." She linked her arm with mine and pulled me closer as we both watched the fog advancing.

We lay in bed in the dark, only the faintest light outlining the curtained window. Neither of us was asleep. "Tasha," I whispered.

"What?"

"Do you think you're bisexual?"

"I don't know. I never really crushed on guys like you did."

"What about Theo Morales?"

She shifted, and the sheets rustled. "I wasn't really into him. I just thought I should have a boyfriend. And besides, I was really into girly things, and I thought lesbians were all tomboys who wore clunky shoes. That's not me."

"No, that's definitely not you."

"But maybe I'm queer."

"Not a lesbian?"

"Can't I just be me?" A pause. "Do you think you're bisexual? You like guys. Don't you?"

"Yeah, I like guys—some guys. I don't know. There's something different about Steph. I mean, I've never felt this way before."

"How?"

"Like . . . when I'm with her, I'm all there. Every part of me."

"That's how I felt with Haley."

I turned to face Tasha. I saw her profile in the near darkness, her eyes turned up to the ceiling. "Maybe she'll come around," I said.

Tasha sighed. "I'm tired of waiting. It's been months." She looked at me. "What are you going to do? I'm saying this to you as a friend, but you know this isn't a good situation."

A twisting inside me. I closed my eyes. "I know."

Tasha reached for my hand and squeezed it.

"Be careful, you might be falling in love with me," I whispered.

She choked on a laugh. "Shut up. Go to sleep."

"Good night, Tash."

"Good night."

In the morning, before I drove Tasha to the Airporter, I took her into the studio to show her the painting. She looked at it, lips pursed. "This is what you've been doing when you're not doing Steph?"

"Oh my God, don't say that out loud!"

She grinned. "If I can't speak the truth, what kind of friend would I be?"

"You've changed," I said. "You never used to talk like this."

"I'm free now," she said. "I can say whatever I want."

"So what do you think about this?" I gestured at the painting. "I don't know what to do with it."

She gave me a funny look. "Why don't you ask your grandma?"

"Because—I don't know. I don't want to bother her."

"Aria, your grandma's a real artist, and you're having an art problem. Why don't you talk to her about it? If you were having—I don't know—a writing problem, you'd ask your dad. Wouldn't you?"

"I guess."

"So talk to your grandma."

"Okay. Fine. But what do *you* think?"

She scrutinized the painting again. "I think you're figuring something out. And maybe it's got nothing to do with this painting."

I leaned against the worktable. "Do you think I'm a bad person?"

Tasha turned to look at me. "No. I love you. You're my best friend.

But you need to take care of yourself, okay? Because I'm not gonna be here to hold your hand every night if you make a bad decision."

I took a deep breath. "I can't stop thinking about her."

Tasha gave me a sympathetic look. "I know."

I smiled and reached for her hand. "Tash, don't go."

She rolled her eyes. "You're gonna forget about me as soon as you have Steph to yourself."

"No I won't. I'll never forget about you."

She smirked. "Now who's falling in love with who?"

J oan stood back from my painting and studied it. She cocked her head, and then went right up to the paper and examined the clumps of orange and red paint.

"What do you think?" I asked tentatively.

She stepped back again, still looking at the painting, and said, "It's not important what I think. What do *you* think? What made you want to paint this?"

"I guess I was inspired by that Bernice Bing poster I saw. I wanted to make something like it."

"Was that your goal? To copy the Bernice Bing painting?"

"Copy? I don't know. Is that bad?"

"Copying can be a great way to learn things." Joan turned to look at me. "Was that your intention?"

"I don't know what my intention was. Is."

She nodded. "Maybe this is about playing. You've spent a lot of time studying math and science. Maybe you want to play."

The word *play* made me squirm. "Like a kid."

"Like an artist. So much comes from allowing yourself to experiment with new ideas, new techniques. And all of this is new to you." She gestured to the painting on the wall. "How many have you made?"

"Just that one."

"You should make more."

"But I don't know what to do with this one. How am I supposed to make more if I don't even know what I'm doing?"

"The only way to figure out what you're doing is to do it." She paused and then asked, "Are you having fun with it?"

"I was at first. No, at first I felt like I knew what I was doing. I wanted to use the roofing paper and that blue paint. I wanted to put it on the wall and make it like—oh, I wanted to paint the water in the Adrienne Rich poem, 'Diving into the Wreck.' But then I did that and I didn't know what to do next, and now I'm stuck. What do I do now?"

"Unfortunately, I can't tell you what to do. You need to listen to the work. What is it telling you?"

"Nothing," I said, laughing. "It's totally silent."

Joan moved a stack of Grandpa's tapes out of the camping chair and sat down. "When I was making abstract paintings in the 1960s, there was always this stop-and-start quality to the process for me. A lot of the beginning was just about making marks on the canvas. Trying one thing and then trying something else, seeing what worked for me and what didn't. Sometimes I'd scrape off layers or cut things up and put them together in different ways. Sometimes I did that for months before I figured out what I wanted to express. It could be extremely frustrating, but the point of it was the process. It was about discovering what my preconceptions were, first, and then moving away from them. Finding something new to express. Figuring out who I was as an artist. It takes time."

"So you're saying I should be more patient?" I asked, trying to sound self-deprecating.

She smiled gently. "Maybe." She picked up one of the videotapes and looked down at the picture of Grandpa on the cover. "You know the painting upstairs, *Southern Cross*?"

"Yeah." It was about four feet wide and depicted the stars of the Southern Cross over a dark ocean. But it was an abstract painting, so the stars were not pinpricks of light but lines cut with a palette knife into a sky layered in shades of dark blue and black. The ocean merged into it in purples and violets, and a few drips of yellow suggested reflections on the water. The painting had a sense of great motion, so that the stars and the sky and the ocean seemed to wheel around the canvas.

"I spent almost a year on that one," she said. "I was really obsessive about it. I didn't know I was painting those stars until six months in, maybe. That's when I realized it was about your grandfather. He was always talking about how looking at the stars was like looking back in time, and how the universe was always getting bigger. I could never quite grasp that mathematically—time and how it worked with the distance between us and the stars—but when Russ talks about it he's so vivid. He uses his hands and gives such an impression of motion. I just wanted to capture that. I was falling in love with him when I made that painting. I spent so much time on it and I could never bring myself to sell it."

She put down the videotape and looked at my painting again.

"An abstract painting is like excavating your emotions," she said. "It's not an easy slap-it-on-the-canvas thing. There are layers to get through before you can uncover what it's about. You're at the very start of the process. There are exercises you could do to jog things loose, and sometimes that can help. Take the painting off the wall and turn it around, see if it looks different from a different perspective. You've used high-contrast colors here, which suggests something dramatic. I don't know what it is, but the more you paint, the more you'll be able to excavate your own emotions." She looked at me. "These are things I tell a lot of my students, but you're my granddaughter. I can see this painting means something to you."

"I want it to." I felt a little uncomfortable. She was looking at me so pointedly.

"It's the first one you've made since you were a child, isn't it?"

"Yeah."

"The thing about *Southern Cross* is . . . you know, I hadn't even seen the Southern Cross when I painted it. I didn't see it till we went to Hawaii over a decade later. I painted these stars that I only knew about because Russ told me about them, so in a way they weren't about the actual stars at all. They were about the way I wanted to incorporate Russ and my love for him into my work. I wanted to express something about the drama of falling in love, but also how we were only a small moment in time. In the scale of the universe, we're just a blip. I don't know if all that came through in the painting. It probably didn't. It probably felt too personal to me and that's why I never wanted to sell it."

She placed the videotape she'd been holding on top of the stack that she had moved to the floor. "I'm telling you this because I've learned over my life that I come back to the same subjects over and over again. Not a repetition so much as a cycling. I think everything cycles around again and again. I come back over and over to the same subjects in my art, but hopefully with a bit more wisdom each time. I'm always making art about time. I don't understand how it works, but I'm always interested in it." My grandmother's eyes were a clear, bright blue in her lined face. "This painting—your painting—its true meaning won't be clear until you make another one, and another one after that. But for now, you should work on it until it's finished."

"How will I know when it's finished?"

"That's a question only you can answer. Has the painting said everything you want it to say?"

"Right now? No."

"Then it's not finished yet."

The first time I really understood why the stars moved, I was ten years old. Dad and I were in Woodacre for Christmas vacation, and on Christmas night, Grandpa and I put together the reproduction of Galileo's telescope. Then we took sleeping bags onto the roof, where we lay down in the chilly, clear night. Grandpa said it was important to let our eyes adjust to the dark before looking through the telescope, so at first we simply gazed up at the star-scattered sky. I saw a point of light traveling steadily across the dark expanse, and when I pointed it out, he told me it wasn't a star but a satellite, something built by human hands that we had put in orbit with a rocket ship. He told me Aunt Tammy built things like that, and though I'd known that before, I'd never comprehended that something she created could fly overhead in the dark, impersonating a star.

"The marvelous thing," Grandpa told me that night, "is that everything you see above you is moving. The satellite is moving around the earth, the earth is moving around the sun, and the sun and the planets in our solar system are moving around the center of our Milky Way galaxy."

"But the stars don't look like they're moving," I said.

"That's a funny thing," Grandpa said. He explained to me that the stars did move—they also orbited the center of the galaxy—but we were so far away from them that to us, they appeared to be still. However, if we watched them all night, we'd see that the stars seemed to rise in the east and set in the west, exactly like the sun and the moon. "That's an illusion," Grandpa said. "It's not really happening that way. The stars only seem to rise and set because our planet is spinning, and as it spins, we see different parts of the sky."

The idea that the earth was actually turning at over one thousand miles per hour was mind-blowing to me. I felt the hard surface of the roof beneath me through the sleeping bag, and although it was barely slanted, I had the sudden fear that I'd slide off the edge as the planet spun. But nothing happened; everything remained as it was. It was astonishing, and I remember it even today: the realization that the world was not as it seemed. That the stars that appeared to hang motionless above me both moved and did not move, because the earth below me was not actually still. That what I saw might not be reality, but that it was possible to understand it through careful observation, through the instruments that scientists had built to peer into space.

When I first looked through the telescope, I expected to see something right away—red Mars or the rings of Saturn. I had thought the telescope was like a television: You looked through it and the image would instantly appear. Grandpa told me I could see big things quickly—the moon and some nearby planets—but if I wanted to see something farther away, stars that were older and bigger than our own sun, I had to wait for a moment of what he called *good seeing*. I had to let my eyes adapt to the darkness. I had to relax the muscles of my face. I had to wait for the turbulence in the air to settle, and finally when everything in motion was in motion together, I might see something amazing.

Late Tuesday afternoon, Joan and I made sauce from a bunch of tomatoes that Tony brought over. I blanched and peeled them; then Joan seeded them over the sink and tossed them into a big pot. While I peeled, I imagined where Steph and I would go tomorrow night. We had plans to meet up because Lisa had to work late. Maybe we'd drive down to San Francisco and get tacos in the Mission. Or we could go the other direction to Bolinas and watch the sunset. Maybe people would look at us and know that we were together. I wanted it to be so obvious from the outside that nobody would question what we were doing.

I'd finished peeling the last tomato and was washing up when the sound of a crash made me spin around. Joan was standing next to the stove with empty hands outstretched, a dazed expression on her face. At her feet the pot of tomatoes was overturned on the floor, red pulp splattered everywhere in a parody of a horror movie.

"Are you okay?" I asked.

I didn't understand at first. I thought she had just dropped the pot with slippery hands. But my grandmother's face looked strange; half of it seemed frozen. Her mouth opened as if she was trying to speak, but the sound that came out was an incoherent moan. The right side of her body drooped toward the floor, and I rushed to her as she collapsed, her hip bumping against the kitchen counter, sliding down into the smashed tomatoes.

"Joan!" I tried to pull her out of the red mess, but her body was heavy and unresponsive. Analemma ran to her and licked her face. Joan was still trying to speak, but her mouth didn't move correctly and I couldn't understand her. Her eyelids fluttered closed and a second later she went entirely limp in my arms. "Joan?" I repeated, but she didn't respond. My brain was clogged by a growing panic. Analemma started to whine. I needed to call 911, but I was pinned beneath Joan's body.

I squirmed my way out from beneath her, laying her head on the floor as gently as I could. Analemma was still licking her face and making those whining noises. I scrambled to my feet to grab my phone, getting tomato on the screen as I fumbled to press 911.

"Nine-one-one, what's your emergency?"

"My grandmother—she collapsed." As I looked over at her, I saw blue flames flickering from the stove top. She must have been about to put the pot on the burner.

"Where are you?" the operator asked.

"I'm at home." I turned off the stove. My hand was shaking. Joan's eyes flickered and Analemma let out a shrill bark that I'd never heard before.

"What's your address? I see you're on a cell phone."

I gave the operator the address, and then she asked me to describe what had happened. I dropped to the floor again, pulling Joan back into my lap and trying to wipe off some of the tomatoes with a dish towel. I only smeared it more over her clothes, and Analemma started to lick the tomatoes off the floor. "Stop it, Ana," I said, but she didn't stop.

"Emergency responders are on their way," the operator said. "What's your grandmother's status now?"

"She's blinking. I think she's going in and out of consciousness.

What happened to her?" I tried to pull Analemma away from the tomatoes, but she was too strong.

"The emergency responders will be able to tell you, but it sounds like she may have had a stroke."

The operator tried to explain it to me, but I couldn't pay attention. I was still tugging ineffectually at Analemma's collar. I'd never seen my grandmother like this before: weak-bodied, limbs flaccid, as if whatever made her who she was had vanished. I felt helpless. Whatever was wrong with her, I couldn't fix it, and I was terrified that I would somehow accidentally make it worse.

In the distance I heard the wail of sirens, and as the sound grew closer I realized I had to unlock the front door for them. I got up, leaving Joan again, and ran out of the kitchen. Analemma sprinted after me, leaving red pawprints across the floor. I grabbed her, aiming her toward my room. "Analemma, come!" She turned to look at me with her big brown eyes, and there must have been something in my face or voice because, to my relief, she obeyed. I led her into my room and shut the door.

Outside I saw flashing lights down the hill. I couldn't see the vehicles, but I heard the gate creak open and then firefighters were coming up the path, dressed in heavy-booted firefighting gear. I was still holding my phone to my ear, and the operator told me I could hang up now, so I did, and I led the firefighters into the house and up to the kitchen. Analemma was barking frantically from my room.

As the firefighters examined my grandmother, they asked me what had happened, and I told them everything I had told the operator. "Is she okay?" I asked.

"She's had a stroke," one of the firefighters said. "When did you notice it beginning?"

More sirens sounded in the distance. "When she dropped the tomatoes," I said.

"When was that?"

I thought back. "Right before I called 911." I looked at my phone and the time stamp on my last call. "A little after six."

The sirens cut off, and I heard footsteps pounding up the porch steps. I went back into the living room to see paramedics carrying a gurney into the house. They rushed past me into the kitchen, where the firefighters moved away from Joan. The paramedics knelt beside her on the tomato-streaked floor and tried to talk to her. She was moving her head groggily but still couldn't speak clearly. The paramedics—a man and a woman—asked me what had happened, and once more I explained while they shone lights into Joan's eyes and fitted her with an oxygen mask.

"Who are you?" asked the female paramedic, looking up at me. She had a dark brown ponytail and was wearing a blue uniform with medical patches on the short sleeves. Her name tag read ORTIZ.

"Aria West. Her granddaughter."

"Do you live with her?"

"Only for this summer."

Ortiz and her partner, an Asian man with short dark hair, lifted Joan in one motion onto the stretcher.

"Are you taking her to the hospital?" I asked.

"Yes," the man said. His name tag read WON. "We need her medical information and her identification. Do you have that?"

"No, I—wait," I said, and ran down to the front closet, where Joan kept her purse.

The paramedics came down the stairs behind me, and Won asked me to get out of the way. I moved aside, and they carried Joan out of the house and down the path toward the street. I hurried after them, and the curving path seemed ridiculous now, a Chutes-and-Ladders kind of obstacle in the way of saving Joan's life. Through the gate I saw a red fire truck and an ambulance, all their lights flashing. At the rear of the ambulance the paramedics lifted the gurney, and it unfolded and refolded, the wheels sliding with a clatter into the back. Ortiz jumped inside, and Won turned to me. "How old are you?" he asked.

"Eighteen."

"Your grandmother isn't able to communicate very well right now. Does she have other immediate family members nearby?"

"No."

Ortiz poked her head out of the back of the ambulance and said, "She's asking for you."

Clutching Joan's purse and my phone, I climbed into the ambulance. Joan was moving beneath the belts on the stretcher, and through the oxygen mask I heard her saying something that sounded like my name. "I'm right here," I said, shoving my phone into my pocket so I could reach for her hand. Her fingers were papery and limp, and her eyes darted from my face to Ortiz's. My grandmother looked frightened and confused. I wanted to comfort her. I squeezed her hand and said, "You're going to be fine," and my voice sounded like someone who was much more confident than I felt. I looked at Ortiz, who was adjusting the IV that had been fitted to Joan's other arm, and asked, "Can I ride in here with you?"

"Yes, you'll need to talk to the doctors at the hospital anyway," she said.

Won closed the doors at the back of the ambulance, and a moment later I heard him climb into the front. Ortiz pulled out a cell phone and made a call; it sounded like she was reporting Joan's status to a doctor somewhere else. The ambulance started down the curving road, and I braced myself on the edge of the bench, still holding Joan's hand. Through the window in the back door I saw the flashing lights of the fire truck like off-kilter Christmas lights in the forest.

At the hospital, several doctors and nurses surrounded my grandmother while one nurse pulled me aside to ask questions about what had happened, whether Joan had any medical conditions or allergies, whether she had insurance. I found Joan's Medicare card in her purse, but other than that, I barely knew anything. I remembered that Joan had felt sick last week, and I told the nurse about it. I should have insisted that she call a doctor then.

"Is there anyone you can call who might know more about her medical history?" the nurse asked me.

I wanted to call my dad, but I didn't have the Deer Bay emergency contact number, so I called Aunt Tammy in Pasadena. She picked up the phone on the second ring and said cheerfully, "Aria! How nice to hear from you."

Her happiness was short-lived. After I explained what had happened, I passed the phone to the nurse, who then asked Aunt Tammy all the questions that I hadn't been able to answer. I sat in the gray plastic chair next to the nurse's station and listened distractedly to the conversation. I felt like a six-year-old lost in the supermarket. Every time the sliding doors to the back of the ER opened, I looked up as if Joan might walk out and say it was all a big mistake, she was fine.

When the nurse finished talking to Aunt Tammy, she handed my phone back to me. "Aunt Tammy?" I said. "Are you still there?"

"Yes. I'm going to call you back in a bit, okay? I have to make some arrangements—" In the background I heard my cousins shouting something, and Aunt Tammy told them to hush. "I'll call you back soon," she said, and hung up.

The nurse I'd been speaking to was entering something into her computer, and I went over to ask her, "Is my grandma okay?"

"She's being treated for a stroke," the nurse said. "You should take a seat over there and I'll be sure to let you know when there's news." I must have looked like I needed more reassurance because she added, "She's in good hands. And there's a bathroom over there to your right. You might want to wash up a little. Is that marinara?"

I glanced down at myself and saw red smeared over my arms. It looked like I was covered in blood. "Tomatoes," I said.

She nodded. "I'll let you know when we have more information."

I swung Joan's purse over my shoulder and headed to the restroom. It smelled of antiseptic cleaning solution that couldn't quite hide the lingering odor of something more unpleasant. I tried to breathe through my mouth as I dampened a paper towel to scrub off the tomato residue. It had dried in sticky streaks on my skin, and it took what seemed like a mountain of paper towels to get it off. My jeans were spotted with it, too, and a long stain went up the front of my MIT T-shirt where I had dragged Joan into my lap. I wiped at my shirt, but that just turned it into a big wet spot. I gave up and went to wash my hands. In the mirror over the sink I looked freaked out, and my hair was escaping from its ponytail. I splashed lukewarm water over my face and blotted it dry with another thin paper towel. I redid my ponytail as the bathroom door opened. A woman rushed inside and slammed a stall door shut. She made a gagging sound, and before I heard anything more, I fled.

I took a seat in the waiting room near a mom with a sleepy kid. The ER looked more like a dentist's office than any ER I'd seen on TV, and it smelled like stale coffee and fried food. There were a couple of moms with kids, a few exhausted-looking older people, and a young couple who seemed extremely agitated, constantly getting up to check in with the nurse. I wasn't sure how long I sat there, staring blankly at the sliding doors. I kept seeing Joan crumple against the counter over and over, the slackness in her face, the confusion in her eyes. The world felt so unstable. Everything had changed in a fraction of a second. My stomach gurgled, but the idea of eating made me feel even queasier. I crossed my arms and legs, hunkering down in the chair as if making myself smaller would help.

Sometime later the mom with the kid was called to the registration desk. After they left, I picked up their abandoned *Time* magazine, but the words swam together on the page. When my phone rang, I nearly dropped it on the floor before I answered.

"Aria?" my dad said.

"Dad," I said in relief. "Aunt Tammy called you?"

"Yes. Are you all right?"

I wished he were here so fiercely I could barely breathe. "I'm fine," I managed.

"Tammy wanted me to tell you she's driving up there," Dad said. "She's going to call you when she knows more about her timing. I'm coming, too, but I'm kind of in the middle of nowhere, so it's going to take me longer."

"Okay," I said, my voice hitching.

"Ari, it'll be all right."

I bit my lip, inhaling through my nose. I didn't want to cry in the ER. I wasn't even hurt.

"When the doctor updates you, call Aunt Tammy and let her speak to him," Dad said.

"What about you?"

"I'm on the landline at the main lodge here. There's no cell reception, but I'll turn on my phone just in case. I have to get on the internet and figure out how I'm going to get out of here. I'll call you when I have my flight information."

I suddenly realized what this meant. "It's that serious?"

He didn't speak for a moment. I heard static on the other end, as if he were moving.

"Dad? Is it that serious? Is she going to—" I couldn't say the word.

"It's serious. But your grandma was very lucky that you were with her when she had the stroke. Without you— You did good. Tammy and I will get there as soon as we can."

I read the whole *Time* magazine and a year-old issue of *People* before the nurse called me up to the desk. "You can see your grandmother now," she said.

I followed her through sliding glass doors to a tiny room where Joan was lying on a hospital bed, the kind with rails on each side. It looked like she'd been fenced in. Oxygen tubes ran into her nostrils, an IV was attached to her arm, and one of her fingers was encased in a plastic clip. A doctor in a white coat stood beside the bed, writing something down on a medical chart.

"This is Joan West's granddaughter," the nurse said to the doctor. She turned to me. "This is Dr. Harrison."

"What happened? How is she doing?" I asked him.

"She's had an ischemic stroke, which means she had a blood clot in her brain," he said, speaking in that very calm, emotionless doctor voice. "We've treated her with a drug to dissolve the clot, but she needs to remain under observation for a while. We're waiting for a bed in the neuro ICU to open up for her. You're welcome to wait here if you'd like, but I don't know how long it'll be."

I remembered what my dad had said, and I pulled out my phone. "I need to call my aunt—her daughter. Can you tell her the situation?"

"Sure."

I called Aunt Tammy and handed the phone to the doctor. While they talked I went to Joan's bedside. Her eyes were closed, and she appeared to be asleep. I pulled up a chair next to her and reached out to touch her hand. I felt the bones of her fingers beneath her warm, dry skin. Only yesterday we had been in her old studio together. *I'm always making art about time*, she had told me. I felt like we'd taken a wrong turn into a timeline we weren't supposed to be in.

Her hand squeezed mine.

"Joan?" I said.

Her eyes opened, but they were unfocused.

"Joan?" I said again, standing up to move into her line of sight.

She looked confused, and as her mouth opened, one side of it still seemed paralyzed. "Le—" she said.

"It's me, Aria," I said, not sure if she could see me.

"Lex," she said. "Lexis? Where's Russ?" she asked, her words slurring together.

My heart seemed to stop. "Grandma, it's me, Aria," I said. "Your granddaughter. My dad—your son is coming soon. Your daughter, too."

My grandmother's confusion seemed to deepen, and at that moment Dr. Harrison handed my phone back to me. "Your aunt wants to speak to you."

I took the phone, and Dr. Harrison left. Joan's gaze followed him briefly, then returned to my face. She looked exhausted.

"Aunt Tammy?" I said.

"I'm driving up tonight, as soon as I can leave here," Aunt Tammy said. "There shouldn't be any traffic on the Five, and I'm hoping to get to Woodacre by seven or eight in the morning. The hospital knows to call me if anything changes."

"Okay," I said. Joan's eyes closed again.

"The nurse I spoke to earlier said you helped out a lot by giving them the time of the stroke," Aunt Tammy said.

I sat down in the chair. My legs were shaky. "It all happened very fast."

Aunt Tammy continued to talk, but I didn't register her words. I suddenly remembered Analemma barking her head off in my room.

"Shit," I said.

"What's wrong?"

"I left Analemma in my room. But I left the front door open."

"You left—are you sure?"

"Yes. I followed the paramedics out—I didn't know what to do. I just ran after them."

"Woodacre's pretty safe. I think it'll be okay. But when did Analemma go out last?" Aunt Tammy's voice was brisk, as if she were working through an engineering problem.

"A long time ago. Maybe this morning. We took her on a hike."

"Okay, you need to go home and take her out. Don't panic, it'll be all right. She's a very good dog."

"But what about Joan? Shouldn't I stay with her? They said they're going to move her somewhere."

"They're waiting for a bed to open up in the ICU. I don't know how long it'll be. They're going to call me when she's moved. I think you can go home." She gave a sudden nervous laugh that showed how tense she was. "In fact, I'd really like for you to go home right now and take Analemma out and then lock the front door."

"I'm sorry. I'm really sorry! I'm so stupid."

"No, no, it was an emergency. Go home and call me when you get there so I know everything's okay."

"Okay." I glanced at Joan again. Her eyes were still closed. I left the room and said to Aunt Tammy, "I'll call you soon."

Back in the waiting room, I explained to the nurse that I had to leave. She didn't seem surprised by this, only checked to make sure they had contact information for me and Aunt Tammy. I headed outside, Joan's purse banging against my hip, when I realized I didn't have a ride home. I halted, the doors whooshing shut behind me. It was dark. The parking lot was lit by regularly spaced streetlamps that shone calmly over rows of cars.

I looked down at my phone. It was after midnight. I'd been in the hospital for five hours. I might not have an Uber account, but I knew I could call a taxi. I'd never seen one in Marin, but they had to exist. The hospital could probably even give me the number for a taxi service.

I called Steph.

Usually, climbing into Steph's truck was like stepping through a doorway into our secret world, but tonight things were different. Our world had crashed into this one. In the truck's dim overhead light, Steph looked worried. "How is she?" she asked.

"Asleep." I closed the truck door and the light went out, leaving us in the glare of the emergency room sign. Steph pulled out of the ER driveway and headed for the hospital exit.

"Your family's coming?" she said.

"Yeah. Tomorrow."

We turned onto a wide, four-lane road with a central median. There was no traffic. In the distance was a big church, the cross lit up on top of its Mission-style cupola.

"Thanks for coming to get me," I said.

"No worries. I hope she's okay."

Now that I was no longer in the ER, I felt completely drained from waiting. I shivered.

"Are you cold?" Steph asked, and she waved her hand in front of the vents. "It takes a while to warm up."

"I'm okay."

She reached over and put her hand on my thigh. I could feel her warm palm through the fabric of my jeans. I leaned my head back against the seat and looked at her profile, outlined by the white lights of the dashboard. She kept her eyes on the road. After a while I laced my fingers with hers. She drove all the way to Woodacre holding my hand, not letting go even when she shifted gears.

The front door was closed—maybe the firefighters had closed it—but still unlocked. As soon as I turned the doorknob, Analemma started barking. "It's okay, it's okay," I called as I went up the stairs, flipping on the lights. Her barking quieted, and when I opened the bedroom door, she burst out wagging her tail. Steph came up the stairs into the living room, and Analemma ran over to her.

Steph knelt down to rub her ears. "Hey, Ana."

I called Aunt Tammy to tell her I was back. While I talked to her, Analemma nosed around the floor, sniffing at the tomato paw prints she'd left earlier. I followed her through the living room, past the *Southern Cross* painting, and into the kitchen, where the tomatoes had made a gigantic mess. There was a clump of them where Joan had dropped the pot, red footprints from the firefighters and paramedics and me, and a big smear where I had pulled Joan across the floor.

Analemma whined as she sniffed around the kitchen, and I realized she was looking for Joan. Then she started to lick the tomatoes off the floor. "Analemma!" I cried, and she looked up guiltily for one second before going right back to what she was doing. I told Aunt Tammy I had to go and pulled Analemma by her collar out of the kitchen.

Steph was standing in the living room, looking at the mess. "This is a lot," she said. "Do you need some help?"

"I'll have to deal with it later," I said. "I have to take Analemma out."

"I can come with you."

I felt a surge of relief that embarrassed me, because I didn't want to be clingy but I also didn't want to be alone. "Okay," I said.

Downstairs at the front door I clipped on Analemma's leash and took her outside. Once we were in the yard she relaxed and started nosing at the plants. Steph followed us out, and then we all went down to the street.

"We don't have to go far," I said, opening the gate.

There were only a couple of streetlights down here, spaced fairly far apart, so the woods were quite dark. Analemma was a deeper blackness against the pavement. I looked up, wondering if I'd be able to see any stars, but they were blocked by the leaves overhead. I could only see a fraction of the moon.

We paused by a curb that seemed to be particularly fascinating to Analemma, and while she smelled every inch of the ground, my thoughts went back to my grandmother in the hospital. She had looked so lost and confused, as if she were no longer Joan West at all.

I didn't realize I'd started shaking until Steph put her arms around me. "It's okay," she told me, her voice muffled in my hair. Her hands stroked my back gently. "It's okay."

It took us a while to clean up the tomato remains. I told Steph she could go home but she said she wanted to help. We worked together in silence. My clothes were already stained, so I did most of the cleaning in the kitchen while Steph wiped up the footprints on the living room floor. Analemma had left paw prints on the floor of my room, too, but she must have licked off most of the tomato because her paws were clean.

By the time we were finished, it was almost two in the morning, and I was covered with even more tomato stains than before. Analemma had fallen asleep in her bed in front of the cold woodstove, emitting faint, regular snores.

"To be a dog," Steph said, smiling.

"If only." I rubbed a hand over my face. "Thanks for helping."

"No problem." Steph tapped a finger against her own face. "Uh, you might want to check yourself out in the mirror."

I went into the bathroom and groaned. I'd gotten tomato on my face, too. "I look like I was in a massacre," I said.

"Why don't you wash up? I'll look around and make sure we didn't miss anything."

"Are you sure?"

"Yeah. Go ahead."

"Thanks."

I closed the bathroom door and turned on the shower. I got undressed, and as I pulled my T-shirt over my head, I realize I'd somehow gotten tomatoes in my hair. I carefully extracted myself from my shirt and stepped into the spray.

I realized, at that moment, that I was alone in the house with Steph. It wasn't as if I hadn't known that before, but I'd been so focused on Analemma and cleaning up that it hadn't entirely registered with me. I was alone in the house with Steph. I was naked in the shower, and she was outside in the living room. It was the middle of the night. She had to go home to her girlfriend, and the only reason she was here was because my grandmother had had a stroke, and in a few hours my aunt and my father would arrive.

Tonight we were alone here, together. I had been tired when I stepped into the shower, but I wasn't tired anymore.

When I finished, I carefully dried myself off, rubbing the towel over my wet hair and combing it back from my face. I looked at myself in the mirror. My eyes were bright, my skin pink from the hot water. I hadn't brought clean clothes into the bathroom with me, so I wrapped the damp towel around myself and opened the door.

Steph was sitting on the couch looking at Joan's catalog, open on the coffee table in front of her. She had her back to me and didn't seem to notice that I'd come out of the bathroom. I told myself I should go put some clothes on, but there was something about the posture of Steph's shoulders, a vulnerability, that made me go over to her.

The catalog was open to one of Joan's self-portraits. She was sitting in a seventies-era kitchen with my dad on her lap. By the year in the caption, he must have been around three. She was holding on to him while he tried to squirm away from her, his legs kicking out in a blur. But her eyes were steady as she gazed at the camera. Behind her I noticed an old-fashioned wall clock, centered like a sun above her head. It was three o'clock exactly.

I sat down beside Steph, still clutching my towel around me. I noticed that her T-shirt was so old it had a constellation of tiny holes in it near the shoulder. The faded print on the front read SAC STATE. I wondered if it was something she normally slept in. My phone call had woken her up. It had made her climb out of bed and leave Lisa behind to come and pick me up.

"What did you tell Lisa?" I asked.

Steph looked at me. Her eyes were rimmed with red, as if she was holding back tears. "I told her Joan was in the hospital."

I took her hand and squeezed it. "She's going to be okay," I said. Then we moved toward one another and her arms went around me as we hugged. Her body was warm, her breath catching in her throat. I felt the dampness of the towel pressed against my skin. A shudder went through her.

When she pulled back, I felt tender toward her. I cupped her flushed cheek in my hand. I wanted to kiss her, but I hesitated. Her eyelashes were damp. For one long, silent breath, we looked at each other, motionless.

I felt the weight of that moment all the way through my body, every nerve alive. I think she felt it, too. We could have made a lot of other choices that night, but we made the only one we wanted to make.

She let me lead her into my room where I lay down on the bed, and she lay down beside me. All I had to do was let go of the towel, and her hands were sliding over my hips, cupping the curve of my ass, her mouth on mine. It felt as though we had abandoned all pretense and were finally acknowledging the truth.

I had never had sex with a woman before, but Steph didn't feel like a woman to me. She felt like *Steph*, this person who had dominion over my daydreams, who made my body turn molten when she touched me, as if she were forging me into a new person. When we kissed, I wanted to devour her.

She did everything right. Her mouth on my nipples, the slightest graze of her teeth on my skin. Her hand sliding between my legs, her fingers stroking me. I was shocked by how liquid I was, an ocean beneath her touch. And then she moved to the end of the bed and knelt between my thighs.

The boy I first had sex with, Zachary, had gone down on me, but he often acted as if he thought of it as a precursor to intercourse—not quite the real thing. With Steph, all of it was the real thing.

I became uncomfortably aware of what she was about to do— her tongue on me, inside me, a great intimacy. I wanted it, but I was also embarrassed to want it, to display so blatantly the degree of my desire for her. I wanted to be cool. Remembering that now makes me laugh. I was so far from cool at that point. She might have been kneeling before me, but I was the supplicant.

I raised myself on my elbows to look at her and said in my cool voice, "You don't have to do that."

She paused. Her eyes were dilated as her gaze swept over my stomach, my breasts, my face. I wanted to take a picture of her looking at me. She said, "I want to."

Her words lit me up inside.

I lay back down. Above me the ceiling was bathed in yellow light from the bedside lamp. I curled my fingers into the coverlet and thought, *I'll have to wash this tomorrow.* And then—

It's not as if I didn't know what was going to happen next, but I was still stunned when I felt her mouth on me. Her tongue, climbing the swollen ridge of nerves at the cleft of my body. Her fingers inside me, that exquisite friction. I closed my eyes but I still saw her face, her hazel eyes. I would see her face for years to come. The way she opened me, as if she had always possessed the key to this lock. A smooth, well-oiled click, the tumblers sliding into place, effortless. And I was there so soon, so fast, shuddering against her mouth, the center of my world. She made me feel transcendent, exceptional.

Afterward she crawled up beside me, her head on my pillow, her hand cupping the warmth of my sex, and I realized she was still completely dressed while I was naked, splayed open for her exactly the way I'd wanted to be.

was sixteen when I had sex for the first time. It was during the summer I lived with my mom in New York while she was performing at the Met. She had a fifteenth-floor apartment in Battery Park City with a view of New York Harbor, and when I first arrived, she was full of plans to show me the city and do all sorts of mother-daughter things, but very little of that happened. If she wasn't at the opera house, she was meeting with her vocal coach or her trainer or practicing Italian with her language teacher. She was rarely at home unless she was asleep.

That whole summer felt like it belonged to someone else, as if I had stepped into another person's life by mistake. New York was huge and it stank in the heat. My mom and I were roommates more than mother and daughter. She had a Puerto Rican housekeeper who cleaned the apartment once a week, and I always went out before she came because I was ashamed to be sitting around doing nothing while she cleaned the toilets.

That's how I met Zachary Chou. He was walking a fluffy white dog through our building's lobby, where I was lingering to make sure the housekeeper had left. Zachary lived two floors up from my mom, and he had an agreement with an elderly neighbor to walk the dog, whose name was Dorothy, in exchange for spending money, even though he didn't need it. Zachary's parents were divorced like mine, and he lived with his mom, too. She was never at home either, although she was an investment banker and not an opera singer.

Zachary was the same age as me, but I had never met an Asian boy like him. He had floppy black hair that he shaved on the sides, and he always wore ripped black jeans, black T-shirts, and roughed-up black work boots. Sometimes he'd accessorize with a black jean jacket, and one time he painted his nails black and then let them get increasingly chipped for the rest of the summer. We would walk Dorothy around Battery Park City together, weaving in between tourists visiting the World Trade Center site, and then head back to his apartment or mine. We started out playing video games together, which I was terrible at, but soon discovered it was much more fun to make out, and then to have sex.

His body was pale but wiry, his chest hairless and smooth. The first time I saw his penis we were in his living room with the window blinds open, and I realized I had never really seen Nathan's because it had been dark in his car. So in a way, Zachary's penis was my first. It startled me with its ugliness, and then with my desire for it.

The first time we had sex, it hurt a little, but it wasn't nearly as bad as I'd feared. The unexpected thing was how strange and even absurd it felt. It was incredibly weird to do this with our bodies, things made of flesh and blood that became engorged and wet and behaved as if they had nothing at all to do with our brains. Right after he entered me, I felt strangely disconnected from the fleshy bits of my body, as if I were observing myself in a lab.

Afterward, I went back to my mom's apartment and heated up some leftover penne alla vodka takeout and ate it while watching *True Blood*. I felt quite calm about what had just happened. I didn't walk funny or bleed excessively or feel different in any way. After Haley had sex for the first time with her boyfriend, she told Tasha and me all about it in excruciating detail. It had sounded so exciting and emotional and adult, but after I had sex with Zachary I wondered why my first time was nothing like Haley's experience. I wondered if there was something wrong with me. Maybe I was emotionally stunted.

Zachary didn't seem to think I had a problem. "You're like a guy," he told me once, approvingly. "Sex is just sex, you know?"

I agreed with him—at least when it came to the sex we had. It was just sex, and I liked it. I liked his body and sometimes I even craved it with a physical urge that shocked me. But I didn't crave anything more from him. At the end of the summer we traded contact information, but I knew neither of us would reach out.

Steph didn't let me touch her the first time we had sex. She told me, apologetically, that she was still on her period. That startled me not only because it reminded me that she was not a boy, but also because I'd never been with someone who didn't seem to need to have an orgasm during sex. She said she was more than happy to have pleased me, that it was more than enough, it was plenty.

Before she left, she spent some time in the bathroom washing her hands and face. She came out with damp hair, and I wondered how she would explain that to Lisa, but I didn't ask. I got dressed in pajama pants and a T-shirt and walked her downstairs. Outside it was still dark. I kissed her good night, and her mouth tasted faintly of my toothpaste. I watched her walk down the path until she went out of sight, and then I heard the creak of the gate as it opened and closed. The sound of her truck turning on was a jagged scratch in the quiet. I stood on the front stoop until the rumble of the truck faded away into the deep silence of predawn.

I couldn't bring myself to go inside. I sat down on the doorstep. I didn't know what time it was, but I guessed it was almost sunrise. I wrapped my arms around my knees, trying to keep warm against the cool air.

I wondered if Steph had lied to me about her period. I wondered if she didn't want me to touch her because we were having an affair, and if I made her come, that would mean she really did intend to cheat on Lisa. As long as she didn't come, maybe that meant she wasn't entirely cheating.

It's not that I didn't want to believe Steph, but in the situation we had created, lies were everywhere.

However, I did want to believe her. I wanted to believe she wouldn't lie to me, and that I wouldn't lie to her. I wanted to believe in the specific uniqueness of what had happened between us, its once-in-a-lifetime wonder. With Steph, I felt more pure and free than I'd felt with anyone else before. With Steph, I felt like I was finally being myself.

I sat on the doorstep as the night waned, and the birds began their early morning chorus. When the sky started to brighten, I went inside. I could sleep until Aunt Tammy arrived. Analemma thumped her tail at me as I went through the living room and back to my room. The bed was rumpled, the sheets thrown back. The wet spot had dried slightly. I sat on the edge of the bed and picked up my phone to check the time. It was almost five thirty in the morning, and there was a text from Steph:

XX

Aunt Tammy arrived a little after eight. When I saw her coming into the house with her suitcase, I was struck by how much she looked like Joan in those photos from the seventies, as if time had somehow folded, but imperfectly, because everyone was in the wrong place.

Dad called to tell us he was flying in that afternoon, and Aunt Tammy designated me to pick him up from the Airporter. She was going back to the hospital that morning, because Joan was being moved to the neuro ICU. Dad and Aunt Tammy agreed that I should walk Analemma and then drive to the hospital by myself later. Within an hour of her arrival, Aunt Tammy had left again.

I took Analemma up to the fire road. I remembered the day I'd hiked up here with Steph. I remembered last night. It seemed inappropriate to think about it now, but she had become a constant desire inside me. To not feel that yearning for her would be stranger than to feel it.

I thought about her while I drove to the hospital. I hadn't paid much attention to where it was last night, and today I was surprised to see it was just off Sir Francis Drake. I had driven past the road to the hospital, marked by a Catholic school and that big white church, multiple times. I remembered Steph holding my hand as she drove me home.

I texted Aunt Tammy when I got to the neuro ICU waiting room, and she came out and led me through several hallways to Joan's room. It was small and bristling with machines and monitors that surrounded Joan's guard-railed bed. She was awake, and today she knew who I was, though she still had trouble speaking. Aunt Tammy and I puttered around, talking to her and to each other in the tone of voice you use on a child who's scraped their knee: *It's going to be fine.*

Time must pass more slowly in hospitals. We were waiting to meet with Joan's doctor, but after a while Aunt Tammy asked if I'd go down to the cafeteria and buy her some coffee. I got lost along the way; every hallway looked the same. I imagined turning a corner and finding Steph there, searching for me. I imagined taking her back to Joan's room and introducing her to Aunt Tammy.

I found the cafeteria and bought two coffees. Mine was so bitter I could barely swallow it, but I drank it anyway because it seemed like that's what people did in hospitals. The doctor came to Joan's room, but I didn't understand what he told Aunt Tammy, who took notes on her phone as he talked. My brain was foggy from lack of sleep, but my body was wide-awake, jittery from the caffeine, and primed for Steph.

At three o'clock I left the hospital to pick up Dad at the Airporter stop in San Rafael. When I turned onto Sir Francis Drake, I glanced at the church on the corner. I wasn't even Catholic, but I felt guilty.

Dad's hair had grown out; it flopped over his forehead in brown waves as he hugged me in the parking lot. He was wearing wrinkled clothes and his glasses were smudged. He looked like this every time he emerged from a writers' retreat, but this time the dazed expression on his face was slightly different. This time he also looked frightened.

Dad hardly ever let me drive if he could do it, but today he didn't even notice that I got into the driver's seat.

At the hospital I took him to Joan's room and waited in the doorway while he went in. I heard her speaking faintly: "Matty, you came all this way . . ."

"I'm here, Mom. I'm not leaving you till you're better."

He didn't have that cheery, forced positive tone that Aunt Tammy and I had when we talked to her. He sounded raw and scared. My dad was no good at faking anything.

Steph texted me: *How's Joan? How are you?*

I went out to the waiting room to write back. *Better. My dad and aunt are here. We're at the hospital.*

We didn't write anything more personal. I wondered if Lisa ever picked up Steph's phone. We had canceled our plans for tonight, and I wondered what Steph would do instead.

I was leaving in two weeks. A gaping hollow opened up inside me as I imagined myself saying goodbye to Steph. Would she come out to Woodacre for that or would we go to In-N-Out one last time? The hollow had pull, like a black hole. I didn't want to imagine this. I wanted to stay—not necessarily in California, and definitely not at the hospital, but in this bubble of time when Steph and I were real, when we were together.

I was exhausted, but I remember feeling a queer sense of clarity, as if a lens had just come into focus, and all at once I could see who I was becoming as opposed to who I once was. I was split in two: my future and my past. I wanted to remain here on the edge between my two selves, doubly exposed, all hunger and heart.

was still in the hospital waiting room when my phone rang. It wasn't Steph—it was Haley. Surprised, I answered the call. "Haley?"

"Tasha told me she told you."

For a second I didn't understand what she was talking about. A couple of seats away from me, an elderly man was sitting alone with a portable oxygen tank.

"Don't tell anyone else," Haley said urgently. "Please."

"There's nothing wrong with it," I said. "Why do you think there is?"

"I don't," Haley snapped. "It's just not me. I'm not gay."

Her voice sounded loudly through the phone, and the man with the oxygen tank glanced at me. I got up and moved toward the exit, passing a woman trying to comfort a little girl with a broken arm.

"Are you there?" Haley asked.

"Yeah."

"What's wrong? You sound weird. Are you weirded out by this?"

"No, I'm in the hospital. My grandma's in the hospital." I made it out of the foyer and through the automatic doors to the covered entrance.

"Oh my God, I'm so sorry. Is she okay?"

"She had a stroke. My dad's here, too."

"Wow. This is a bad time. I'm sorry."

I walked toward a bench just outside the portico and sat down, looking at the parking lot. "It's okay," I said. "I've been meaning to call you. I'm just waiting right now anyway."

"Tasha said she visited."

"Yeah." I imagined Steph's truck pulling into the parking lot. I imagined seeing it from a distance, glimpsing the shadow of her face through the windshield.

"I'm sorry I didn't tell you," Haley said. "I feel like this has messed everything up. I didn't mean for this to happen. Tasha's misinterpreting everything."

"I thought—she said you hooked up."

"Whatever it was, it's over." Haley sounded irritated. "It was only a couple of times anyway, and it's not like we had sex."

"What do you mean? Tasha said—"

"You want me to go into detail?"

"No," I said quickly, although I was confused.

"Look, I'm sorry it's ruining my friendship with Tasha. I don't want it to ruin our friendship, too."

A surge of anger went through me. Haley and I had barely talked since graduation. "This is completely fucking over Tasha," I said.

Haley sighed into the phone. "I don't know what to do about that, okay? It's not like I don't love her, I just don't *love* her. Can't you get her to understand that? I can't change the way I feel."

Haley sounded so frustrated and desperate that I wanted to reassure her, but I also remembered Tasha's face when she told me what had happened. I didn't respond.

"Please, just make her understand," Haley pleaded. "She won't talk to me anymore, and I don't exactly blame her, but it's not like I don't want her in my life."

"I can't make her change her feelings either. You should understand that."

There was silence on the other end. A white woman with frizzy brown hair came out of the hospital and lit a cigarette. I stared at her, perplexed.

Finally, Haley said, "I know. I guess we're stuck then." She gave a brief, pained laugh. "I never thought it would end like this. You have to believe me. I had no idea. It wasn't supposed to be like this. Tasha and I—we're supposed to be friends."

The word *friends* sounded so tortured, a tangle of confusion and disbelief.

"I miss her," Haley said. She spoke so softly I almost couldn't hear her.

"Then why don't you tell her?"

The woman was still smoking under the portico, glaring out at the parking lot.

"I can't." Haley sniffed, and I wondered if she was holding back tears. "If I say anything like that, she'll never get over it. I need her to get over it. I'm sorry, but I can't be more than friends with her. It was a mistake, and I don't know why she doesn't get that. I really tried to explain it to her, but this has been really hard for me, too."

"How can you say that?" I asked. "Tasha's one of your best friends. How could you say it was a mistake? Don't you know how that makes her feel?"

"How do you think it makes *me* feel?"

"I don't know!" I exploded. "I think you're in denial."

I heard Haley catch her breath on the other end. "That's what you think," she said coldly.

I knew I should apologize. There was a ding on my phone and a text from my dad popped up.

Where are you?

I made a frustrated sound. "I have to go," I said. "We can talk later."

I ended the call and headed back toward the hospital doors. As I passed the smoking woman, I said, "You're not supposed to smoke here. It's a hospital."

"Mind your own business," she snapped.

I turned to look straight at her. I wanted to get into it. But she looked so defeated—bags under her eyes, her hair a mess, a stain that looked like coffee mixed with ketchup on her shirt—I was ashamed I had chastised her.

wasn't supposed to be at home alone on Friday when Steph came over to do the yard work. Dad and I were supposed to be packing up some of Joan's clothes to prepare for her transfer to a stroke rehabilitation center in San Rafael, but Aunt Tammy had called early from the hospital and asked Dad to join her there. The appointment they had with Joan's doctors had been moved up from the afternoon.

He left just as Steph arrived. I was standing on the front step as she came up the path, and my stomach lurched in anticipation.

"My dad's gone for—I don't know, a while," I said instead of hello. "My aunt, too. We're alone."

She kissed me as if we had nothing to hide. "I still have to do the yard work," she said, but I heard the smile in her voice.

"Later," I said, and kissed her again.

She called in sick to work. I told her I didn't want her to lose her hours but she insisted, and said she didn't know when we'd get this chance to be together again. It sounded so adult, so responsible, even though she was shirking her duties for me. I didn't protest for long. I wanted this stolen time for us.

I led the way to my room, holding her hand. I sat down on the edge of my bed and she stood in front of me, a hesitant expression on her face.

"Are you still on your period?" I asked.

She seemed a little embarrassed. "No."

"What's wrong?"

"Nothing."

"You don't want to—"

"I want to," she said, cutting me off. She kissed me before I could say another word.

She pulled my T-shirt off over my head, unfastened my bra. I reached for her blue T-shirt and tugged it up. She was wearing a black sports bra. Her stomach was pale and firm, dotted on the right side with three tiny black moles. She took off her shoes and we moved back on the bed. I wanted to feel her skin on mine. I slid my fingers beneath the straps of her sports bra and whispered, "Help me with this." She looked hesitant again, and I wondered if she was shy. I moved my hand away and lay back. "Only if you want to," I said.

I reached up and cupped her cheek in my hand, my thumb rubbing against the fullness of her lower lip. She looked at me for a long moment as if she were trying to decide what to do, and then she lowered her mouth to my throat while her hand slid along my body, down to my shorts, unbuttoning them.

"Wait," I said. "I owe you one. Let me—"

"Ladies first," she said. She shifted; her breath was a tickle on my breast. Her hand slipped between my legs and I couldn't speak after that, not for a long time, not until she slid up my sweat-dampened body and nestled her head in the crook of my neck, her face smelling like me.

We lay together on the bed, breathing together. I was naked again and she was warm against my side, still wearing her shorts and sports bra. She pulled the sheet over us and wrapped her arm around me. I felt the rise and fall of her chest in a gentle rhythm against my body.

After a few minutes I asked, "What did you mean, 'ladies first'? You don't think of yourself as a lady?"

"I'm definitely not a lady."

"You don't think of yourself as—as a woman?"

She stiffened, and the comfortable intimacy that had cocooned us evaporated.

"I'm sorry," I said immediately. "I don't know how to talk about this." She separated herself from me and I turned on my side to face her. She looked as if she were trying to decide whether or not to be offended. "I'm sorry," I said again.

She closed her eyes as if not seeing me would help. "It's complicated," she said quietly. "Some people don't get it."

"I get it."

"Do you?"

"Are you . . . genderqueer?" I had looked up the word after Tasha said it, but I didn't fully understand it. Steph didn't speak for a moment and I worried that I'd just made it worse. Then she opened her eyes and smiled at me.

"You sound like you're speaking a foreign language," she said.

I exhaled. "I guess I am. I've never had to think about this stuff before."

"That's what worries me. What if you see me and you don't like what you see?" She looked anxious. Her cheeks flushed. "I'm not a boy. Maybe you wish I was."

"I don't," I said emphatically. "I definitely don't wish you were a boy. I like *you*. I want *you*."

Her hazel eyes reflected the light from the window; they reflected me in a tiny dark image. They grew bright, and I saw a teardrop swelling in one corner. Before it spilled out, I caught it with my fingertip, and then I kissed her mouth softly.

She kissed me back. Gently at first, and then harder, until she pushed herself up to peel off her sports bra. She had small breasts with dark pink nipples. She unbuttoned her shorts and took them off along with her underwear. Her lanky torso curved into rounded hips, a thin line of brown hair leading from her belly button to the curly patch between her legs. I felt like she had given me a gift in allowing me to see her.

I touched her, and her skin was warm. I pulled her closer, wanting to feel her pressed against me. She moved on top of me, skin on skin, breast against breast, her legs straddling my hip, and her breath quickened. It was amazing to be beneath her, to have this effect on her. She moved against me more rapidly, and I felt the slickness between her legs on my thigh. I wanted to make her come, but I wanted to do it with my mouth. I wanted to do for her what she had done for me. I asked, "Can I go down on you?"

She stopped moving, breathless. "Are you sure you want to?"

"Yes, but you'll have to tell me if I'm doing it wrong."

She hesitated, her face flushed, and then she rolled off me, and I went to kneel between her legs. I lowered my head, my hair cascading over her inner thighs. She was pearlescent, lustrous, the whole of her body poised alive on the tip of my tongue. I didn't know what I was doing, but I knew what I liked, so I tried to treat her the way I'd want to be treated. It occurred to me that I was applying the golden rule in a way that might not be intended, and I almost broke into laugher with her thighs around my face, but then she began to rock against me and I forgot everything except her, the sounds she made, my hands cupping her backside as if I were holding a drinking bowl to my mouth.

She tasted like saltwater oysters. I was in love with all of her. I was not myself anymore; I was hers.

On Saturday, we moved Joan to the rehabilitation facility in San Rafael. It was only a few blocks away from Steph and Lisa's apartment.

At the facility, Joan would have several daily sessions with speech and physical therapists, with time off for rest in the late afternoons and evenings. She had to relearn how to speak clearly, how to use her right hand, how to walk. The doctors told us that with the proper rehabilitation, she could regain much of her normal life, although she was now at increased risk for additional strokes.

Joan's room had a few dents on the edges of the furniture and scuff marks on the beige walls where wheelchair tires had bumped. I wondered who had lived there before her. The blue-and-beige-patterned curtains were depressingly institutional, and I made a mental note to bring in fresh flowers and photos of Grandpa and the family. Maybe some art supplies or the catalog of Joan's work to remind her of who she was, because it seemed like sometimes she still had trouble remembering.

Before we left her on the first night, she asked me, in her slurred speech, to bring the last box of Grandpa's papers so she could sort them. "I'm going to be bored out of my mind here," she said. "Keep me occupied with something."

"I will," I said, and I bent down to hug her before we left. She smelled like the hospital.

I googled nearby camera stores and found one in San Anselmo stuffed between a boutique and a bookstore. It looked like it had been there since the 1950s, and when I went inside, an actual bell jingled against the door. The interior was meticulously clean, with shelves of cameras neatly lined up on the wall and a spotless glass counter spanning the width. Behind the counter, a white woman with curly brown hair sat on a stool looking at a MacBook.

"How can I help you?" she asked.

I took Joan's Rolleiflex out of my backpack. "I want to buy some film for this."

"Nice camera," she said. "You into retro photography?"

"It belongs to my grandmother," I said, setting it on the glass counter. "She's an artist. She hasn't used it in a while, though. Do you think it still works okay?"

She took the camera out of its leather case and removed the lens cap, popping open the viewfinder to look through the lens. She moved a lever, pressed a button that clicked, and then twisted something on the camera that caused the bottom to flip open. "It's in pretty good shape," she said, closing the bottom after she'd looked inside. "You should just try it out. Do you want color or black-and-white film?"

Joan's art photography was all black-and-white. "Black-and-white," I said.

The woman got up and went to a cabinet behind her, returning with a couple of small rectangular boxes. "There are twelve exposures per roll, so I'd buy two to get started. That's twenty dollars."

I took my wallet out of my bag. "I don't know how to load it."

"I can show you," she said, taking my credit card. "Who's your grandmother? Would I know her?"

"Maybe. Her name is Joan West."

"I'll look her up." She handed me my receipt. "We can develop the film when you're ready."

I met Steph for lunch on Monday. I hadn't seen her since Friday, and when I spotted her in the garden center talking to a customer by the potted plants, time seemed to slow down and speed up all at once. It felt like a year had passed since we were together, and yet I could still feel her at my fingertips.

I hovered in the background until she saw me. The way her smile lit up her eyes made me feel invincible.

When she was finished with the customer, I went over to her. "Hi," I said. I wanted to kiss her right there, but I was afraid her coworkers might notice.

"Hi." She reached out and touched my arm with the tip of her fingers. "I'm almost done."

She let me follow her to the stockroom where she put away the tools she had been using. It was dim in there, lit by a couple of bulbs hanging from the ceiling, and the shelves and walls were crowded with garden equipment, piles of pots, sacks of fertilizer. We kissed in the corner behind a piece of wooden trellis, my hands sliding beneath her tee, her hands slipping beneath the waistband of my shorts. I would have let her touch me right there, I wouldn't have cared if anyone walked in, but she stopped, breathing heavily, and said, "We can't."

"Why not?"

She pressed her forehead to mine and laughed. "I work here. That's why."

We went to In-N-Out and ordered burgers and fries, sitting in the cab of her truck overlooking the marshland, in full view of the bright afternoon. We talked about Joan and the next Madchen gig, which

Roxy had booked at a bar in San Francisco in September. Steph was going to do it. I would be gone by then, but neither of us brought that up.

Monday night at the rehab center, I brought out the Rolleiflex. "There's film in it," I said, putting the camera on the bed next to my grandmother. "I went to this camera store in San Anselmo and they helped me load it."

Joan touched the camera with her left hand, her fingers moving over the case as if to convince herself it was there. "This is so thoughtful of you," she said.

Dad looked surprised. "I haven't seen that camera in years."

Joan lifted it up and set it on her stomach, but her right hand fumbled with the lens cap. "Can you help me?"

I reached over to remove the cap. She started to lift up the focusing hood but her hand was trembling.

"I'm too shaky now," she said. "Matty, will you take a picture of me and Aria?"

She walked my dad through focusing the camera and setting the aperture and shutter speed, and then told me to move the lamp and adjust the curtain for better light. While she instructed us, she seemed like her old self again.

After Dad had taken a couple of pictures of me and Joan, she had him push the tray table out to the foot of the bed, where he could set the camera and use the self-timer. He ran back to us after he pressed the shutter release, perching on Joan's other side just in time for the click.

She felt so small between us. I could feel the flutter of her pulse in her wrist as I held her hand.

On Tuesday I didn't see Steph.

Dad and I bought peach tarts from a bakery in Fairfax and brought them to Joan at the rehab center.

On Wednesday after work, Steph and I drove out behind the loading docks again. There was nowhere for us to be together except in her truck, and I felt a rising desperation inside me. I was leaving in one week.

Joan showed me how to take out the exposed film and load the camera with a fresh roll, and talked me through taking a couple of pictures. Through the viewfinder, Joan's flipped image floated, mirage-like, on the speckled focusing screen, as if the camera were a door to a different time and place.

Thursday morning when I went into the kitchen for breakfast, Dad was sitting at the table, motionless. He looked up at me when I entered the room. His face was drained of all color except for rims of redness around his eyes, and instantly I knew something was wrong.

"What happened?" I asked.

"Your grandmother died last night," he said.

I stared at him. "But she was getting better," I said, as if this were an argument.

Deep lines appeared in his cheeks as he grimaced. "She—"

He didn't continue, his shoulders heaving as a ragged breath came out of him. I went around the table and pulled out the chair beside him, sitting down. He wiped his hands across his eyes, leaving streaks of wetness on his face.

"She had a hemorrhagic stroke," he said. "It was probably because of her previous stroke. She died early this morning. Tammy's there now. I wanted to be here to tell you when you woke up."

It made no sense to me. We had been taking pictures the night before. Today I was going to take the rolls of film to that camera store to have them developed.

Dad put his arm around me. He was shaking, his whole body an earthquake. I turned in my chair to hold him, and the landslide of his grief overwhelmed me. My father wasn't supposed to cry like this, not in front of me. I didn't know how to react. Was I supposed to comfort him? I couldn't breathe.

Analemma came into the kitchen, nosing at Dad's knees. Every day since Joan went to the hospital, Analemma had repeatedly gone upstairs looking for her. Every time she'd come back down sniffing, sniffing, as if she couldn't accept that Joan wasn't in the house somewhere. Now Analemma sniffed Dad more and more insistently, until he dropped his hands from his wet face and started to stroke her ears. She nosed her way closer and closer, and finally with a short laugh he got out of his chair and knelt on the floor, and Analemma pressed her head against his chest, a faint whine coming out of her.

It was the whine that did it. There was no way to tell Analemma what had happened. Joan had disappeared with no explanation, and Analemma would never see her again.

I would never see her again.

My eyes were burning hot, spilling over.

I got down on the floor, too, and Dad put his arm around me, pulling me close. Analemma was warm and muscled and solid between us, and I still remember the scent of her—a toasted, earthy liveness—and I buried my head in her neck, my tears soaking into her silken black fur.

A unt Tammy came home from the rehab facility before noon with a suitcase of Joan's things. After Grandpa died, my grandmother had written out explicit instructions on what she wanted to happen after her death. Grandpa had been cremated and his ashes were scattered in the Marin Headlands; she wanted the same thing.

"We'll have the private memorial service a week from Saturday," Aunt Tammy said, drinking another cup of coffee in the kitchen, where we had gathered to discuss the funeral plans. My father had become alternately quiet and angry, and Aunt Tammy had turned into an efficient planning machine. "Almost everything is booked up with gay weddings, but I was able to rent the Fairfax Women's Club, and I've contacted the Buddhist teacher Mom specified for the service. I have to go back to Pasadena after that but I should be able to get some time off in September when we do the public memorial at her gallery in San Francisco. Matt, if you can come out for a week, we can try to get the house in shape to put it on the market."

"I'll work it out," Dad said. "Are you taking Analemma with you?"

"Yes." Aunt Tammy turned to me. "Aria, we should change your plane ticket to fly back next Sunday so you can be here for the memorial but still get back in time for freshman orientation. You can come back for the public memorial if you want, and we'll scatter her ashes after that."

I suddenly remembered Tony Merritt. "We have to tell Tony."

"Who's Tony?" Aunt Tammy asked.

"He's her friend. He lives in Woodacre. I got the impression he—they were special friends."

"I thought he was just a contractor," Dad said.

"She didn't always tell us everything," Tammy said.

"He's not in the instructions," Dad said.

"I'll tell him," I said. I didn't want Tony to show up with Goldie to take the dogs on a hike and find out that way.

"You shouldn't have to do that," Aunt Tammy said.

"I can tell him," Dad said. "Do you have his number?"

"Neither of you knows him," I said. "And I don't know his number. I only know where he lives." The house seemed to press in on the three of us—it felt too small—and I was overwhelmed by the need to get out. "Can I borrow the car?" I asked, standing up.

"Doesn't he live in Woodacre? Do you need to drive?" Dad asked.

"I need to get that film developed," I said. "Where's her camera?"

"In the suitcase," Aunt Tammy said.

Dad looked unhappy. "Be careful," he said.

Goldie started barking as I unlatched the gate to Tony's yard. He opened the front door before I got there, and Goldie ran out to greet me, her tail whipping back and forth.

"Aria," Tony said. "This is unexpected."

"Hi," I said, bending down to pet Goldie's back. By the time I straightened up, the expression on Tony's face had turned serious.

"What happened? Is it your grandma? She hasn't answered my calls for a couple of days."

Haltingly, I told him. He looked away, and then down at the ground. Goldie went up to him and nudged her nose against his knee. He crossed his arms. I was afraid he would cry like my dad, and I didn't know what I'd do if he did.

But he didn't cry. We stood there in silence for what felt like several minutes. He finally raised his head and looked at me. His eyes were dry, but his face was grave, all the lines around his eyes and mouth drawn down.

"Thank you for telling me," he said. "Are you alone up there?"

"No, my dad and my aunt are here."

He nodded. "I'll come and pay my respects later. I'm so sorry."

And then he turned around and went back inside. Goldie gave me a glance that could only be described as anxious, and followed him into the house.

I drove to the garden center. I knew Steph was working and she might not be able to take a lunch break with me, but I had to see her. She'd want to know about Joan, and it wasn't something I wanted to tell her in a text message.

I found her outside the stockroom, where she was dealing with a pallet of potting soil. She was surprised to see me. "Hi! What are you doing here?"

I didn't know how else to say it. "Joan died this morning."

She looked at me blankly for a second, then put down her clipboard on top of the potting soil and pulled me into a hug. "I'm so sorry," she said.

I wrapped my arms around her waist and buried my face in the crook of her neck. I took a deep breath. She smelled like plants and soil, alive. Joan should still be alive. She hadn't finished whatever she was making in Grandpa's old office. When Grandpa had died, it had been awful but expected. He'd had cancer and we had time to say goodbye. This was different. It felt like a mistake. How could she be dead? I hadn't seen her body. I couldn't think of her as a *body*.

Steph's hand stroked my hair and I pressed myself closer to her. I was crying, my tears dampening the material of her T-shirt. There was a deep ache in the pit of my stomach, and I knew it would become a convulsion, a retching up of my disbelief if I didn't control it. I had to control it; I was in public. I crumpled the back of Steph's T-shirt in my hand. I shuddered in her arms, and she held me tighter until the shuddering stopped. I raised my head from her neck and she ran her thumb across my tear-streaked cheeks.

"I'm so sorry," she said again. Her eyes were wet. She kissed me gently.

I kissed her back. Softly at first, and then I became aware of the pressure of her breasts against mine and the slightest suggestion of her tongue against my lips. The kiss deepened. I felt as if kissing her were the most vital thing in the world. I needed to do it, to taste her open mouth, and I only had to push the tiniest bit for her to respond.

It became a hungry kiss. My teeth on her lips. Her hands in my hair, holding me to her. The world disappeared, and there was only this connection between us, so real it felt like a physical creature, ravenous. All we could do was feed it.

And then like an ax shattering glass, Lisa's voice behind us: "What the fuck are you doing?"

Steph pulled away first, her face flushed, her eyes panicked. The connection between us felt like a phantom limb. I was still reaching for her as she said, "Lisa—"

"What the fuck are you doing?" Lisa demanded again.

Steph jerked away from me. I snapped back into this world.

Lisa was standing ten feet away in her Safeway vest, one hand gripping her car keys, the other her phone. Her face was red, and it only grew redder as she looked from me to Steph.

"Joan died," Steph said, and I knew as soon as she spoke that those words were the wrong ones.

"You were *comforting* her?" Lisa demanded.

"No, I—" Steph stepped between me and Lisa as if to defend me.

I saw the rage on Lisa's face change into something much worse. Pain.

"I'm so sorry," Steph said, reaching out to her.

Lisa stepped back, her bottom lip quivering. Fat tears began to leak out of her eyes. "Get away from me," Lisa said. "Don't touch me."

"Please, let me explain."

"What could you possibly explain? Are you sleeping with her?"

Steph didn't answer, and Lisa's face was beet red now.

"I can't believe I trusted you. You said you were just friends." Lisa looked beyond Steph at me. "Do you know what she told me? She said you were confused, that you needed some help dealing with coming out. I felt sorry for you! I guess she helped you."

I still couldn't seem to speak. In the background I saw some customers glancing in our direction.

Lisa suddenly advanced toward me. "You were in our house." She looked at Steph. "Did you fuck her in our house?"

I flinched.

"No, no, we never—I would never do that," Steph said.

Lisa came closer and Steph stopped her, grabbing her arms. "Let go of me!" Lisa screamed.

"Please, let's go home. Let's talk about it at home," Steph pleaded. Lisa's arms were flailing and Steph was flailing with her in a bizarre interpretation of patty-cake.

"Get the fuck away from my girlfriend," Lisa snarled at me.

"Lisa," Steph said. "Lisa, please."

All of a sudden Lisa backed away, raising her hands as if she were surrendering. "Whatever," she said. Tears were running freely down her face now. She turned around and stalked out of the garden center, leaving Steph and me behind.

I reached for Steph, but she rebuffed me. "We can't do this now," she said curtly. She went after Lisa, running through the garden center.

I was left standing beside the pallet of potting soil. A woman with a baby stroller was staring at me, and when she realized I had seen her she turned away, her face reddening. I didn't know what to do. I sank down onto an overturned pot. I was shaking. I was hot and freezing at the same time. I dropped my head into my hands, forcing myself to take several breaths. I was in public. I was mortified.

The strains of eighties pop wafted through the garden center, a man singing about jumping. A voice said over the intercom: "Jennifer to checkout. Jennifer to checkout." I pushed my hair back from my face, trying to smooth it out. I wiped my eyes; to my surprise they were dry. I picked up my purse from where I had dropped it on the ground near the potting soil. I put on my sunglasses and left.

M y mom called while Dad was out picking up dinner.

"Your father told me," she said over the phone. "I'm so sorry."

In Hong Kong, it was tomorrow, just after nine in the morning. I was in my room, where I'd been hiding since I got back from the garden center.

"Your grandmother was a great artist," Mom said.

I remembered Joan saying *Your mother is an artist*, and for a split second the connection between Joan, my mother, and me seemed crystal clear, revelatory. I knew I should understand who they were and who I was and why all this had happened—but the moment vanished as quickly as it came, and I was in the guest room in Woodacre, and Mom was in Hong Kong, and Joan was gone.

O n Friday morning, I learned that Steph had called very early and told Aunt Tammy she was sorry about Joan, and she could no longer do the yard work.

I called her, but it went straight to voicemail. I left a brief message, trying to sound rational, cool. "Please call me back. We need to talk."

Dad changed my plane ticket to leave after the memorial service, so now I had an extra four days in California. The irony wasn't lost on me.

Steph hadn't called me, so I texted her.

I just wanted to check in on you. Are you okay?

If you don't want to talk, just tell me.

Eventually, Steph responded: *I can't talk right now. I'm really sorry for your loss. I need some space please.*

I stared at her message. There was no opening for me to follow up. I deleted it.

Tasha told me I was in shock. "You do this," she said over the phone. "After the thing with Jacob, remember? You went to class and acted like everything was fine. Have you ever even admitted that it wasn't fine?"

I didn't remember.

"This is going to come back to kick you in the ass," Tasha said. "You need to talk about it."

"I don't have anything to say." I was blank inside, erased.

I went to the studio, where I pulled down the unfinished painting and stared at the bare wall beneath it.

I went back to bed. The sheets were cool against my bare legs. I hadn't opened the curtains and sunlight glowed around the edges. I remembered being here with Steph, the warm skin of her body against mine. Her mouth on my breasts, between my legs. Her fingers in me, curved like an invitation.

My feelings had shut off, but my body had not. My hand slid beneath my underwear. She was with me, her face a ghost above.

G uilt is a shape-shifter. It can fester like a sore, burning for attention, or it can lurk like a beast in the dark, always there but never clearly visible. If you don't look at it directly, it can seem as if it's gone, and the only proof that it remains is the shadow it casts in the corner.

My guilt comes out late at night or early in the morning, a specter that hovers over me as I drift into or out of sleep. Sometimes I like to see it. It can be seductive if it wants to. It knows exactly what I like. It knows precisely which memories to recall.

Sometimes I hope it will never go away.

called Mel. When she answered the phone, it sounded as if she had done so reluctantly. "What's up?"

It had been one week since Lisa found me and Steph at the garden center.

"Steph won't take my calls," I said. My voice was cool, as if I were an aggrieved secretary.

Mel knew what I was talking about. "You've got to give her some time."

"I'm leaving soon. We have to talk now."

"I can't make her do anything."

"You're her best friend."

"Yeah, well, I'm not her boss. Look, I shouldn't even be talking to you."

"Why not?"

Mel sighed. "Because I was Steph's friend first."

I played my last card. "Tell her my grandma's memorial is on Saturday at two. At the Fairfax Women's Club. Please tell her. Joan would've wanted her there."

Mel didn't respond at first. I didn't push her. Finally, she said, "I'm really sorry this happened."

I knew I should be sorry, too.

My mom called again the night before the memorial service. I took my phone into my room and closed the door, sitting on the edge of the bed.

"How's your father?" she asked. "Are you watching out for him? I know he takes things hard."

"He's okay," I said, even though he wasn't. He had taken to writing late into the night on the living room couch. I could see the light from beneath my door while I lay awake well past midnight, checking my phone repeatedly as if I were a rat trained to push a button. In the morning when I came out to the kitchen after a few hours of restless sleep, my dad was often drinking coffee alone, red-eyed and drained, and I wondered whether he'd slept at all.

"Promise me you'll keep an eye on him," Mom said. "He's not like you and me. He needs people like us to keep him grounded."

"People like us?" I said stiffly.

"You know what I mean," she said, as if we shared a secret. "We get things done when we have to. Make sure he gets something to eat besides coffee."

How had she known he wasn't eating?

A memory rose: Mom rolling out scallion pancakes. I was small enough that I needed to stand on a chair to reach the counter. She poured oil over the dough and sprinkled on salt, telling me to spread it out with my fingers. It felt like slippery sandpaper. The scallions smelled fresh and sharp. *These are your dad's favorite*, she said.

"... emailing you an article from my cousin Eddie," Mom was saying. "I'm sending it now."

"What?"

"I'm sending you something from cousin Eddie," Mom said again, sounding strangely patient. "I thought you might like to see it. I was really surprised because I met them both, but I guess I didn't understand at the time."

I had missed something, but before I could ask what it was, Mom was saying goodbye.

"I have to go now. Make sure you eat something, too. I'll call you after the memorial."

A moment later my phone vibrated. A surge of hope—but it was just the email from my mom. The subject read: "FWD: Just married . . . finally!"

I opened the email.

Dear friends and family,

Congratulations are in order! I'm happy to share the news that my beloved sister, Lily, has finally married her longtime partner, Kath Miller. They celebrated their nuptials last week in a beautiful small ceremony (photo attached). I'm also forwarding an LA Times story about many of the same-sex marriages that have taken place this summer, which includes Lily and Kath! They have not registered for gifts because as Lily told me, "We already have everything!" But if you're inclined to give, she invites you to donate in their name to Lambda Legal. Lily advises me that both brides have chosen to keep their names.

With much joy,
Eddie Hu

I clicked through to the *LA Times* article, which was a long feature about several couples. I scrolled down to the section about Lily, which was subtitled A MATCH MADE IN HEAVEN. It began with a photo of two older women—one white, one Asian—standing in front of a small airplane on a sun-drenched tarmac. The white woman, whose silvery hair was cut as short as Steph's, was dressed in khakis and a white shirt with rolled-up sleeves, and she was giving the Asian woman a fond smile. The Asian woman, wearing a black-and-white wrap dress, had gray hair worn in a retro style, and she looked directly at the camera with a laugh. I felt a little flip in my heart looking at the photo. Lily was so joyful, and Kath obviously loved her. I scrolled down to read the story.

For years in their early twenties, Lily Hu and Kath Miller kept their love alive via monthly flights. Miller would fly a small plane from Oakland, where she worked as a flight mechanic, to Pasadena, where Hu worked as a computer at the Jet Propulsion Laboratory. The couple first started dating in high school, and Lily wasn't initially sure whether their relationship would last.

"I thought for sure she'd forget me," Hu notes, laughing.

"I would never forget you," Miller replies, putting her arm around her lifelong love.

This summer, they celebrate their fifty-third anniversary, although they like to debate about whether several years in the middle count. The couple's commuting relationship went through some turbulent times in the early 1960s, when Miller focused on training for an experimental program to send women astronauts into space. Hu says she was able to weather the separation because she understood Miller's dream. After all, Hu was part of the team responsible for building many of JPL's robotic spacecraft, including Voyager.

"A mutual friend helped us find our way back to each other," Hu says. The two reconnected in the mid-1960s, and Miller moved to Pasadena in 1968.

"We've been together ever since," Miller says.

They bought a little house in Pasadena, and Miller launched a flight school at a local airport, where she continues to teach a few enthusiastic young pilots today during her retirement. Hu retired from JPL ten years ago after a long career first as a computer and then as an engineer, but she still keeps up with the space program through a network of JPL friends.

Hu says she and Miller never felt the urge to tie the knot before the Supreme Court decision this summer. "We had friends who had commitment ceremonies, but we didn't feel like we needed it," she says. "We were committed to each other privately, and it didn't seem necessary until there were real legal reasons to do it."

"I bought her a ring in 1969," Miller says. "And she wore it, but we never made a big fuss about it."

In early August, the couple held a small wedding ceremony in their own backyard, with just a dozen friends and family members in attendance. But the most meaningful part of the event, Hu says, was going to City Hall to get the marriage certificate.

"I feel recognized by my country," Hu says. "I never dreamed this was possible when I was younger. I can't describe how wonderful that feels."

The photo that Eddie attached showed the two women standing arm in arm in front of a stucco wall covered with climbing vines, surrounded by a number of people I didn't know. The man next to Lily was probably Eddie, her brother, but the rest of the people I wasn't sure about. On Kath's side were several white people who could have been her relatives, and a few children stood in front. Some of them were half Asian, like me. Everyone was smiling, but none looked as happy as Lily and Kath, who were gazing at each other rather than the photographer. I zoomed in on Lily's and Kath's faces, feeling an unexpectedly vivid connection to them both, as if I could sense the love between them glowing like a radiant sun. After so many years, they could show their love to the world at last.

was flying out super early on Sunday morning with my dad after the family memorial service, so I had to pack before. My new boots wouldn't fit in my suitcase, so I found an old duffel bag in the basement and put them in there. Dad and Aunt Tammy agreed that I could have Joan's camera and her catalog. I added those to the duffel bag along with my broken telescope. I rolled up my unfinished painting and wedged it in, too.

I almost threw away the Madchen CD and postcard, but at the last minute I slid them into the suitcase's interior pocket.

I put Steph's copy of *The Dream of a Common Language* in my purse so I could give it to her if she came to the memorial.

Dad and I arrived early at the Fairfax Women's Club, but Aunt Tammy was already there, along with Uncle Brian and their kids, Luke and Noah. They had set up a table at the back of the room for photos of my grandmother, which were lined up in chronological order. Joan as a blond child, as a teen girl in a 1950s dress, in her wedding gown with Grandpa. The young couple with their kids in Boulder. A big family photo taken at a reunion in the 1980s. There was one that included my mom and me as a baby; a shot of my grandparents when they were older, on a ship in the ocean; me and Joan and Dad on a summer vacation a couple of years ago.

The rest of the family began to arrive. Grandpa's younger brother, Rob, and his wife, who drove up from Santa Barbara. Great-Aunt Margaret, Joan's sister, had flown in from Chicago with her husband. She looked so much like Joan that I had to stop myself from staring at her.

I had brought some photos to add to the memorial display. A picture of my grandparents at Cornell that I'd taken from the wall in Grandpa's old office. The self-portrait that usually hung on the guest bedroom wall. And one of the photos we'd taken at the rehab center: Dad, Joan, and me, our arms around her. The film hadn't advanced properly, so the three of us were on the bottom half of the picture. The top half showed a skewed image of the wall above the bed lit by the bedside lamp. I liked the way our heads were half transparent, merging into the lamp with the light shining up.

This was supposed to be a personal memorial service for family and close friends, so only about a dozen others came. A few of Joan's artist friends and their partners; a couple of Grandpa's best friends and their wives; Tony Merritt, who squeezed my shoulder. A couple of women I might have seen at Spirit Rock, who came with the Buddhist teacher, Susan Douglas. She had short gray hair and kind eyes, and she carried a Tibetan singing bowl on a small red cushion.

The public memorial in September would be much bigger; Aunt Tammy was calling it a celebration of life. There would be an exhibit of Joan's work; there would be speeches from her proteges and peers. Today's gathering was small and intimate. Today was for grief.

There was no sign of Steph.

I sat in the front row next to my dad and didn't allow myself to turn around to see if anyone had slipped in after the memorial began. During the opening meditation, I closed my eyes so I could better listen to the silence in the room. Breathing, the creaking of chairs, muffled coughing. The door at the rear of the building opened and closed. The desire to look was an itch between my shoulder blades, but I held still.

The singing bowl rang out, low and resonant, three times. Bodies shifted in their seats. Susan Douglas stood up. Behind her was an altar, where Joan's ashes were contained in a ceramic urn made by a friend. A small bronze statue of the Buddha was placed nearby, along with several bouquets of flowers. My mother had sent white lilies. I looked up at the vaulted wooden ceiling while Susan Douglas invited us to remember Joan West. She spoke about rejoicing in the positive ways Joan had contributed to the world. Others got up to speak their memories: Great-Aunt Margaret, Aunt Tammy, Dad. I felt like I should say something, but I was terrified I'd do it wrong. My ears were full of a buzzing noise; I couldn't listen to my dad's eulogy. I saw the tears on his face. I saw Joan in the studio, telling me she was always making art about time. *I don't understand how it works, but I'm always interested in it.*

Susan Douglas was speaking. "All conditioned things are impermanent; they arise and pass away. Understanding this deeply brings the greatest happiness, which is peace."

Joan had left detailed instructions on the way her ashes were to be scattered. In September, after the public memorial, we would hike out to the Marin Headlands with the urn and a photographer friend of hers. Joan wanted the ashes scattered in a circle, and she wanted the scattering to be photographed.

My hands were so cold.

"Joan's physical body may be gone now, but who she was is not gone. She was more than her body, just as we are all more than our bodies. She was connected with all of you. You influenced her, and she influenced you, and that influence continues."

The urn was beautiful. It had a round belly and an elegantly curved neck and a perfectly fitted lid, and it had been glazed in some way that left brilliant sea-green streaks and dark blue flecks on the surface. As if the sea had been burned into the clay.

My stomach was a hollow inside me.

"Everything that Joan taught you goes on. The thoughts that arise in your mind when you think of her are still influenced by her."

The hollow was growing. I would become a sinkhole.

Susan Douglas lit a candle on the altar. A thin trickle of smoke rose from the match. "Earth returning to earth, fire returning to fire, wind returning to wind, water returning to water."

When it was over, I stood up and turned around. Steph was leaving through the door at the rear of the room.

My stomach lurched back into existence. I grabbed my purse and went after her.

Outside, the late-afternoon light was shining through the pines and redwoods that nestled up close to the brown-shingled building. Steph was walking down the path toward the street. She was leaving without saying a single word to me.

"Steph," I called. It was quiet here; I heard the sound of children playing in the park nearby, and I knew my voice had carried.

At first I thought she would pretend she hadn't heard me, but then she turned around. She was dressed all in black—black button-down shirt, pants, shoes. It made her seem older. Like a stranger.

I caught up to her on the sidewalk. "You were just going to leave without talking to me?"

The expression on her face was unreadable. "I didn't think it was the right place."

"Is the sidewalk better?"

She shook her head just slightly. "Don't make this worse."

A hot rush of anger. I pulled *The Dream of a Common Language* out of my bag and thrust it at her. "I wanted to give this back to you."

She accepted the book unhappily. She took a quick breath, then looked past me toward the park. "Let's go for a walk."

She headed for the trees without waiting.

I followed.

"It was a mistake," she said.

She had led me down the block to a wooded picnic area. She sat down on a bench and stared at the woodchip-strewn ground. I stood in front of her, arms crossed.

"You can't mean that," I said.

"I do mean it. It was wrong. I'm sorry." She wouldn't look at me.

"But I thought we had a—a connection." I heard the words emerging from me like the lines of a soap opera.

She looked frustrated. "Yeah, we had a connection, but it wasn't the kind that lasts."

"How do you know? We haven't given it any time."

"There's no point. There's no future for us." She was twisting *The Dream of a Common Language* into a tube.

"Are you still with Lisa?"

She took a deep breath. "No."

Everything I'd never allowed myself to hope for surged up inside me. "Steph—"

"Don't," she said, finally looking up at me. Her eyes were full of pain. "I'm not right for you. I'm just a stop on your journey. We could never begin a relationship—a real relationship—the way we started this. It's all lies."

I sank to my knees in front of her. "I never lied to you."

She shook her head, looking past me.

"Please," I said. "What I feel for you is the most honest thing I've ever felt."

I reached for her hand, and she was so startled that she let me take it. The book fell out of her grasp. She seemed to struggle with something inside herself, and for a moment I thought I had won, but then she said deliberately, "You're leaving. You're going to MIT, for fuck's sake, and I'm staying here."

"We can keep in touch—"

"That's not the answer. We can't—I can't." She wrenched her hand out of mine.

Humiliated. My legs trembled as I got up. I would leave. I would walk away, and she would never see me again.

But if I left, I'd never see her again either.

She hadn't moved. Her jaw was clenched tight as she stared down at the ground. Red splotches grew on her cheeks. I heard the kids shrieking in the park nearby.

I couldn't leave like this. I sat down beside her, letting my bag slide off my shoulder onto the bench.

I felt so small.

"Did you even like me?" I asked. The words hurt.

"Of course I liked you," she said immediately.

My heart in my throat.

"Don't even—" She stopped, exhaling. "Look, I've been with—I was with Lisa for three and half years, and I loved her, but it wasn't working for a long time. And then you came along, and you—" She rubbed a hand over her face. The black cuff of her sleeve was rolled back, and I saw the tail of the koi tattoo curling over her wrist. "You were new, and you liked my music, and you liked me. I felt like you saw me. I really needed that."

"I do see you," I said thickly.

"But I need to see myself," she said, meeting my eyes.

Like diving into the deep.

"I don't know who I am anymore," she said quietly. "I hurt Lisa so much, and I never wanted to do that. Like Joan said—" Her voice broke. "I have to do what my heart desires, and I don't know what that is anymore. For so long I told myself I loved Lisa more than I wanted to make music, but I was lying to myself. I always knew I was lying. What kind of person wants something they might never have more than the person who loves them?"

I ached for her. "People have dreams," I said. "They're not wrong."

"How do I know it's not a fantasy?" she asked.

Joan would know the answer, but I did not. My eyes went hot.

"I have to figure my shit out," Steph said.

"You will," I said. "I can be here for you."

"No," she said sadly.

I remembered the first time she had touched me, her fingers plucking the oak leaf from my hair. I remembered the look in her eye, just like the one she had now, and I realized she had been afraid from that very first moment that something like this would happen.

"You're right," she said. "You never lied to me, but I lied to you. I used you, and I can't be with you knowing that I did that to you."

No ground beneath me. "But I'm in love with you," I whispered.

"No, you're not," she said gently.

Plummeting.

"You think you are," she said, "but one day you'll realize this was just a door opening for you. I promise."

She picked up *The Dream of a Common Language* from the ground and stood up.

"I'm so sorry for your loss," she said.

I couldn't watch her leave.

D ad found me sitting in Joan's car, crying.

"Where were you?" he asked through the window. "I called you."

I shook my head, unable to answer. I didn't have any Kleenex and my face was a mess of tears and snot.

He opened the door and crouched down and gathered me into his arms. "It's okay," he said, holding me close. "It's going to be okay."

I couldn't stop crying.

Afterward, there was dinner at a restaurant in Fairfax, where nobody had an appetite, not even Luke and Noah. Then there were awkward, extended goodbyes as people scattered to local hotels. Aunt Tammy was staying in Fairfax with her family since there wasn't room for them all at Joan's house. Tomorrow they'd come and get Analemma before they drove back to Pasadena. Dad and I would be gone before then.

As we walked through the dusk to Joan's car, I realized I'd have to stop calling it *Joan's car* and *Joan's house*. Soon they would be sold to new owners, and the car and the house would belong to them.

Analemma was happy to see us, although she still seemed confused by Joan's absence. Dad took her out while I put away the pictures I'd brought to the memorial service. I hung the self-portrait back in the guest room, and I took the photo of my grandparents up to Grandpa's office. All the photos would have to come down eventually, but for now I felt like this one should go back where I'd found it.

The stairs creaked as I climbed up to the third floor. There was my grandparents' carved wooden bed with the handmade quilt on it, the bookshelf below the long window that opened onto the roof, Dad's suitcase open on the floor. The house was so quiet I could hear the wind in the trees outside.

I opened the door to Grandpa's office and went in, turning on the light. The built-in desk was still covered with stacks of papers, and the project that Joan had been working on was still covered by a canvas at the end of the room. When I had come up here to find a picture for the memorial, I'd been focused on the wall of photos, but now I noticed several shoe boxes full of paper cubes on the counter. I stuck the picture of my grandparents back on the wall and went to look more closely at the cubes. They were about a half-inch square, and there were letters and numbers on them, sometimes typed and sometimes handwritten. I recognized Grandpa's handwriting. Joan had made these cubes from his notes.

I looked over at the canvas-covered form. While Joan was alive, I would never have peeked, but someone was going to see this sooner or later. I crossed the room and carefully pulled off the canvas. Beneath it was a sculpture made of hundreds of those paper cubes. It was shaped like a head.

Downstairs I heard Dad and Analemma return. "Aria?"

"Up here," I called.

The structure of the sculpture was so intricate, each cube fitted precisely into the ones around it. In one area, a math equation in Grandpa's handwriting had been constructed across several cubes.

Dad and Analemma came upstairs and into Grandpa's office, and Dad paused in the doorway.

"I think it's a statue," I said.

Dawning comprehension came over his face. "It's my father. Come over here—you can see it better."

I went to stand by him, and with more distance, the tiny paper cubes became part of a whole. I had been too close to see it clearly. Now I recognized Grandpa in profile: his high forehead, his prominent nose, even the shape of his hair.

"She wasn't finished," Dad said. "The back of his head isn't done."

He was right. It looked as if Joan had gotten about three-quarters of the way through the project, and the lower back portion of Grandpa's head was missing.

"It's over there," I said, gesturing to the boxes of cubes. "That's the rest of him."

Dad picked up a cube and examined it. "I wonder if she was going to paint the sculpture, too."

"It would cover the handwriting. So probably not, right?"

He went to the sculpture and turned it to face us. From this angle, you couldn't see the missing portion of Grandpa's head.

"It's perfect as is," Dad said. He came over and put his arm around me. Analemma sat down at our feet, leaning against my legs. Night had fallen, and the overhead light turned the windows into mirrors. Our reflections were partially transparent, so I could see the outline of tree tops through them, as if we were floating out in the dark. I felt as if we'd accidentally stepped into one of Joan's photos. I felt her with us, pressing the shutter.

2023

The Pearl Gallery is brightly lit against the March evening. Outside the floor-to-ceiling windows, the darkness of Mass Ave is streaked with traffic lights. Dad brings me a huge bouquet of tulips; his wife follows with a bottle of Veuve Clicquot.

"I'm so proud of you," Dad says, and he almost crushes the flowers as he hugs me.

"Thank you," I say, and then I'm clutching the tulips and the champagne as more people arrive. I can hardly believe this is happening. So much was delayed during the pandemic, and now it feels like everything is happening at once. Tonight is the opening of my first show, and in three weeks I'm supposed to defend my dissertation. My brain is leaping from my paintings to Mars and back again.

Tasha texts to say she's looking for parking. She drove up from New York for this. I haven't seen her since her engagement party at New Year's. Someone takes the flowers and champagne away from me. Fatima and Jing and Aaron, who are also in my PhD cohort at MIT, arrive together. They bring me peonies and hydrangeas.

Jess Wong, the gallery's event coordinator, comes up to me and asks, "Are you ready?"

I've written down a brief speech, and I'm suddenly seized with nerves. But I nod anyway. I follow her toward the center of the gallery space, where she stands right in front of the biggest painting of the show. It's called *A Scatter of Light*.

It's an abstract work in mixed media: acrylic, oil, polycarbonate, aluminum, roofing paper, and postcard on board. In the center is a red sphere thickly textured with impasto. I'm really pleased with the effect; in some places it looks like a topographic map. Oranges and reds emanate from the central sphere, and fragments of shattered polycarbonate and aluminum are embedded in the paint. Toward the edges of the painting the colors transition into blues and purples and blacks. I've cut in hard-edged lines radiating out like dark rays. Within the rays are shards cut from a postcard. They show a tiny hand, the neck of a guitar, a leg. I have hidden the face.

I wish my grandmother could see this.

Jess Wong turns on a wireless microphone and gives me an encouraging smile. I pull out the piece of paper on which I've printed my speech. The words swim before my eyes. I'm thinking about my research into the microbial life that might exist on Mars. I look around the room, at the people who have gathered to see my art. Even Skylar's here; they raise a plastic glass of wine to me. And then the gallery door opens and Tasha hurries inside. She catches my eye immediately and smiles.

"Welcome, everyone!" Jess says. "Thanks so much for coming out tonight. Pearl Gallery is committed to supporting and uplifting exciting new local artists, and I'm so thrilled to introduce you to the talented person behind the incredible pieces you see tonight: Aria Tang West."

Applause. I see Dad holding up his phone. Mom is watching over FaceTime from Geneva; it's the middle of the night there. Jess holds the microphone out to me, and after a deep breath, I take it.

I've probably had too much champagne. I feel the bubbles in me, and I wonder if defending my dissertation will feel this good. I haven't had a chance to talk to Tasha all night and now she finds me, pulling me over to *A Scatter of Light*, and we stand still together, in front of it.

"What's the title mean?" she asks me.

"It's not literal," I say.

She gives me a patient look. "Humor me."

"Okay, so think about the sunset. Sometimes it's red, right? But the sun is actually white—it's all colors at once. If you were looking at the sun in space, it would be white. We see the sunset as red because particles in the air like dust or smog scatter away the blues and violets, so we only see red."

"Okay," she says, and I can tell she wants more.

"What I'm saying is—" I hesitate. I don't like to explain this stuff to people. I just want them to see a painting and experience how it makes them feel, but Tasha is my best friend. So I say, "The sunset is beautiful to us but in many ways we're seeing an illusion. The sun isn't red. It isn't even setting."

"But it's still beautiful," she says.

"It is. But what are we not seeing?"

She raises her eyebrows. "Blue?"

I laugh. "Don't think about it too hard."

She points up at the painting. "What are those pieces of paper?"

"They're from a postcard."

"What postcard?"

"A postcard of this band I used to know."

"What band?"

I don't tell her. Instead I say, "Remember when you visited me in California the summer after high school?"

She looks suspicious. "Yeah."

"That's when I started working on this piece."

She stares at me, and then I see her get it. She puts her hand on my arm. "Is this the painting you showed me in your grandma's studio?"

"It's under there."

I've buried it beneath layers of paint, but I can still see it in faint outline because I know where to look. The edges of the roofing paper. That bleeding egg, still marked by the impasto. For years, I had no idea what to do with the painting. It stayed rolled up in one closet after another. I thought about throwing it away so many times, but I could never let it go. It was still speaking to me. I just had to learn how to hear it.

ACKNOWLEDGMENTS

I began thinking about this novel in 2012, and I started writing it in 2013, which means it's been alive in my imagination for ten years. It had a difficult journey from my mind to the printed page, but every step along the way I've had the support of my best friends, who read a very early (terrible) draft and always remembered that this book existed, even when I thought it would never get published. Aimee, Betty, Cameron, Hye-John, Lesly, Nicole, Sarah, Sarah, and Vincent: This book is for you.

For those who are familiar with Marin County, California, I'd like to acknowledge that the In-N-Out in this book doesn't exist in reality. I moved the In-N-Out from Strawberry Village in Mill Valley three miles north to the Trader Joe's shopping center in Greenbrae. I claim poetic license.

George Dutton generously donated to the Kidlit Against Anti-AAPI Racism Auction in 2021 and won the opportunity to have a character named after a loved one in my next book; that character is Talia Dutton, named after his daughter. The character of Sarah Franco was inspired by my friend Sarah Pecora, who also named her.

Thanks to Laura Langlie, who started this book on its publication path. Thanks to M-E Girard, Karla Yancy, Anushka Fernandopulle, Kate Cochrane, and Laura Chandra for their guidance on medical issues, Buddhism, and Martha's Vineyard. Any errors are mine. Thanks to Cindy Pon, who waited very patiently to read this! Thanks to artist Feifei Ruan for translating my vision of Aria's journey into a beautiful cover image. Thanks to my agent, Michael Bourret, who always helps me see things in perspective. Thanks to my editor, Andrew Karre, who somehow understood what I was trying to do with this book even before I did.

As always, thanks to my wife, Amy, who has endured my angst about this book for a decade and truly deserves a prize.

CREDITS

DUTTON BOOKS AND PENGUIN YOUNG READERS GROUP

ART AND DESIGN
Anna Booth

CONTRACTS
Anton Abrahamsen

COPYEDITORS AND PROOFREADERS
Rob Farren
Anne Heausler
Jacqueline Hornberger

EDITOR
Andrew Karre

MANAGING EDITOR
Natalie Vielkind

MARKETING
James Akinaka
Christina Colangelo
Brianna Lockhart
Felicity Vallence
Shannon Spann

PRODUCTION MANAGER
Vanessa Robles

PUBLICITY
Elyse Marshall

PUBLISHER
Julie Strauss-Gabel

PUBLISHING MANAGER
Melissa Faulner

SUBSIDIARY RIGHTS
Micah Hecht
Kim Ryan

SALES
Jill Bailey
Andrea Baird
Maggie Brennan
Trevor Bundy
Nicole Davies
Tina Deniker
John Dennany
Cletus Durkin
Eliana Ferreri
Becky Green
Sheila Hennessey

Todd Jones
Doni Kay
Steve Kent
Mary McGrath
Debra Polansky
Colleen Conway Ramos
Mary Raymond
Jennifer Ridgway
Judy Samuels
Nicole White
Allan Winebarger
Dawn Zahorik

SCHOOL AND LIBRARY MARKETING AND PROMOTION
Venessa Carson
Judith Huerta
Carmela Iaria
Trevor Ingerson
Summer Ogata
Megan Parker
Rachel Wease

LISTENING LIBRARY
Rebecca Waugh

DYSTEL, GODERICH & BOURRET

Lauren E. Abramo
Michael Bourret
Andrew Dugan
Nataly Gruender
Gracie Freeman Lifschutz